EIGHT SECONDS

FRANCES DALL'ALBA

Poinsettia
Publishing

Also By Frances Dall'Alba

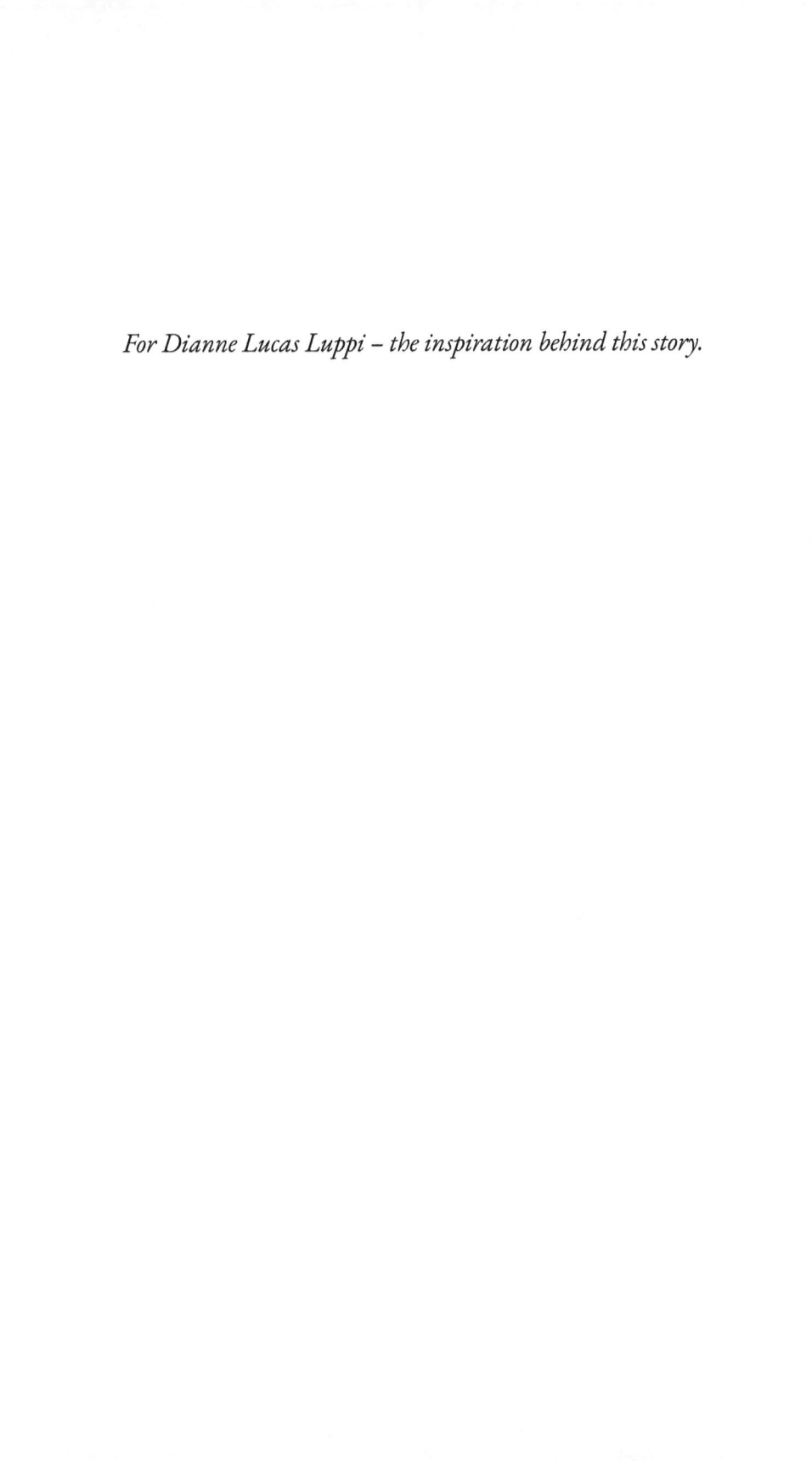

For Dianne Lucas Luppi – the inspiration behind this story.

Chapter 1

1966 – 12 Years Old

Grace Maree Lucas pushed on the pedals of her second-hand bike, the basket in front long since gone and only a few tattered ribbons still attached to the handlebars. She wound her legs as fast as they would go, glad she was strong and lean from riding her bike and horse often. The wind whistled through her short, blonde hair, its early morning briskness nipping at her skin as she rode against it.

She inhaled a lungful of the sweet air, her knuckles frozen to the handlebar as she gripped them tighter over the bumps and potholes in the road. She couldn't wait to spend time with her horse, Megaton.

Riding along the eucalypt-lined dirt road weaving between farms, she hoped to spot a kangaroo or even a blue-tongued lizard along its edges. Wary of snakes, though, she rarely stopped in case they tangled with her wheels.

She was panting by the time she reached the neighbour's poultry farm. It was eight miles from the outskirts of Kalamunda, an outer suburb of Perth, and where her horse stayed. She wheeled the bike around the back of the chook shed and spotted Liz finishing her chores. "Hi, Liz," she called out, dropping the bike haphazardly and sprinting towards Liz who stopped and leaned on her broom. "How much time do I have before we leave?"

"About forty minutes. The boys are nearly packed, and I started work early this morning. Make sure you and Megaton are back by then."

Forty minutes! Yes, yes, yes. Liz was one of the few people who understood her obsession with horses. One of the few people who cared what she thought. Her gut clenched again at the reminder of her father's anger the night before. Asking for a second-hand saddle had put him in a foul mood. Asking anything of her father always ended badly. If only she were more like her older sister, Annette. He always made time for her.

She pushed all that to the back of her mind and raced past Liz towards the fence behind the sheds, calling out, "Megaton! Megaton!"

Megaton's ears pricked at her voice, and he bolted across the yard towards her. She had her arms out wide and hugged him when he reached her, joy surging through her chest. He might be the ugliest horse, with short legs and a weirdly misshapen nose, but he was hers to ride whenever she wanted. There was nothing else she ever wanted as badly.

She never left home without sneaking a carrot or apple from the fridge. Today was no different. She straddled the fence and pulled out the chunky carrot from the pocket of her faded jeans and the hobble strap from around her waist. Megaton gobbled it up while she tied the strap around his neck and used the fence to climb onto his back.

Grace threaded his matted mane through her fingers, gripping it tightly as she squeezed her legs against his flank and rode bareback. Megaton whinnied and trotted through the open gate. "Let's go, boy," she whispered into his ear. The cool breeze barely raised a goosebump under her loose skivvy as she cantered down the packed dirt road away from the sheds, the thumping of hooves blending with the morning call songs of the cockatoos.

Nothing mattered when she was with Megaton. Except for her best school friend, Diane who loved riding too, Megaton was the only other friend she had. He didn't laugh at her when she mixed up her letters and words. He didn't laugh at the shoddy second-hand clothes she was lucky to snare from her older sisters. No, Megaton loved her as she was. Grace nuzzled her nose into his mane; the dusty, horsy smell tickled her nose as she hugged him tighter around his neck.

The patch of eucalypt forest loomed ahead, her laughter getting caught up in the surrounding breeze. Colourful displays of spring wildflowers dotted either side of the track, their mixed colours always delighting her. She loved mornings like this. She'd do anything to be near, or on, a horse. It's what she lived for.

It was also the one place her father rarely intruded.

Slowing to a trot, she pulled on the strap, guiding Megaton into a gentle turn before squeezing her knees again for the ride home. She didn't want to miss the trip to the Peaceville Valley Rodeo with Liz and her three sons. It wasn't her fault that sometimes she wished she lived with Liz's family who treated her like she belonged with them. Instead, she shrugged off the sharp jab of pain every time her father reminded her they would've been better off if she'd never been born.

Yeah, he wouldn't notice if she was gone for most of the day. More likely relieved she was out of sight. Not used to feeling sorry for herself, she closed her eyes and rested her cheek against the horse's neck, the rise and fall soothing her sadness. Megaton would take her back to the sheds. He did it every other time. She soaked up the smell of his soft and velvety hide, vowing to forget about home for a day.

Grace dismounted and led Megaton to the feed bucket and water trough. The pungent smell of chicken poo drifted towards her. She batted away the smell like an annoying blowfly and untied the hobble strap. Leaving Megaton, she went into the small tack room and rummaged around for the horse brush. A rub down would make Megaton feel better. Who knew when she'd be back for another ride?

"Hey, squirt, ready to go?"

Liz's oldest son, Larry, was nearly eighteen and so tall and grown-up. She loved it when he called her squirt. Even though she thought she was very grown-up at twelve, she liked that Larry acted like her older brother and taught her things about horses and bikes.

"Just give me a minute. I want to give Megaton a quick rub down."

He ruffled her hair when he walked past holding a saddle. She was the youngest in her actual family, and except for her brother Robert, no one ever took much notice of her, let alone spent time with her. She and Robert usually fled from their dad's temper and belt.

She used long brush strokes around Megaton's girth, resting her ear against Megaton's flank, enjoying the sounds of his pounding heart. "You be good today. I'll be back soon." There was nothing better than the early morning fog rising around them as the sun peeked over the trees. Megaton was hers. Liz had gifted him to her as they had no use for him, and she could ride him whenever she wanted. He wasn't going with them that day, but at every pony club event that happened within cooee of Kalamunda, somehow, she got herself and Megaton there even if she had to ride him.

"Ready, Grace?"

Grace looked up. Liz was locking up the shed. "Coming." She gave Megaton one last brush over his back end and a hug around the neck. "See you soon," she whispered in his ear when he whinnied back. Leading him back to the paddock, she sent him off to graze before running back to put the brush in its proper place.

"Don't forget your bike," Larry reminded her.

She smiled sheepishly, taking a right turn towards where she'd left it lying on its side in a patch of dewy grass. Larry never got cranky with her but was strict about leaving equipment and bikes lying haphazardly around the yard. The constant reminder that someone could trip over it and hurt themselves was something she should've learnt by now. "Sorry, Larry."

"You'll get it one day if you ever put horses last on your list of importance."

Well, that would never happen, Grace mused as she opened the door of the Dodge truck and hopped in.

The rodeo campground was bustling with floats, horses in every size and colour and crowds hiding under cowboy hats. Strains of a Loretta Lynn song came through the speakers, and barbequed onions and bacon made her tummy rumble. Grace jammed her clenched fists inside the pockets of her jeans to stop them from shaking and shut the door of the Dodge with her shoulder. "What do you mean?"

Liz strolled around to her side of the Dodge and, with a kind smile, asked, "Do you want me to enter you in the poddy competition? I reckon you can do it."

Grace's stomach dropped. Her usual fierce desire to hop on anything and hold on tight went walkabout. It usually applied to horses, but could she do the same with a small calf? No one had asked her before, and she'd never considered it. She'd been to many rodeos and had fond memories of one when a cowboy enthralled the crowd with his whip-cracking tricks.

Liz patted her on the shoulder, and Grace's jolt to attention must have looked like a nod.

"Is that a yes?"

She nodded again, not sure what she was getting herself into.

"There are kids who do this sort of stuff all the time. I have a feeling you're as good as any of them. Sometimes it's all about the balance and not being scared. I think you have it, Grace. What do you think?"

Scared? She was never scared of climbing on top of a horse. A poddy, well, how much different could it be? She supposed now was as good a time to start not being afraid. She didn't like being scared. "What do I need to wear?"

Liz put an arm around her shoulder and walked with her to the back of the Dodge. Lifting an Esky, Liz looked her up and down. Her gaze slid over her worn jeans, cotton long-sleeved shirt and scruffy sneakers.

"You'll do just fine as you are. Come on, let's organise our camp for the day, and I'll put in the nomination."

Larry clapped her on the shoulder. "You can carry the tarp, Grace."

Larry and his two younger brothers were unloading the rodeo gear needed for the events they were taking part in. Grace reached for the tarp still sitting in the back tray of the Dodge that Larry would tie between some trees to give them a bit of shade. He was always doing thoughtful things for his mum.

She followed Liz to the rear of the fenced area, behind the rodeo grounds, where families set up for the day. Crated trucks were parked haphazardly under shady eucalypt trees, messily surrounding temporary pens. Different pens separated calves, steers, horses and bulls. She never tired of looking at animals and they never intentionally hurt her.

With only an hour before the rodeo started, cowboys and organisers mingled outside the main arena. A booming voice tested the PA system, and music played intermittently. Others carried clipboards and were writing names and confirming nominations.

Grace almost changed her mind and was about to stop Liz from nominating her when something made her halt. The only way to stop being scared was to give it a go. If she was still scared afterwards, she didn't need to do it again.

She walked up to the pen holding the meanest bulls and eyed the one standing closest to the railings. The bull snorted at her. In a flash, she was back in Mount Gambier, where her family had once lived. She was out picking mushrooms with Robert and Annette when a bull with the longest horns came out of nowhere and chased them. They made a mad dash through a barbed-wire fence, leaving the bull on the other side stamping its front hoof and snorting with rage. With legs shaking, Grace had stared at it and remembered thinking: one day, I'm not going to be afraid of you.

Those words kept running through her head, and the confidence to ride her first poddy settled comfortably inside her. She just had to hold on tight for eight seconds. How hard could it be?

Grace waited with the small group of kids the same age as her, conspicuously devoid of girls. She was often mistaken for a boy even when riding along the roads *and* wearing a halter-neck top. It confounded her. Obviously, she dressed like a girl, but her short-cropped hair was as far as people went.

Anyway, what did she care about how she looked, despite some girls at school already sporting sizeable breasts and wearing bras. Peering down at her chest, she checked just in case they'd magically grown in the past couple of hours, catching her out for wanting to ride a poddy with the boys. She shook her head at the silly thought. They were the same as yesterday—flat as a board and unlikely to change in a hurry.

She didn't know any of the kids from Peaceville, and nobody talked to her. The other boys stood in clusters, and she didn't mind being ignored. Instead, Grace followed some of their excited chatter about previous rides and best times. It didn't sound like any were newcomers to poddy riding and the muscles in her stomach clammed up. The pain worsened when the chute boss bellowed from atop the fence rail.

"Okay, kids, line up. Your event is on next. For those who make good time and impress the judges with good points, we'll call your number and get your details after everyone's had their turn."

Grace bit her bottom lip, her hands clenching and unclenching. Should she barge up to the front and get it over and done with, or have her go last? Her feet were frozen to the ground, so that decided for her.

One of the marshals neatly dressed with a press-button cowboy shirt sidled up alongside them and ticked off numbers on his clipboard, assigning which chute they would ride from. Liz had pinned her number thirteen onto the back of her checked long-sleeved shirt, and it flapped

against her back when the breeze raised the square piece of material held
by safety pins.

The announcement of their event sounded over the PA system, and she
licked her dry lips. *Eight seconds. That's all I have to hold on for. How hard
can it be?* Larry assured her she could do it. She hoped he and his brothers
Geoff and Greg were watching as she wanted to make them proud. Some
days they all went to a lot of trouble to make things easier for her.

When the first boy climbed onto his poddy, Grace tried to peer over the
others and into the tiny chute where they readied themselves. She couldn't
see a lot, but her heart leapt when the chute gate opened and the calf burst
free. With a better view of the arena, the young boy lasted only half a
second before he was thrown off.

Entrants two, three and four didn't make it to four seconds. *Holy
Shoot.* Eight seconds was feeling like a very long time, *and* those boys were
experienced.

Grace watched in dismay as each boy struggled to make it to the eight
second time limit. There were only three kids ahead of her and her stomach
decided at that moment to play up with a cramp across her lower tummy.
She swallowed a couple of times, hoping to settle it. Her eyes darted around
the yards searching for a tap. She needed a swig of water—but no such luck.

"Number thirteen," the marshal called out.

She had no idea how long the last few entrants stayed on; she was busy
stewing with her worries.

"Up ya get, mate."

Grace climbed up into the chute and was helped onto the poddy by a
cowboy. With the rope wound around the poddy's belly, it bucked against
the confines of the pen. She swallowed back a lump of fear.

"Here, give us your hand."

Mesmerised, she watched as they wound the scratchy rope around her
palm. She gripped it tight once they finished and held it against her pelvis as
Larry had instructed. The boisterous noise from the rodeo crowd mingled
with the announcer's voice coming through the PA. She blocked it from
her mind. For the stalled seconds before the chute gate opened, it was just

her and the poddy. Adjusting her body and gritting her teeth, she nodded to the officials, and they opened the gate for her.

The poddy let loose and bucked its way into the arena. Every buck transformed her movements into a dance, her free hand flailing for balance, never once touching down. Every muscle tensed and strained as she poised for the next bone-jarring buck. Not a single shred of fear ravaged her mind. Only a new sense of freedom—until the eight second siren sounded and her body jerked her hand free of the wound rope.

She had time to anticipate the landing and protect herself once the poddy threw her off. Falling face down into the dirt wasn't pleasant, and she coughed out a mouthful as she rolled over. Those eight seconds were the longest of her entire life, but she would never forget them. And on her very first poddy ride! Something new buzzed through her veins.

A pickup man was by her side within seconds, helping her up. Accepting a pat on the back, she dusted her jeans and sent a huge smile in his direction. Applause and whistling filled the arena ... for her. She straightened her shoulders, standing tall and proud. Walking back to the exit gate, a new lightness burnt brightly in her chest, buoying her up. She'd never experienced anything like this before. Could never have imagined it. She was hooked, and she'd be back.

Chapter 2

Grace was thrust into the centre of the group by the jostling boys, as names and ages were recorded for the winner's announcement. The other kids looked her up and down and whispered amongst themselves. The only words she could pick up were 'where'd he come from?' Annoyance wedged itself inside her chest.

She was the only rider to make the eight second time. The next closest competitor had made it to six seconds. Unsure of how to handle the curious stares, unlike her cheeky self, she kept her mouth shut. If she had the best time, it was better to let her actions speak rather than her words. Sometimes they came out garbled, and people laughed, worsening the situation.

With the adrenalin kick easing off, her heart no longer pounded inside her chest. She leant back against the rough timber railing—just outside the main arena—to wait for the announcement. She inhaled the distinctive smell of animal poo and eyed the old ringers sitting atop the arena rails with worn Akubras pulled low.

The next event was the under eighteen's saddle bronc rides, and they would announce the poddy winners after that round finished.

She lifted a knee and hitched her foot behind the railing, hanging her arms along the top rail, a little bored as they matched numbers to names. The marshal moved through the bunch of kids, one by one, filling in his form and informing each competitor what points they scored.

"Name," the marshal asked when he reached her.

Grace unhitched her foot from the railing and straightened. "Grace Lucas."

The marshal's smile froze. Silence punctuated the air for a few moments. "As in Grace? A girl?"

Grace nodded before clenching her teeth. Now she was full-on infuriated. So what if her hair was cropped short? It was how her mother cut it, and honestly, Grace couldn't care less. It was easier to manage, and it never flicked in her eyes when she rode Megaton. Then she frowned, more concerned she might be in trouble. Surely Liz wouldn't let her do anything wrong?

"Ah ... we might have a problem here." The marshal scratched his head and looked around like he was hoping someone would come up and solve it. Grace had no idea what the problem was.

"Is she a girl?" one of the other boys asked, pointing a finger at her chest.

"Wait a sec. I'll be right back."

The marshal walked away towards the officials, leaving Grace confused and surrounded by boys staring at her. Should she have competed? Being a girl had never stopped her from doing anything before. It hadn't stopped her father from flogging her as much as he did Robert. Why would being a girl be a problem?

After what felt like an hour but was probably only about five minutes, the marshal and other organisers made their way back to the group of teenagers. What Grace didn't understand was how the nominations worked. Didn't Liz give them her name? What was all the fuss about? Was there a separate girl's competition she should've been in?

When the marshal and others reached them, the band of teenage boys gathered closer.

"Ah ... Grace, we have a problem. Apparently, the rules are girls are not allowed to compete against boys. I'm sorry, luv, but we can't give you the first-place prize," the marshal explained.

Something stirred inside her chest, but first, she had to check. "Was I supposed to compete in a girl's category?"

"Not possible. There weren't any other girls," one of the organisers threw in.

"But what was I supposed to do?"

The marshal shrugged, his teeth digging into his bottom lip. This was obviously an issue for the too-hard basket.

"I'm sorry, Grace, it's against the association's rules. We'll give you a mention, but we can't officially give you the first prize."

"But I won." Steely determination set in, and Grace was not prepared to give up her first prize. Suddenly, all the excitement in making time seemed like a waste of time. Why could boys enjoy doing this but not girls?

"Give it to her, you lousy buggers. She rode the best out there today, and you're gonna take that away from her?"

Grace, along with the marshal and officials, looked up to the old ringer sitting atop the arena rails.

"But ... but it's the association's rules," one marshal said.

"Big ass is what they are. If that was my daughter who'd just ridden that poddy like this young thing did, I'd be fighting for the first-place trophy. Give it to her. She was your best rider today."

The ringer turned his wrinkled face in Grace's direction. Every line and scar told a thousand stories, but his dimpled smile would stay with her forever. She smiled back, grateful someone had stood up for her. Grace didn't know who he was or what hold he had over the marshal and officials, but they nodded, conferred amongst themselves, then walked off. Would she receive the first-place trophy?

With the marshal gone, Grace didn't want to wait around and find out what the boys thought of a girl taking first prize. All she wanted was to find Liz and Larry. Maybe they could explain to her what this rule was all about. Why had Liz entered her in the poddy competition if girls weren't allowed to ride?

She trudged off towards their camp, her heart no longer in the beauty of the animals and atmosphere surrounding her. She switched off to the sound of the voice coming through the PA system and the music that intermittently played between the announcer's words. It'd be a long day to hold her disappointment when she would rather be home with Megaton. *He* didn't care if she was a girl.

The camp was empty. Liz and the boys were nowhere to be seen. She didn't expect anything else. They would be sitting on the grandstand waiting for the results to be announced. It was a pity her name wouldn't be called out to receive the first-prize trophy. They would've seen her eight second ride and would expect her to receive it.

Grace yawned, suddenly spent. The anxiety leading up to the ride, the adrenalin kick, and the pounding heart, followed by the disappointing news, made her limbs feel all floppy. She lay down on the rug Liz had spread out, rested her head on a rolled-up oilskin jacket and closed her eyes.

"Grace! Grace!"

Her eyes flickered open. Larry was barrelling towards her. Bewildered, she sat up.

"Get out there and accept your first-prize trophy. Hurry up; they've been calling your name for ages."

Grace was on her feet in a flash. She raced to the arena and clambered up the railings. Jumping down the other side, she hurried towards the centre.

"Do we have Grace Lucas?" The announcer searched the crowd.

"Yes, that's me," she puffed, reaching his side with a smile stretching across her face. Her sneakers stirred up the dirt, and dust rose in the air.

"I believe this belongs to you." She shook the man's hand and took the trophy. "Give this young lady a big round of applause, ladies and gentlemen. I've never handed a first-place trophy to a girl before, but I thoroughly enjoyed watching her ride today. Did anyone else enjoy Grace's ride?"

Grace looked down at a miniature eight-inch saddle trophy, and her heart swelled when the crowd's applause doubled in intensity. Liz was somewhere in the crowd, and she hoped she'd done her proud. She also hoped her dad might be proud of her when she showed him her first ever trophy.

Chapter 3

Present Day

Erin Blackwater tripped on the edge of a paver in her haste to reach her car. She bit her lip when her ankle twisted dangerously but righted herself just in time before any damage was done. She tossed her bags into the boot of her smart little Honda, always reluctant to leave the tranquil acreage property where her grandparents lived.

She closed the boot with a rushed slam and raised her hand to shade her eyes against the morning sun. Scouting around, she smiled when twigs snapped and the forest brush rustled in the small pocket of rainforest hugging the winding creek. With two fingers in the corners of her mouth, she sounded a piercing whistle, laughing when Lacey came bounding towards her. She'd seen her race off in that direction only minutes earlier. Most likely chasing a white-tailed rat.

"Come here, rascal." She crouched on the lush, green lawn and hugged her border collie. Lacey jumped up, her paws on Erin's knee and pink tongue lolling out of her mouth. Her tail swirled like a windmill. It always pained Erin to leave her behind, but the city was no place for a dog. As a kid, she'd pined for any pet, but to no avail. When her grandparents eventually suggested they had room for one, there was no rescinding on that promise.

Erin rubbed her nose into Lacey's shaggy black and white fur, inhaling the doggy smell mixed with the crisp early morning and rainforest leaves. A smell she couldn't get in the city. It made the freedom of these crazy weekend dashes to the high mountain property even more special. Some days, nothing else mattered.

How did she keep everyone happy about how she wanted to live her life? With her grandparents, parents and boyfriend pulling her in different directions, it was the time she spent with Lacey that kept her sane.

"I've got to go, my darling. Be a good girl for Grandad, okay."

Lacey barked, racing off and spinning on the lawn, chasing her tail. Erin laughed, her heart squeezing at the simple love having a pet gave her. If only she could live here forever, just her and Lacey. Life would be a lot less complicated.

Erin rose and turned towards the house, calling out, "Grandma, I have to go."

Her grandmother emerged from the side door of the kitchen. "I figured you were close to leaving. When I heard your laughter, I didn't have to guess who you were saying goodbye to."

"Oh, Grandma, I want to stay here forever. Why does growing up have to be so difficult?"

"There's a time and place for everything. Now off you go so you don't have to rush on the road."

Erin hugged her grandma. "Say bye to Grandad. I'll see you next weekend."

"Didn't your dad mention some function they wanted you to attend?"

Erin groaned. "Actually, it's the following weekend." Damn, she'd forgotten about it. Nicholas, her boyfriend, had talked it up too, reminding her how important it was for both their careers. She opened the car door and shook her head. Why?

She reversed on the gravel drive, giving her grandmother one last wave and resigning herself to the hour-long drive down to the coast.

If she hated anything, it was trying to find a free car park. She wasn't a swearing kind of person but give her an impossible situation, and she could let fly with enough expletives to embarrass anyone within earshot. She tapped her foot on the brake and indicated as a car reversed from a park under a mango tree. The rich, fruity smell from the over-ripe mangoes scattered over the grassy verge rose to meet her nose when she stepped foot from the car. Loaded with ripened fruit, the overburdened tree looked ready to topple over. One little puff of wind and she might come back to find its branches lying on her car's bonnet, dents and all.

She pushed the worry to the back of her mind. The agreed time for the initial interview had come and gone ten minutes ago. She didn't enjoy being late for anything. It wasn't like her to be tardy, but the traffic on the winding mountain road had been slow and frustrating to drive behind.

She scowled when the mid-morning sun bit into her skin. It was a grim reminder of one of the reasons she hated the prickly heat of the tropics. It would only take minutes for sweat to form and soak her clothes. Time to get into the air conditioning before she changed her mind and drove back in the direction she'd come from.

Walking quickly across the road in front of the Cairns Base Hospital, she flicked through her old messages on her phone for details of the patient's ward. A horn blared on her right, and she jumped. *Shoot!* That was all she needed—to be the centre of an accident. If she wasn't killed, she would die of shame for looking down at her phone. Wasn't this the complaint about every millennial these days?

Inside the building, she located the lifts; the tension eased from her shoulders as it climbed to the third level—the cool air giving her a shiver. The world was okay again, except she was twenty minutes late.

With no idea of how unwell the patient was, this trip could be a waste of time. She might be asleep or in too much pain. God almighty, why was she chosen to do this task? She was more than happy to sit behind a desk for the next twelve months, doing brain-dead data entry that wouldn't incite any stress. A year off from all pressure.

The lift pinged, and the doors opened to an empty corridor, bar a few trollies of linen and a line of portable blood pressure machines against the wall. Concentrating on the arrows and directions to different wards, she navigated her way to the patient's ward. Another thirty metres and she stood outside room 23. She squared her shoulders and took an extra deep breath before knocking gently. When she pushed on the door, she stumbled on the castors of a trolley left awkwardly in the way and muffled a groan. She almost laughed at how comical she must've looked. Instead, she straightened and surveyed the room. There was only one patient in the three-bed bay, and thankfully, there was a glint of amusement in her eyes.

"You must be the medical researcher?" the patient said, a small smile playing at the corner of her mouth.

Erin returned the smile with a sheepish one and stepped towards the bed. "Sorry I'm late. You must be"—she glanced at her bundle of notes for reassurance and then looked at the name on the whiteboard above the bed—"Mrs Grace Luppi?"

Grace nodded gently, like any effort hurt to do so. She pressed the remote control to lift the head of the bed higher and shuffled to sit up. "Yes, come and take a seat."

Erin sat in a plump leather recliner, which seemed out of place, and organised her notes on her lap. She'd read through them a few times and had a vague idea of how she would approach the interview, but she took a moment to organise her thoughts with a steadying breath.

"So, what would you like to know?" Grace asked kindly.

Erin forced her hands to stop moving by knotting her fingers and met Grace's patient eyes. From her notes, the patient was sixty-four years old. Her skin was amazingly smooth for someone of her age and the medical trials she'd suffered through. With a few grey strands amongst her short-cropped blonde hair, her welcome smile was what Erin needed to relax.

"The research company I work for want me to document your recovery after everything that's happened to you. From what they've noted here, how your body recovered and gave you back some kidney function was a very rare thing."

"I'm no longer on dialysis, thank goodness. I hated it so much. Mentally, it was killing me faster than what a failed kidney was doing."

"How are you feeling today? You need to tell me when you've had enough and want to rest, okay."

"I'm all good. Actually, I'm being discharged next Thursday. They told me I can go home."

Erin frowned. "How is that possible?" She flicked back a couple of pages and skim read the report. She looked up. "Weren't you admitted about three weeks ago with a blood clot, then um ... some inflammation around the heart and lungs? And that caused your lung to partially collapse? That can't be good."

Grace just smiled back. "Sometimes there's more to life than what's happening inside your body."

Erin wanted to argue this point. After taking six years to complete four years of a medical degree, she knew enough to know that what happened inside a person's body usually defined what was happening in a person's life.

"How did you end up in a job like this?" Grace asked.

This jolted Erin out of her ruminations, and she managed to laugh. "Hey, I'm the one supposed to be asking the questions."

Grace chuckled. "You have an infectious sounding laugh. Has anyone ever told you that?"

Erin's smile slipped. She'd been told lots of times, but lately, a lot of reasons to laugh had been missing from her life. It seemed only Lacey could get it out of her.

"I'm sorry. I didn't mean to pry. If we're going to be meeting once a week over the next few months, it might be nice to know a little about you too."

Erin forced a smile, liking how forthright Grace was. "Not too much to know. I'm a med student with two years to go, but I needed some time out. So, I've taken a year off, and I'm working for a medical research company. I love the less stress for a change. Sounds like your case might be super-exciting, though. The professor who recommended this study thought it was worth doing."

"What sorts of things do they want to know?" Grace asked.

"My job is to delve a little into your past. Find out what sort of health you experienced growing up and any outside factors that might've contributed along the way. Those sorts of things. Then they want me to document your recovery. What you've done physically since your first lot of surgery, ahh ..." Erin glanced again at her notes and flicked back a further couple of pages. "... which was to the nerves in your lower back after they were crushed."

Grace nodded and took a mouthful of water. "You'll know I'm recovered when I can get back on my horse. It's what keeps me going. That and my family. They mean the world to me, so I want to improve and get better. Do your notes tell you how I had to learn to drink, eat, write, roll over, sit up and walk all over again?"

"There are notes here about your rehabilitation, but sometimes words lack the emotional trial a person has to go through to recover. With research projects like this, they want me to delve deeper into a person's emotional state and what gets them through the ordeal. But we won't do that on the first day."

Erin closed the folder and sat it on her lap. "My notes tell me you live up on the mountains. My dog, Lacey, lives up there on my grandparent's property. It's so beautiful."

"Then you'll have to visit me and meet my horse, Eve. Have you ever ridden one?"

Erin sat back and relaxed by rolling her shoulders. She would start on the serious stuff the next time they met. The research coordinator advised her to only chat during the first interview and connect with the patient. Make sure they were relaxed enough to open up and talk naturally. "No, I've never ridden a horse. Owning a pet was a big no-no as I was growing up. My parents were too busy and had no time or space for one, but it never stopped me from wanting one."

"But you own a dog?"

"Only in the last six months."

"Would you like to learn?"

Erin's eyes opened wide. A thread of excitement worked around her body until she closed it down and clamped hard on her jaw. "I'm sorry, Grace. This is supposed to be about you, not me. I have to concentrate my research on your life, not mine."

"Well, to do that, you'll have to understand how horses, and anything else I could climb onto, have brought me to this point in my life."

"What do you mean? Have horses always been important to you?"

Grace smiled serenely. "You could say that."

Chapter 4

Present Day

"Good morning, Grace. How are you feeling today?"

"Ready to climb walls if I don't leave here soon."

Erin chuckled as she settled on the same leather recliner as last time and noted Grace was still the only patient in the room. Someone had brought in a large bunch of sunflowers that stood tall in a glass vase on the window sill. Erin stared at them in fascination. The intricacy of the delicate petals and how they emerged from the hub of seeds in its centre was fascinating. "What a beautiful bunch of flowers."

"My daughter knows they're my favourite. Such a happy flower, don't you think?"

Erin had never heard a flower referred to as 'happy' before, but it perfectly suited the sunflower. She smiled. "I agree wholeheartedly, now—"

"I'm being discharged tomorrow," Grace cut in. "How about you come over this weekend and meet my horse? I won't be able to ride yet, but she'll enjoy anyone on her back."

Erin curled her fingers tighter around the pen she held. This weekend she was supposed to attend the medical foundation fundraiser dinner. Her conscience wavered. As someone in the profession, where everyone in her family were founding members since the days of the ark, it was the right thing to do. But oh, to be offered the opportunity to ride a horse, something she'd dreamt of since her preteen pony-obsession days, was such a big ask to give up.

Erin rolled her shoulders and relaxed her fingers. "Thank you for the invite. I'll have to check whether I can back out of somewhere I'm supposed to be." She turned to a new page in her notebook. "Now, let's go back to the nitty-gritty of your health as a child and when things went a little pear-shaped about a year ago."

"Hmm." Grace smiled thoughtfully. "Pear-shaped is a good way to describe how close I came to dying. As a kid, I was always getting colds and sore throats. Sometimes I would get abdominal pain or severe nausea, landing me in hospital a couple of times, but no one could ever tell me what was wrong. Only recently was I finally diagnosed."

When Grace paused, Erin was compelled to say, "and—?"

"Biliary Dyskinesia."

"Oh, okay. I know a little about the disorder. It affects the gallbladder and sphincter, right?"

"Yes, but it's never stopped me from living the life I wanted. Only now am I learning more about it. It disrupts the normal digestion system in the body, and all the pain I used to ignore in my abdomen was because of it. I used to put up with it because feeling unwell was not going to hold me back. Until my first lot of surgery a year ago. This time, it was more than just the disorder. It was a combination of many things, but of all the challenges I've faced, this would have to be the hardest."

"Why's that?" Erin asked as she adjusted the volume on the audio recorder.

"I had no control over it. It was as though my body had a mind of its own and wouldn't listen to anything I said. When you lose control over your body, you start to wonder if it's all worth it. Why keep fighting? Why not just give up and let it finally rest? It was supposed to be straightforward surgery to the nerves in my lower back until the complications started and—" Grace deflated back into her pillow. Was the discussion tiring her or bringing back painful memories?

"We can stop if you like," Erin suggested.

"No, it's okay." Grace raised a hand in surrender. "Sometimes they say it's better to talk about it. So, I may as well." She sucked in a deep breath, sighed and shrugged. "So, after four days, I was raced back to hospital with a very high temperature. They took me straight into surgery again, and they found a perforation in the bowel, which they repaired. They also did a colostomy and tracheostomy and put me in an induced coma for three weeks. During this time, I suffered from septicaemia and kidney failure. Not a bad run, hey?"

"Wow. That must have been a traumatic and scary time for you. How long did you remain in hospital?" Erin scribbled down details. Later, she would compare her written notes to the audio of Grace's experience.

"Eighty days in ICU. Seventy-three on life support. Then a further six weeks in rehab."

"This must have been a worrying time for your family."

Grace nodded. "When I wasn't unconscious, it felt like I'd lost control of my body, and I was doing everything possible not to lose my mind. I worried I was fighting my health for nothing. Take control of your life, Erin. Don't cave in to what others want. I haven't always been able to choose the direction my life was going. Then one day, you wake up and realise it's going off onto the wrong path."

Erin swallowed, put her pen down and sat back. Grace's warning about taking control of her life hit a raw nerve. If only she knew how.

Grace fussed with her pillow, looking a little agitated. Erin reached into her bag for her water bottle and drank a mouthful, giving her a moment to settle. "Okay, for something different, tell me a happy childhood memory. One that doesn't involve being sick."

Grace settled back against her hospital pillow, and a serene look came over her face. "I had a great friend when I was about twelve. Her name was Diane, and we spent every weekend together."

"Doing what? Getting up to mischief?" Erin asked, raising an eyebrow.

"No, nothing like that. Every weekend there was a pony club event somewhere close. We'd clean our gear the night before, and it was nothing to wake up in the dark to ride to it."

"You didn't have a float to transport your horses?"

"Nah, nothing that fancy. Walliston Horse and Pony Club was only three miles from where we kept our horses, but it wasn't unusual to ride eight to ten miles to attend a meet."

"What was your horse like?"

Grace's smile stretched wider across her face. "Sammy was an ex-pacer, and I was lucky enough to be given him after my first horse died. He was jet black and fifteen point one hands high, with a white heart on his head." She chuckled and directed her gaze back to Erin. "He was a bit crazy and used to rear up a lot at the start of a novelty event, but I loved him. If Diane and I weren't at a pony club meet, there were gymkhanas once a month. Our horses always came home covered in ribbons."

"Sounds like you had a great childhood."

Grace grimaced. "I had a very cruel father, and I copped a bit of abuse from him. So, the more time I spent with Diane's family, the better. If we had a free weekend, we would ride for miles. Sometimes as far as Bickley Reservoir or Orange Grove, where they had a lake you were allowed to cool your horse in. We swam, we picnicked, and whenever Diane's family came too, her mum would always make us braised steak and onion jaffles. I loved them. Since I copped it from my father if I was under his feet or if I wasn't there, this was one way I could avoid him."

"Oh, I'm sorry. I didn't realise."

Grace tried to sit up, but exhaustion won, and she flopped back. "I don't often think about those days, but yeah, going to Diane's house most weekends saved me from a lot of pain. I have much to thank her family for."

Erin hadn't stayed too much longer at the hospital. She hated the idea of stirring up old memories that weren't all pleasant. As excited as Grace was about leaving the next day, there was still a long road to recovery, and Erin made a mental note to concentrate on more positive questions.

Grace tired easily, and Erin wanted to use what energy Grace could muster to discover other avenues relating to her health. Hopefully, they would come to light as the weeks progressed. The research needed to centre on her medical journey, but her private life had to fit in there somewhere too. What a person did during their lifetime sometimes contributed to what happened to their health in later years. That's what her study's outcome would determine.

After the interview ended, Erin had returned to the office at the research centre but not before promising Grace a visit to her property that weekend for the long-awaited horseriding lesson.

Now she paced the living room of the plush townhouse she shared with Nicholas. Grace's words about taking control of your life kept spinning in circles around her head. Why couldn't she do what her family wanted? Everyone on her dad's side were doctors. Her father, grandparents and great-grandparents. Not a single broken link. When her mother met her dad shortly after graduating as a doctor, it added to the importance of their heritage. Her brother, James, with his fourth year almost wrapped up despite being two years younger, was the icing on the cake.

Some days it irked her that she didn't conform. Maybe she was a throwback from her mother's side. Except she knew nothing about them.

When Nicholas's car pulled into the garage, she swallowed roughly. The start of a headache lingered in her temple. Could she be strong enough to take a stance? Two years after completing his medical degree, Nicholas was everything her parents idolised in a boyfriend. He fit their mould perfectly.

She glanced nervously at her packed weekend bag sitting by the door. She'd committed to visiting Grace. Now she had to follow through with it.

"Hi." Nicholas dumped his briefcase on the sofa without noticing where she stood and made for the kitchen. He looked a little dishevelled in his rumpled clothes and he often liked a mellow red wine to help unwind, especially on a Friday night.

She should've been dressed by now in the gorgeous jade creation she'd purchased from the best store in Cairns, made for families just like hers. It followed her neat curves and would make her look stunning if her honey-brown hair and make-up were done right. At nearly six in the evening, she was still in jeans with her hair tied back in a ponytail. Her feet were in her most comfortable Crocs—her favourite pair, which irritated Nicholas every time she wore them. *When you're a doctor you have to dress the part. Start practicing now,* was his usual line.

"How was your day?" Standard issue question when you didn't want to know the intricacies, the stresses, the problems. She'd heard them all her life.

When Nicholas turned, his hand froze somewhere near his mouth. His wine glass was half full; he'd already enjoyed a couple of sips. A flash of anger crossed his face as he looked her up and down. "You're not ready. We have to be there in a little over an hour."

Her stomach churned. Why so much foreboding between two people who loved each other? Didn't she? A prickly flush raced across her skin. *What did I just think?* They met in their carefree college days when despondency hadn't attacked her yet. Everything had seemed so right then. Now? She wasn't so sure.

With sudden bravery, she blurted, "I'm sorry to tell you this so late, but I won't be going to the function tonight."

Nicholas slammed the glass down. Wine sloshed over the edge and left an angry red puddle on the marble benchtop. "What the heck is that supposed to mean?"

"I'm driving up to the Tablelands now. I have a commitment tomorrow."

"Bloody hell," he spat, "because of a stupid dog?"

The word 'stupid' hardened her resolve and managed to control the thumping inside her chest.

"You don't think you could've mentioned it yesterday or last week?"

And what? Wear me down until I gave in and agreed to come?

Her back straightened. "I'm sorry, but it's part of my job," she said without flinching. Nothing had been right between them since deciding to take time off from her studies. The work she did with the medical research company didn't interest him, and they were spending less time together.

"Bitch," he spat, striding past and shoving her sideways towards the edge of the door so it dug into her hip.

She winced but bit her tongue and swallowed her cry. It wasn't the first time he'd used his extra weight to inflict a bruise here and there.

Her eyes stung with moisture. She swiped at them and breathed deeply. Her parents, Rosemary and Brian, would agree with Nicholas that she should've told him days ago. She got all that, but if discussed earlier, they would've ground her down until she gave in and lost the argument.

Now she could run away and breathe easier. She liked running away from what was expected of her. She'd been doing it all her life.

Chapter 5

14 Years Old

The slap across her cheek stole her breath away. Grace didn't understand what provoked it. She'd been flogged and tormented by this man many times, but this was different.

"You told me to clean the lounge room. I did it." In fact, she was pleased with her efforts. She wasn't a slacker, and hard work never worried her.

Another slap to her cheek; her head jerked sideways from the force, and this time it set her back a step, her hand automatically coming up to touch the spot that stung. Something had triggered her father, and she was being punished for it.

"I told you to use the vacuum." His face scrunched up in anger as he towered over her.

She was the daughter he never wanted. Two long years ago, she'd come home from winning the poddy race, and he'd been proud of her saddle trophy. Grace glanced past her father and could still see it on the shelf where he'd placed it that glorious afternoon.

She ground her jaw. Things had changed, and she hadn't grasped it, deteriorating little by little. The shock that she only realised now had her senses on full alert. She was not taking this. Not anymore. "You told me to clean the lounge room, and I did." She said through gritted teeth.

"You didn't use the vacuum." His voice bellowed an octave higher. No doubt the neighbours would hear it too. Not that they ever did anything.

She'd cleaned the lounge room no better or worse than what her sister Annette would've, so how it looked wasn't the issue. It was also something their mother usually attended to. Why would her father care how clean it was? No, today it was something else. Grace bravely jutted her chin out and spoke with a firmness that belied her fourteen years. "You told me to clean the lounge," she said in a firm voice, refusing to allow a single quiver to escape.

Smack! He attacked the other side of her face, and this time Grace tasted blood. Her fingers curled tightly inwards, her nails biting into her palms. "You told me to clean the lounge room."

Smack! Again and again, her father's huge palm connected with her face, and in the background, her mother screamed, "Digger, don't. Don't, Digger." She was in too much shock to move an inch to defend herself. Why didn't her mother come and help her? Stand between them. Take the blows. Why was she allowing this to happen to her daughter?

Grace had heard enough times from her father that he regretted she'd been born. She'd closed her heart around that pain a long time ago. But it hurt worse for her mother to stand back and do nothing.

Blood dripped down the side of her face from her nose. She straightened her shoulders and stood as tall as she could, finally ducking away from his swinging arm. She wasn't going to take this treatment anymore. Through the lump in her throat, she said, "You told me to clean the lounge room. I did it." She glared at her father. "Hit me once more, and I'm leaving."

Smack! Hard enough for blood to splatter along her arm and for her to see stars. When her mother appeared by her side to comfort her in her arms, she snapped. Grace shrugged her off and stormed away, her father yelling at her mother getting lost in the daze enshrouding her.

Tears began to fall and mingle with the blood still dripping off her face, but she didn't care. She ran down the passage to her room and shoved some jeans, shirts and underwear into the duffle bag she used when she went to pony club meets and gymkhanas. She could sleep anywhere and wouldn't need much, but she wasn't sleeping another night under this roof.

Unexpected fear threatened to overwhelm her, but she swiped at her face with a towel she'd not hung in the bathroom and attempted to keep it at bay. No way would she cry tears over her father.

Despite her impulsive nature, she slumped onto her bed and took a few deep breaths to calm down and think things through. Her heart pounded inside her chest, which didn't help as she took one last look at her pokey bedroom. Usually kept tidy, there was stuff strewn all over the floor after her hasty scramble for clothes.

Whether they didn't believe her threat to leave or didn't care, neither of her parents appeared before she slammed the front door shut. Once outside, she mentally flicked through her friends from school and pony club, working up the courage to choose which one to approach first.

There wasn't really a choice to make. She already spent most of her weekends with Diane's family. The one best friend she always relied on to go horseriding and compete together. Even though she debated whether their new friend, Jackie and her family, was an option. One look at the mess her father had made of her face, and she doubted neither would turn her away.

⚜

The sudden braking of the bus to Port Hedland caused Grace's head to slump forward, awakening her from her dozy state. Disorientated, she sat up straighter in the seat, unsettled by the memories of what happened three months ago. Diane's family took her in, and she began working at the local grocery store. Whether they'd tired of her or wanted her gone, Diane's parents found her a job on a station in Marble Bar. For that, she was grateful.

The bruises inflicted by her father had long since disappeared, but the emotional hurt only intensified. The police never questioned her father. As a soldier who served in New Guinea, he was heralded a hero. How could a father be cruel to one child when her sister was treated so differently? What had Grace done so wrong in her short fourteen years to make her father hate her so much? Yes, she was cheeky and very stubborn, but how was that bad?

What baffled Grace even more was how an ex-Dominican nun could stand so mute beside her husband and let him do this to their child. But the three years her mother spent training as a nun had brought no spirituality into their household. Grace had no idea who God was.

The only story she remembered her mother telling them was how she'd been made to lie flat on her stomach, reciting the Hail Mary for two hours, after accidentally breaking a teacup. Many times, her mother had bitterly recounted how she'd left the seminary soon after the incident. She never spoke of God anymore.

The red bulldust landscape streaming past her window hadn't changed since falling asleep. The only things she knew about Marble Bar was that it was the hottest place in Australia, and it took a day and a half on the bus to get there. She shuddered at the remoteness and the terrible heat she would need to deal with if the stuffiness inside the bus was anything to go by.

Standing up to slide open the small window above the sealed-in pane, she coughed as a blast of hot air raced into her lungs. Sweat laced the back of her shirt that stuck to her skin. She tugged at it, hoping to create any whiff of breeze, but it didn't make any difference. Plopping back onto her seat, she turned to the middle-aged woman sitting beside her. "Sorry. I thought it might cool things down."

"That's okay, dear. I thought about doing it earlier, but you were sleeping peacefully."

Grace smiled in response and turned back to facing the front, her mind wandering back to the animals she'd be working with instead.

Having never travelled to a working sheep station before, she hoped that being surrounded by horses again would quell any fears of being so far from anyone she knew. If only Liz and her family hadn't recently moved away for work. Things might have turned our different for her.

Leaving behind her precious Sammie, the ex-pacer given to her after losing Megaton, had also been hard. She'd managed to sneak in a goodbye the day before. Her throat thickened, and she swallowed back the unshed tears. She couldn't guarantee Sammie would be properly taken care of or ridden for exercise. Being parted from Sammie was the worst form of punishment imaginable.

Maybe if she were a better kid, her father wouldn't hate her so much, and she would still be living at home and able to spend every afternoon with Sammie. Instead, she'd worked long hours at the grocery store, forced to give up going to school.

She sighed, pushing her short fringe away from her forehead and leant against the warm window, the vibration lulling her eyes closed. Being around horses was the catalyst for accepting the jillaroo job. She'd imposed herself long enough on the good graces of her friend's family, and not being able to ride Sammie every day had hurt more than being banished from her family.

If she could manage the work and the heat, she'd suffer through anything if her job involved riding horses.

❦

Grace wiped her brow with the cuff of her shirt, now grimy with dust and sweat from where she'd constantly wiped it. She pushed the old battered and grubby Akubra hat—which she'd found hanging on a peg outside her sleep-out—lower down her head. Had she swapped one form of abuse for another? As the youngest paid staff at the remote station, they made her do everything and anything. Cleaning water troughs in this heat was surely the idea of a sadist.

Rolf, the property owner, was in deep discussion with another stockman by the feed shed. A rough-speaking German, there was something about how Rolf leered at her that made her skin crawl whenever she caught his gaze.

She made a point of never giving him any excuse to pick on her. Out here, where the possibility of making friends was limited, it was a relief Margi, the station manager's wife, took pity on her and had taken her under her wing like a mother would. She was also friendly with a couple of the Aboriginal jackeroos and often rode together.

In the afternoon heat, Grace emptied bucket after bucket of water out of the troughs that needed cleaning, cleaned them as she was told with the particular curved brush, and did her job well.

"Hey, Grace, we need you to do some dirty work."

Grace didn't miss the double meaning from her boss, and she tried to hide the shudder when Rolf flicked his gaze up and down her body, lingering on her chest and hips.

"Do you want me to finish this trough?" Maintaining her composure, she stood up tall. Her sudden growth spurt had her at nearly eye level with Rolf even though she was still flat-chested and far from looking like a woman. Dressed in loose jeans and a hand-me-down pair of brown work boots, she looked like a gangly teenage boy. The old Akubra finished the picture off perfectly.

"Get in"—he pointed over his shoulder to the rust-eaten ute—"and we'll drive out to the dam on the west side. A couple of sheep are stuck in the receding water."

Grace's heart pumped painfully. She grabbed her water bottle, an old cordial bottle, and headed towards the ute. Sheep stuck in the dam meant a lot of mud to wade through. She'd do that until the day she died rather than be left alone with Rolf so far from the homestead. When Edgar, one of the friendly Aboriginal jackeroos, got in too, relief swamped her tired limbs, and she nearly fainted. The heat would've been blamed for it if it had happened, but Grace knew better.

Okay, I can do a bit of sheep retrieval. Another dirty job she was accustomed to, but it was all worth it. Out here, she had free rein to ride the horses whenever there was spare time, and she was riding every day. Life was manageable if she kept away from Rolf.

⁕

"So, do you have a nice dress to wear to the dance?" Margi asked, looking her up and down from the steps of the small cottage she shared with her husband. Grace smiled cheekily. "What, can't I go in jeans?"

"Darling, the Coongan Races are the biggest thing out here. I take it that's a no?"

Grace nodded, not really worried. She was planning on going for the racing and the novelty events. Dancing hadn't been an option.

"You're taller than me, but I'll find you something."

Grace's eyebrows shot up. "Really?"

"You're a very attractive young lady," Margi said. "I bet your mum didn't get a chance to teach you how to shave your legs either?"

Grace twisted her mouth in a wry grimace. There were a lot of things her mother hadn't taught her.

"Let's go to the water trough in the backyard. We'll have you shaved and looking your best within the hour. There's a trick to how you run the razor up your leg. Think you can manage it?"

Grace laughed at her lighthearted teasing. Despite the heat pressing down on her every day, Margi and her stationmaster husband, John made her laugh often when only the presence of a horse could usually manage such a thing.

Grace peered down at the length of her legs. They were long. Longer than most women she encountered. She doubted an hour would be enough time, but she was game enough to try. She had the weekend off as everyone within a five-hundred-kilometre radius prepared to drive to the races. It was the biggest event on the social calendar when heat, drought and hard-working days meant little time for social pleasure. "Okay, thanks, Margi. And I'd love to borrow something to wear."

"Done. I have plenty of old dresses hanging in my cupboard, and they need to be worn occasionally ... if only we had enough places to wear them."

Margi chuckled, making Grace curious about how a normal mother-daughter relationship would be. Margi's kids were long gone and living their own lives. She had a handful of them scattered far and wide. Grace had only met one son and his wife when they called in to visit a couple of weeks ago. But Marble Bar wasn't the place you'd choose to drop by. By all accounts, there were more arriving for the Coongan Races, hence Margi's infectious excitement about the coming weekend.

Grace was yet to receive a single letter from her family, and they all knew where she'd gone. Her mother loved to write letters, so why the silence? Would she have preferred Grace to be home to cop more abuse from her father?

Margi was a breath of fresh air, and Grace absorbed everything this woman taught her. She vowed to be different if she ever had a daughter.

Chapter 6

Grace checked the studs were done up on her borrowed pressed-stud shirt before shoving more newspaper inside her boots. They were her first ever riding boots, even if they were a little big for her slim foot. She'd never been so proud of owning something before. Margi had given her some boot polish, and they outshone the hot Marble Bar sun, if that was possible.

The rodeo and novelty events were in full swing at Coongan, and she was up next in the novice barrel racing. Hugging the matted brown station horse to her chest, she smiled. She was in her happy place. He was her favourite horse since arriving at the station. A natural connection had developed between them, and she always picked him over the others. On his back, she was just the passenger, he the motor. She spent every spare moment allowed fine-tuning their skill and speed together.

They'd done this cloverleaf pattern of barrels a hundred times before. This horse was agile and fast, and she planned on getting a darn good time without knocking over any of them.

All the pony clubs and local rodeos had never dampened her enthusiasm to compete. Its compelling lure continued to drive her to do her best. There weren't always a lot of females competing, but it never stopped Grace from wanting to do more and more.

As long as she didn't hurt herself or get sick. The thought always sat quietly in the back of her mind because she'd been in and out of hospitals as a kid. They were mustering five to ten thousand-acre paddocks in a few weeks' time, and she didn't want to miss any of the action.

She looked up when the horse whinnied near her face. "Shush. We're nearly on. You ready to fly around this course?" They spoke in their own language, and the horse pressed his muzzle against her cheek.

Closing her eyes and resting her face against the horse's muzzle, she recalled that day as a small child being stuck in the hospital. Looking out the window, she had spotted a horse in a nearby paddock. She never forgot her resolve to get better, so she could be near horses.

There was nothing ailing her today, and her heart pumped joyfully in her chest with the usual adrenalin rush she experienced before events. She was doing everything she had promised to her young self. Despite never being given a diagnosis as to why she got sick sometimes, life wasn't bad when she could ride a horse. In a few minutes, she'd be doing just that, and for this reason alone, she didn't mind the blistering sun beating down on her.

Grace steadied her horse as she leant forward to whisper in his ear, letting her soothing tones calm him. The crowd was especially loud that day, and she didn't want him spooked. Within seconds, her time would start, and then there'd be just her and her horse doing their stuff.

When the hooter sounded, time stilled for Grace. Everything happened in captured time frames. Graceful swings and sudden turns, the rise and sway of the horse's movements as it traversed the tricky course. Grace likened it to opera, no different from the music Margi occasionally played from her living quarters. The horse knew what to do, just needing the slightest touch or pressure from Grace. Not a single barrel was knocked down, not a single second wasted. When she completed the course and the crowd showed their appreciation by clapping and shouting, Grace steadied the horse, giving herself a moment to catch her breath. Only then did the calm of confidence settle over her, knowing she'd done her best.

"Grace Lucas, is that you?"

Grace was leading the horse away from the arena towards the temporary stables when her name was called out. She turned in the voice's direction.

"Larry?" A small part of home was in this god-forsaken place. Having just been told her time wasn't the best for the day, she was doing her utmost not to let it sting. The sight of Larry was almost her undoing.

"What's up, squirt? I knew you were somewhere in these parts. When I heard them call your name, I couldn't believe it. That ride was pretty bloody special."

Grace let the disappointment of her time show. "It wasn't the fastest time, though."

Larry put his arm around her shoulders and squeezed her. "Do you have any idea who you were up against? I think every single one of them is older than you, with a hell of a lot more experience. I'd say you did pretty amazing."

"If you say so. I'm still not happy, though."

Larry chuckled, the familiar sound helping her feel better. "Let me guess. The old Grace I know hasn't changed a bit. Always determined to beat the field, stubborn, and pigheaded enough to keep trying until she did."

Grace elbowed him in the ribs, trying not to laugh at the description he drew of her. It was close to spot on. She was never satisfied with second place. In fact, she'd never be happy until she could compete in any event in the rodeo and female be damned.

"Thanks, Larry. It's good to have a familiar face here. It's so far away from home."

Larry grimaced. No doubt he'd heard the story about why she left her family. She'd broken down to Liz one day and wouldn't be surprised if Liz had suggested Larry look her up.

"Are you going to the dance tonight?"

Grace's eyes lit up. "I sure am." The dress Margi loaned her made her look so feminine. For someone who lived in jeans and long-sleeved shirts, this would be her first time wearing a dress in years. With her hair longer than how she usually wore it and with newly shaved legs, she was ready to dance.

"Good. I'll keep an eye on ya. As your official older brother here, I'll call it my duty to keep all those boys away from you. No getting up to any mischief tonight either."

She sniggered at the tone Larry had taken on. She didn't mind one bit. "I can't. I want to race tomorrow, and I'm going to win."

Larry shook his head. "Of course, why else would you want to race? Is this the lucky fellow who's going to join you?"

Grace tugged on the lead rope and continued to walk towards the stables. "He sure is. He's the best I've raced in a long time."

Larry followed by her side. "Let me help you with him, and then I'll buy you some food. Are you hungry?"

Grace rolled her eyes and grinned her hardest. "I could eat a horse." Her disappointment had taken a back seat. She was with an old friend and wasn't surprised when he laughed at her joke. Grace's appetite was legendary around Liz and her family. There'd been occasions when Grace had eaten more than Liz's three boys had at the dinner table. Unlike her family, the more she ate, the happier Liz was.

Her active lifestyle made it a full-time job filling up all the spaces her nonstop growth spurt created, and Larry knew this. So, she'd feast alongside Larry and have the time of her life. She hadn't realised how lonely her time at Marble Bar was. For Grace, being around horses was always enough. But when someone like Larry turned up unexpectedly, it brightened her day and made her appreciate that special people were important too. Whether Liz suggested he look her up or not, it didn't matter. He was a familiar face to share the weekend with, and she hugged the thought close.

⁓

Larry hadn't joked and followed her every move at the dance the previous night, sending her back to her camping quarters and bed well before midnight.

"You're only fourteen, young lady. Time for bed."

She'd done her usual scowl, confident it wouldn't end in a beating. She'd danced with no one in particular but had clowned around with kids her age and danced in groups to the music of Dolly Parton and Johnny Cash.

Grateful for Larry's intervention and refreshed from a good sleep and a breakfast of bacon and eggs, Grace sat upon her mount and eyed the straight race track before her, the steady breeze stirring up the red bulldust. There were no starting cages here; instead, a line had been drawn in the dust to show where they began. She swiped once more across her brow. Boy, it was hot, with nowhere for the midday sun to hide.

Other riders jostled into position, the announcer raising his voice to be heard. Crowds lined the dirty brown rail running the length of the track, and Grace didn't doubt the punters were spending their money quickly before the race started. She was now a lot savvier to many things in life that other fourteen-year-olds would never be exposed to.

Grace looked neither left nor right but spent the precious seconds before the race soothing her horse. No one asked her name or age. It was simply an open event for any takers. Grace never let an opportunity pass her by, especially when age and sex demanded she didn't compete. Dressed up as she was, she easily passed as a young stockman. Grace smiled. *All the better.*

When the starter's hooter sounded, Grace climbed inside her own bubble where only she and the horse existed. Her supple body moved in time with the horse's racing strides, and Grace almost whooped for joy when she realised she was leading the pack of racers. A shadow fell across her periphery, startling her. Reacting to the sudden movement, Grace snuck a look to her right as the rider kicked her horse in the flank.

The secure bubble exploded. She was flying in the air as her horse continued to gallop without her. The last thing she recalled was hitting the dirt hard. Someone—maybe it was her—screamed in pain.

Grace slowly came to and winced as her body jolted. She tried to stretch her legs, but a wall of some sort stopped them. "Where am I?" she croaked.

A hand, then a cool cloth, pressed her temple. Its immediate effect was a balm to the pain running riot. "Shh, honey. I'm Jenny and a nurse. We're driving to Port Hedland to get you seen to."

Ah, that made sense. She was in the back seat of a car as it bumped along the road, her head resting on the nurse's lap and pounding. With a nurse sitting beside her and stroking her hair, tears welled. She was in safe hands, even if her knees were squashed up against her chest.

"And before you ask," the nurse growled, "the pilot was too damn drunk to fly. Sorry honey, it's not the most comfortable ride, but we'll get you there."

It hurt too much to nod, so she gave up.

Consciousness came and went, along with sips of water, waves of nausea and the ever-present gentle touches of the nurse. At one point, when she was feeling more lucid, the memory of how she came off the horse flashed before her. Anger boiled in her veins. She was winning that race; damn him to hell. She had nearly reached the finish line. But it was too late now, and she was exhausted. Her legs ached from being curled in the back seat, and every bump sent pain through her body.

Feeling slightly better and grateful for the caring nurse and knowing she wouldn't be flogged by her father, she relaxed her exhausted body and willed herself to sleep.

After a few minutes, she realised it wasn't going to happen. She kept thinking of the rider kicking the flank of her horse, trying to picture his face. Grace understood the desire to win; it ran strong in her too. But to cheat? To risk the safety of a rider and horse?

"Did anyone see what happened?" She asked.

"I don't know, honey. I wasn't watching the race."

"What about my horse? Was Edgar or John looking after it?"

"Shh, I'm sure they are. Don't worry about it for now."

Her chest ached as she worried about her horse. As far as she could remember, she'd only been thrown off. So hopefully, the horse hadn't stumbled.

With her concern under control for the time being, she took a painful sigh, closed her eyes and tried to relax. It was another life lesson to learn: not everyone competed fairly and honestly if they could get away with it. It wasn't the first time she had been exposed to this behaviour. She made a silent vow to herself before slipping back into oblivion—one day, she would ride again and win if it was the last thing she did.

Chapter 7

Present Day

Erin spotted the sign for the road, its words covered in thick lichen, the letters beginning to fade. Her instructions were to follow the narrow drive for about one kilometre until she reached a gate with stencilled horses on it. Grace had reminded her to close the gate after so the horses didn't stray.

She drove up the steep incline, doing her best to dodge the potholes on the gravelled road. Her Honda Civic had never been off-road before, so this was a new experience for her car, too. She smiled at the way she treated her car as if it had feelings and patted the dash as the gate came into view.

She braked and left the car running while she went to untangle the intricate looped chain before dragging the gate back against the fence. Once she was safely past, she hopped out again to close it. The sprawling homestead was only a hundred metres away at the end of the gravel driveway, placed neatly on an open green paddock with small shrubbery dotted around it. Busy gardens bordered the house and vibrant colours greeted her arrival.

When three horses meandered towards her and started sniffing at the Honda, she pulled back the speed, worried she might hurt them.

The horses towered over her little car, and she gulped. *And I agreed to climb on top of one of them?* Maybe she should've gone to the function last night after all? Suddenly, she wasn't so sure about this idea. Her parent's numerous messages had continued to beep on her phone until she switched it off just before leaving her grandparent's place. As the car crawled forward, she shrugged. There was plenty of time to listen to their tirades of disappointment in the coming days. As for Nicholas ...

Once the car was parked near the homestead, she turned off the ignition. Her hand drifted down to her hip, rubbing the tender spot which now sported the beginnings of a bruise the size of her fist. She'd think about him later, too.

Attempting to dismiss Nicholas from her thoughts, she reached the back seat and grabbed the muffins she'd cooked that morning. Her grandmother's home was the only place where she succumbed to her passion for cooking sweets. Nothing thrilled her more than losing herself in making something sweet and pretty.

Her mother had always been too busy to cook. Birthday cakes were always ordered from a bakery or cake shop. Only since her grandmother's retirement had someone with time on their hands shown her the ropes around a kitchen. And all in the past six months. Talk about a turning point in her life. A long-awaited pet and a desire she never knew she had were all coming to fruition. What else was around the corner?

She held the vintage Tupperware container—with no lid as the muffins were too high—and stepped out of the car, pushing the door closed with her butt. A horse appeared from behind her shoulder and swooped down to the muffins.

She gasped. "Hey, no, these aren't for you."

Erin backtracked, waving the horse away with her free hand. "Shoo, shoo," she said, eyeing the front patio and the knee-high fence which looked a thousand metres away. Another massive, chocolate-coloured horse with white patches sidled up to her other side, nudging her hand with its nose and demanding the muffins. "No. Get back, you two," she hissed, spinning around, fingers trembling. "Where is everyone?" She tried to step towards the blue ute parked near a stable with a veterinary service logo on its side, but the first horse blocked her path.

As terrified as she was of the giant animals looming over her, she laughed. A big belly laugh. What a comical sight this would be to anyone watching. It wasn't long before her laughter caught the attention of someone. A man poked his face around the corner of the stable and headed in her direction.

His smile was the first thing to disarm her when dimples appeared out of nowhere. "Hey." Removing an arm-length plastic glove from one hand, he manoeuvred himself between the horses and reached for a handshake. "You must be the med student doing some research on Grace?"

She took his hand in hers, its warmth surrounding her. "Yes, I am." Erin looked over his shoulder and took a step back when a third horse trotted over and started nibbling on the young man's collar.

She choked with laughter again. Three horses, two humans and many, many hooves on the end of long legs which risked trampling her delicate feet.

"What a laugh," he said, chuckling along with her.

His gaze caught hers and held. She'd been told before that her laughter turned heads. It wasn't something she did on purpose. When it happened, it was as natural as breathing. The way his gaze landed softly on her felt like another compliment.

"Tom, by the way," he said, gently pushing the horses away. "C'mon, you lot, get out of here."

"I'm Erin. Nice to meet you." They started walking towards the house, the horses following. Maybe she should've brought carrots instead. "Do ... do you work for Grace?"

He shook his head. "I moved up north a couple of months ago and work for the local vet. Grace is a terrific lady, and I've been doing a bit extra for her on the weekends."

"Oh, okay, well, nice meeting you. I'm sure Grace is waiting for me inside. I hope she's feeling well enough today."

"Well, that's just it." Tom ran a hand through his scruffy light-brown hair. "When she knew I was coming over to give her horses their monthly injections, she asked if I could hang around. She's not feeling the best and is still in bed. She asked if I had time to give you some beginner riding lessons."

Erin's heart began to beat erratically, and a tingling heat crept up her neck. Grace had mentioned that her husband would be happy to help hoist her on the horse, but she hadn't pictured anyone else being around.

"Ah ... that's not necessary. I don't want to hold you up from your weekend. You must have a thousand other things to do. I can always come back another day."

Awkward silence punctuated the air when Tom continued to look at her, vivid green eyes staring and assessing her. He cleared his throat and thrust a hand in the pocket of his jeans.

"I tell you what. How about you go inside and put the kettle on? I'm sure you'll find your way around Grace's kitchen. We'll all enjoy a break and then a horseriding lesson. I'm only new to the area, so I haven't met many people yet. Today I have a bit of time on my hands."

"But—"

"I'm doing Grace a favour. She mentioned you were keen, and I'm happy to help if ... ah ..."

Huh?

"... if you're happy to share that cooking. No wonder these brutes want one too. They look delicious, and I'm starving."

He turned and wrapped his arms around one of the horses and mock play-fought with it. The horse whinnied back at him and cantered off towards the paddock. Tom patted the others gently on their rumps, and they followed too.

Erin stood, her mouth agape. How did he do that? Within a matter of seconds, it was only her and Tom.

"That's all you need to do for them to leave," Tom said with a smile that reached the corner of his eyes. "Now I don't have to share the muffins with them."

She burst out laughing again as he turned her around and pointed to the door leading to the kitchen. He muttered, "That laugh is something," and a tingle of excitement crept along her arms and a silly grin spread across her face.

From the first step inside the richly timbered homestead, Erin forgot about finding the kettle. She was struck instead by the horse paraphernalia the home contained. Her steps led her past the kitchen and into the vast living room, where she inspected many horse-related items.

Everyone had an interest or a hobby, but as kids, they usually outgrew them. Grace hadn't outgrown this passion. When she'd told Erin that horses were special to her, she hadn't said it lightly. The rug on the floor had horses on it. The shelves carried all manner of horse-related knickknacks. There were trophies, framed photos of Grace with different horses, show jumping events, and—a photo caught her attention. The image was a little grainy, and she couldn't tell who it was, except whoever it was, was on the back of a bull—not a horse. Maybe it was her husband?

Erin was startled and turned when a voice called from the bedroom.

"Erin, is that you?"

She'd never walked into some stranger's house and felt so comfortable before. Like she wanted to sink into the comfortable-looking dark couch and put her feet up. This wasn't some sterile home. It was filled with things and love, and it showed in every nook and cranny. "Yes, I'm coming."

Erin navigated the hallway and passed various closed doors, keeping her ears tuned to Grace's voice she could still hear. Entering the bedroom, she found Grace sitting up in her bed, still in her pyjamas, looking tired. She smiled, despite her pale and drawn face.

"I'm sorry, Erin. I overdid it yesterday." She looked towards the man in the room, standing in front of the expansive windows overlooking the lush garden, and made the introductions. "This is my husband, Peter. He has an errand to do today, so I've asked Tom to give me a hand. You don't mind, do you?"

Peter shook her hand, kissed Grace on her cheek, and then left them. "No, no, of course not. As long as I'm not putting anyone out."

"Tom said he didn't mind; otherwise, I would've sent him on his way if he was busy."

"Oh, thanks. Now, I've brought some muffins; they're in the kitchen. Tom said you'd enjoy a cuppa with them."

"He's a good lad, and I certainly would. Why don't you bring it in here and join me?"

Erin looked around the spacious bedroom and out the window overlooking the green, rolling hills. In the short distance was an expanse of forest that surrounded the famous Lake Eacham.

"It won't tire you?"

"No, of course not. It's my own fault. I got Peter to take me to the lake yesterday, and I insisted on kicking 300 metres with flippers on."

Erin's eyes widened in shock.

"Yeah, crazy, I know, but I wanted to give my core and legs a good workout. All I need is a couple of days of rest." She smiled wistfully. "And then I'll do it again."

"Are you sure you should?"

"Absolutely. Lying around won't fix me."

Erin looked at this aging woman whose body had been to hell and back but didn't see an invalid. What she *could* see, she wasn't so sure of. "Right, that cup of tea. I won't be a moment."

She walked from the bedroom and slowed her steps again as she took in all the horse-related trinkets, trophies and ribbons placed around the house. When she reached the kitchen, Tom was there with the kettle in hand.

He filled it, plugged it in, and then turned to look at her. It lent warmth to the good feelings she was experiencing just being in the house. Studying the image on the horse calendar on the fridge, she said, "She sure loves horses." Inwardly, she rolled her eyes. What a complete goose stating the obvious.

Tom chuckled. "She's an amazing woman. Remarkable, in fact."

Erin fumbled with the first cupboard door. Looking for mugs, she found them behind the third one. "Why do you say that?"

"You don't know what she's achieved in her life?"

She straightened with three mugs tangled in her fingers. "No, I don't. I've only been told to concentrate on her health, and we only met a couple of weeks ago."

Tom's lips turned up at the edges. "Then I suppose you'll have to ask her."

"Okay. I will. If I pick up one trophy, ribbon or photo at a time, I'll ask her to talk about it when we're not doing official research stuff."

Tom took the mugs from her and set them on the bench. "That's a good idea. Now, what are you drinking?"

"White tea, thanks, with one sugar."

As Tom busied himself, Erin studied him. She licked her dry lips when it registered that she liked what she saw. He towered over her, his shoulders straining the long-sleeved blue shirt. With dimples to distract, his face spoke of strength and boldness with the odd freckle smattered on his lean cheeks. She itched to touch them.

"Good luck with getting your research done. She has a thousand stories to tell." Tom turned around, and she flicked her gaze away from his face, down his torso towards the mugs.

"Thanks. I'll keep that in mind." Picking up a mug, she added, "You go ahead. I'm going to choose something on the way. Can you manage the muffin container too?"

Tom nodded and left the kitchen. Erin stopped in the living room and took a moment to look about. She spotted a bright red ribbon curled around a mantle clock that didn't appear to be working. She picked the ribbon up, stirring some dust. In bold white print, it had 'Biloela Show 2009 – 2nd Place' on it. *This'll do for starters.*

Tom had already eaten a couple of muffins by the time she got back to the bedroom, and his mug was empty. He hovered by the door. "Thanks, Erin, they were delicious. I've got to go back to the stables and finish before I ready the horses for riding."

Honestly, he'd taken five seconds flat to eat two of her muffins, and she loved that someone enjoyed her cooking. It buoyed her flagging spirits. She was in enough trouble for choosing horseriding over a medical function.

When he was gone, Grace pointed to the comfortable-looking armchair beside the bed and reached for a muffin. Erin made herself comfortable and sipped her tea.

"What's that you have in your hand?" Grace asked through a mouthful of muffin. "These are delicious, by the way."

"A ribbon. I'm guessing you rode in show events?"

"Which show is it from?".

Erin straightened it on the blanket that covered Grace.

"Oh, the Biloela Show. Lots of wonderful memories there. I used to compete around the Brisbane area for a few months, then follow the show run out to Roma and up the central highlands. One year I did the show run from Rockhampton to Cairns, picking up places in the D and C grade jumping and six-bar jumping."

"That's a long time away from home?"

"Oh, you know, so many good times and funny stories with some fantastic friends that it didn't matter how long you were away from home. Showjumping sort of happened by accident."

Grace took a couple of sips of her tea and another mouthful of the muffin before continuing. "It started when I bought a grey gelding called Uncrowned King. I didn't like its name, so I changed it to 'I'm A Skite', because its sire's name was 'Bit of A Skite'."

Erin chuckled, saving a muffin crumb from falling on the floor.

"Yeah, you can have so much fun naming a horse. Anyway, he had a natural jumping ability, so I enrolled in showjumping lessons with this fellow called Guy Creighton whenever the club got him up our way to do teaching schools."

Erin touched the ribbon again. "Second place is pretty special."

"I won and placed in many events over the years. My best with I'm A Skite was at the Tully show when he cleared 1.67 metres. God, I loved that horse. He had a great temperament, but I had another beauty I'll never forget."

"What was its name?"

"Rosez, Pearl of a Girl. I was so lucky to breed and own that beautiful mare, and not a day went by that I didn't appreciate her."

Grace put her finished mug down and sat back. "It was at the Biloela Show that I remember how remarkable Rosez was. We were in a D-grade grand prix, and I cleared the first round. But during the second round, I got in front of her movement."

"What does that mean?" Erin asked, wrapping her hands around the warm mug.

"I left the saddle before Rosez left the ground. I had an unforgiving saddle, and the minute I did something wrong, it hit me in the behind and spat me over the front."

"Ugh, that sounds painful."

Grace chuckled. "It could've happened that way, but instead, I landed six inches in front of the saddle. Rosez kept cantering and put her head down. I slipped back down her neck because I was up around her ears somewhere."

"You're lucky you managed to stay on."

"Trust me, I didn't want to hit the ground. Not only would it mean elimination, but at my age, there's no bounce, just a splat effect and then it hurts."

Erin cringed. "Falling off doesn't sound like fun."

"No, it's not, but there's more to come. Unfortunately, as I pushed back into the saddle, the bridle slipped over her right ear. I saw this but thought we could still do it, so I clicked her on towards the last fence, which was a treble. Wazza, an old mate, called out to me that I'd lost my bridle. I knew this, but at that stage, I was using voice encouragement, saying, 'come on, Rosez, come on'. When she jumped the first log fence, the bridle hit her in the chest. After jumping the second verticle, she stopped without losing forward motion. I was still saying, 'come on, darling, come on,' and then she chipped two tiny strides, ballooning the last fence. Four final strides and she was past the finish flags."

Erin's brow wrinkled. *Ballooning?* She didn't understand the technical terms Grace had used, but she got the gist of what'd happened.

"I couldn't believe my five-year-old mare had tried so hard. All I had to do was keep riding, and she kept jumping."

Grace picked up the ribbon and studied it. She looked lost in her memories, so Erin settled back in the armchair and didn't disturb her. Instead, her thoughts wandered over to where Tom was readying the horses. Unexpected nerves swirled in her stomach, and she pressed her hands there to quell them.

"What about you, Erin? What interesting stuff have you done with your life so far?"

Erin looked up, startled for a moment. "Ah ... my life's not that interesting. All I've achieved is a botched attempt at completing a medical degree and—"

Graced waited as though giving her time to sort out her thoughts.

"And ... you know what? I'm not so sure about it anymore."

Finally! She'd aired something which had been disturbing her for a while. With her heart beating that little bit faster, Erin squirmed in her seat. Was Grace going to pry some more? Was she going to reveal some home truths she'd kept buried for quite some time?

⁂

"You're not going to let go, are you?" Erin sat atop Grace's horse. Her heart sent vibrations thundering inside her chest.

Tom held the reins and stroked Eve's nose. "She's not going anywhere unless we tell her to. Try to relax because she'll sense if you're not."

"*You* try relaxing when you're three stories off the ground," she cut in. "This is so high up."

Tom chuckled as he walked to the side of the horse. "Hold the rein like this." He placed the smooth leather into her hand and curled her fingers around it. "And gently pull back. This'll tell the horse to stand still. We're not going to do much more than some simple walk and stop commands. You can do this around the enclosed yard. We'll leave the cantering for next time."

Erin's fingers tingled where he'd touched. There was so much thumping, thundering and tingling in her body; no wonder her emotions were scattered everywhere.

Tom brushed up against her legs. "I'll adjust the stirrups; give me a sec."

She looked down at Tom from her dizzying height and possibly swayed a bit. A hot flush travelled up her neck when his hands rested on her leg and then ankle. *Horseriding, girl, concentrate!* But her awareness of him only increased tenfold when he moved to her other side to adjust the other stirrup.

"How does that feel?" Tom was looking at her expectantly and with his dimples on full display. "Extra points if you answer with that special laugh of yours."

"Sorry, but I'm not feeling any laughter vibes at the moment." Her stomach tensed, riddled with nerves.

"You will soon," Tom coaxed. "We'll have you smiling and laughing in no time at all. Now ... get Eve to take a few steps before you pull back on the reins, and then repeat. Think you can manage that?"

"I'm not sure if my arms will move."

"Not even one walk and stop command?"

Did the frown on his brow mean she was a lost cause? What was wrong with her? Her childhood dream was coming true, and she was not coping?

"Here, I tell you what I'm going to do. I'll climb up behind you, and we'll go for a short walk to ease you in."

Behind me? He's joking, isn't he?

Before she could splutter a response, Tom removed her foot from the stirrup and replaced it with his.

"Scuse me," he said with a lopsided smile as he hoisted himself over in a smooth motion and nestled Erin against his chest. A hint of earthy male aftershave wafted past her nose. Her skin tingled at his closeness and her body was now responding to more than the fear of getting the animal to move.

"I want you to loosen the reins and do this." He placed his hands on hers, and she noted his actions as Eve started to walk. "Now, pull like this, and she'll stop. You can also squeeze your thighs, clip your heels or click your tongue. They'll all work to encourage a horse to walk. Here, you have a go."

She did as Tom instructed, over and over, and after about twenty minutes, the tension in her shoulders had eased, and she settled back in the saddle. All she had to do was walk five metres and then stop. On repeat. She was getting the hang of this.

"Now talk to her. Let her know you're enjoying this."

A shiver went up Erin's spine when Tom whispered near her ear. She'd almost forgotten he was behind her, so engrossed in her walk and stop commands. "What do I talk about?" she asked, breathing in deeply and feeling more relaxed as she inhaled the familiar smells of horse and human which circled her.

"It doesn't matter, as long as it's soothing and calm."

Right! Soothing and calm. She could do this. Actually, she was enjoying this premature control she had over the horse. "Ah ... hello, Eve. It's um ... me, Erin here."

"How long have you wanted to ride for?" Tom prompted.

"Ever since I was a girl."

"Talk to the horse, Erin, not me."

"Oh, bloody hell," she spluttered, and only then did she laugh. Tom stiffened behind her.

"I think you're relaxed enough now." He slid off and ran his hand along Eve's neck. "Let's have you do some walk and stop commands on your own."

Erin gulped but straightened. Why was she suddenly missing the warmth behind her back? With some trepidation, she took control of the reins and circled Eve around the small fenced yard, aware that Tom's gaze never left her.

Within a few minutes, the strangest thing happened. She didn't feel so far off the ground anymore. With Tom only metres away, she spoke freely to Eve and expressed her joy at being allowed to ride her. She even reached down to her neck and rubbed like she'd seen Tom do.

Exhilaration spread through her limbs. She was actually on a horse and riding. *Woohoo*, she wanted to shout. There was also one very hot and good-looking vet helping her, but she had to plug that thought fast.

A wide smile spread across her face as she directed Eve towards Tom.

"Feels good, doesn't it?" Tom took the reins and patted Eve on the neck.

"It does. Thank you for taking the time out today."

"Let me help you down first before you thank me."

Standing beside the horse, Tom reached up and secured his hands on either side of her chest, showing her how to slide off and which foot to land on first. Heat rushed up her neck at the intimate way he held her. When she was on the ground, she spun around to thank him again and nearly collided with his chest. She muttered a quick thank you.

He took a rapid step back. "Any time, Erin. I enjoyed it too."

Her breathing was shallow, and it was only when Tom patted Eve on the rump and she trotted off that Erin could step back further and breathe again. "Um ... thanks again, Tom. I better say goodbye to Grace and make tracks to leave. Do you need a hand unsaddling her?"

"I'll teach you how to do that in your next lesson."

"Ah ... right." She nodded and raised her hand in a poor attempt at a wave.

So, there was going to be a next time?

Chapter 8

Nearly 15 Years Old

"You did good, Grace."

Grace rolled her sore shoulders and smiled at Edgar, who hadn't left her side these past weeks. A few years older than herself, he'd taught her so much. Her instructions from John had been to stick by his side. Leaning on her broom, she gave herself a moment to appreciate that she *had* done good. Having never worked so physically hard before, in her books, she'd grown-up and all without the help of her family.

Being able to handle the work and heat was enough of a challenge. If you didn't drink enough water, you'd faint within minutes. She'd come close a couple of times, and for some reassurance, she leant the broom against the door and walked across the shed to her water bottle. She guzzled a good bit of what remained, satisfied it'd get her to the end of the afternoon.

Edgar was an excellent horseman, and it didn't take long for her competitive nature to shine through. She'd often egged him to race her across a paddock when they should've been concentrating on the muster, leaving him laughing at her antics.

This gentle man, who lived on the station in a separate mission camp with his family, calmed her. Grace had been to their camp twice with Edgar, shouldering the weight of carrying meat, flour, sugar and tea.

Escaping to the muster was what she'd needed. It'd taken her most of the week after the Coongan Races to recover from her fall. If it hadn't been for Margi's insistence, Rolf would've had her cleaning the shearing sheds before the muster. After a few days, her headaches disappeared, and by the time the mustering started, she was her usual self again.

Being able to ride for such long hours every day buoyed her spirits and dampened the disappointment of not winning that race.

The stockmen on their motorbikes did the river paddocks first, doing the woolly muster initially for all those sheep that evaded a couple of shears. The remaining stockmen then concentrated on the main paddocks, moving the herd from the far left and far right, pushing them together. Gradually, the sheep were funnelled into one large herd and driven towards the homestead.

She smiled, remembering how some sheep got an easy ride. If they fell in the oppressive heat and didn't want to budge, a stockman would hoist it up on his motorbike and carry it home.

"Come on, you lot. I don't pay you to stand around and talk. This shed needs to be swept up. The shearing's over for this year, so get a move on."

Grace ground her jaw. Rolf walked in on the very moment she was doing nothing. A first since the muster began. Where was John? He was a pleasure to work around. Being in Rolf's presence left her unsure of many things she didn't understand. While Edgar had been raised in a different world, she sensed he could read her thoughts and would often turn up by her side when she needed someone. For that, she was grateful, so she threw Edgar a lopsided smile and picked up her broom.

One day, she'd like to try shearing, she mused as she worked the broom from one end of the shearing shed towards the open doors at the other end. She inhaled a lung full of the unique oily smell of a shearing shed, having enjoyed the hustle and bustle of the shearers and the whizzing of their machines. They were all friendly to her and she'd snuck as much time as she could watching the skilled shearers in between sweeping the wool scraps and penning the sheep. The first time the shearer's blade skimmed a strip along the sheep's belly and then removed the entire fleece in one piece like a piece of art left her spellbound. She had a lot to learn. Meal breaks were the other good times. Shearers laughed and joked, and ate plenty of food cooked and prepared by Margi and her helpers.

She rolled her shoulders to ease the pain, knowing very well why they hurt so much. Hours on the end of a broom only added to it. For once, she wouldn't complain when it was time for bed. For someone so young and inexperienced, she'd been darn good at throwing a fleece, and the older stockmen told her repeatedly.

Once the shearing began, her chores involved penning the sheep near each shearer, picking up the fleece from the board where the shearer left it after completing a shear and throwing it onto the table—this required skill and strength. Being young and with lots of energy, she was the quickest to walk around the fleece, pulling off the edges of any dirty wool, leaving the wool classer to decide on its quality and which bale it would go into.

The days rushed by, but it was a relief when the last piece of shorn wool was lifted onto the classer's bench. She wasn't experienced at classifying the quality of the wool, but she reckoned she'd have a much better idea by next year's muster.

She looked down at the pile of woolly debris she was gathering with her broom. Very little was wasted. Even the scrappy stuff was baled separately and sold as lesser quality wool. Only dust remained in the shearer's shed and a few scraps of stray wool. They'd done good at this year's muster, and she was excited about the next one.

⁕

After another day of riding and checking fences with Edgar, Grace put the saddle away in the tack room, brushed down her horse and topped up its feed and water. She used the sleeve of her shirt to wipe her brow, smearing more sweat. Often they raced each other back to the stables, and being able to laugh into the breeze restored her energy and sense of purpose. The heat had a way of oppressing the very goodness of life.

She turned with a smile on her face at the familiar yelp of Rolf's dog, a Doberman Pinscher. He'd taken to her from the day she'd arrived, and she never missed an opportunity to take time out with the homestead pet. Never hearing its name, she adopted the generic one 'Dog', which worked well enough. A thick stick was firmly wedged in his jaw, and he politely dropped it at Grace's feet.

"So, it's like that, is it? You want to play?" She picked the saliva-covered stick up and walked outside the stable, giving it a good fling towards the open dusty paddock. While Dog bounded after the stick, skidding as he picked it up, she leant back against the stable and took in the setting sun, which captured the red foliage of the weeping red mulga and made a lie out of those who said there was no colour in Australia's outback. For Grace, she appreciated colour in everything.

While the station's landscape verged into rough, red-dirt rocky outcrops, the blazing sun brought out the colours in rocks, plants and small desert flowers that took your breath away when in bloom.

Dog returned with the stick and dropped it at her feet. He sat patiently, tongue lopping from the side of his mouth. "Good boy." She scratched under his jaw. "You want to play fetch again?" Dog's tail wagged in the dust. "Are you ready?" Grace picked up the slobbery stick and threw it as far as possible. "Go!"

She was nearing six months on the station, and in that time, Rolf and Edgar, and Margi, had schooled her impatient and stubborn ways to reflect patience, persistence and knowledge beyond her years. The freedom of earning a living and making her own choices sometimes left her wishing for her carefree childhood where a prepared meal waited for her every night.

She enjoyed learning all about station life. Every day was different, with an opportunity to have a go at something new. Her motto to never let fear stand in her way helped her survive everyday life in Marble Bar. Nothing would stop her from doing something once her mind was set. Yep, her pigheadedness hadn't abandoned her to the vast and empty landscape that stretched for miles.

Giving Dog one last hug before flinging the stick a final time, she made
her way to her room — a small sleepout attached to the rear of the main
homestead — to prepare dinner and have a shower.

⬥

There weren't too many people to socialise with at the station, and Margi
told her Rolf's wife had gone to Perth for a few weeks. While Grace
had little to do with the fair-skinned German woman living in the main
homestead, she often heard quiet conversation and classical music. Instead,
Grace relied on Margi. She was easy to approach and spoke English. A
mother figure Grace desperately needed.

But the station manager's cottage where Margi and John lived was a
good half mile away from the main homestead, making it less likely that
Grace could drop in for a chat at any hour. When Edgar returned each
day to his family's camp, a couple of miles away, it left only a handful
of stockmen close by. They slept in separate quarters near the stables,
leaving Grace relatively alone in the corrugated sleep-out attached to the
homestead.

Someone had left an old radio in her room, and after preparing and
eating her dinner, she would often listen to the only station she could
access. It aired a mix of classical and modern music only broken by news
segments. It wasn't much, but it was better than listening to the crickets,
night animals or the lonely howl of a dingo. Apart from a rickety single bed
with a lumpy mattress, and a paint-chipped chest of drawers, and a small
wooden table and chair, there wasn't too much else to keep her amused in
her room.

A tepid shower —directly outside her room with an adjoining
outhouse — did nothing to lessen the sweat continuously coating her skin,
but after so many months, she was acclimatising, and it wasn't so hard to

sleep. The window could be kept permanently opened when needed as it was barred and screened. The front door was always locked.

She was in that zone between awake and asleep when the doorhandle rattled. Alarmed, she sat up but didn't turn the bedside lamp on. She waited for her eyes to adjust to the dark. Who was trying to get inside her room? Holding her breath, she tiptoed to the door. If someone was breaking in, she would surprise them and dash out the door at the same time. She'd make a run for it to the station manager's cottage. Even in the dark she wouldn't hesitate to find safety in Margi's arms.

Releasing the trapped air slowly out of her lungs, she listened carefully, making sure it sounded like someone was trying to break in.

"Grace, open up!"

Her heart slammed against her chest. That thick German accent. She'd tried every tactic to ignore the warning signs every time Rolf looked her over. The hairs on the back of her neck shot up, and she squeezed her hands into balls to stop them from trembling. Heck, what were her options?

The door rattled harder, sending her beating heart into another spin. Would the rusted bolt hold? Would he try and bash the door open? She didn't have a weapon to defend herself.

"I'll be back in a few minutes. You open up the door then," he hissed.

With his wife away and no one else close by, he must've thought it a good time to … she didn't want to think about his intentions. She listened to the sound of his retreating steps on the concrete path. She had to make a run for it.

Sliding across the pad bolt, she turned the doorknob and pulled the door open enough to stick her head out and check the moonlit yard. Taking a step out, she almost stepped on Dog. "Shit! What are you doing here, boy?" Afraid Rolf would hear her and return, she grabbed Dog by the ear and pulled him into the room with her. Damn! She should've run to Margi's cottage, but it was too late. Rolf's returning footsteps were stomping down the path.

Slamming the door shut and bolting the pad bolt across, she added the security chain. Then she collected a sturdy chair from around the table and secured it underneath the handle.

Dog seemed to sense her fear and sat to attention by the chair. Resembling a statue, he didn't move a muscle or make a single sound. Grace gathered her pillow and knelt beside Dog, comforted by the warmth and strength of the guard dog. Rolf eventually swore and cursed, his words coming through the door sounding slurred. When he eventually walked off, he kicked the door once before stillness surrounded it.

Thank goodness for Dog. While she tossed and turned, her sleep disturbed and uncomfortable, she was relieved to have taken the time to get to know him. With Dog by her side and eventually on the end of her bed, she felt safe.

By the time the sun peeked over the distant ranges and the station woke, she'd left the Marble Bar property. She wouldn't, no, couldn't stay, not while Rolf owned it. She'd found a stockman going to Port Hedland and begged a lift. Then caught a bus to take her home. She didn't have to tell Rolf anything. She didn't owe him a thing. He could damn well go to hell for all she cared.

She would tell Margi the truth one day, though. It was the least she could do since Margi had befriended her. Why did men have that sort of power over women? Dressed in jeans and Akubra, she resembled a bloke, but Rolf had seen past that and spied her curves and growing boobs.

There was no choice but to return home and face her father or find a new job. Neither were appealing.

Chapter 9

16 Years Old

Grace meandered along the makeshift fence housing the Sole Bros Circus. It'd set up camp on the outskirts of Kalamunda the previous week, and she longingly gazed at the animals that belonged to the troupe. The giant, majestic elephants and the palominos casually grazed on the surrounding grass and bales of hay. Barred cages held a lion and lioness secure. They paced up and back the length of the gate, watching, waiting. Monkeys were causing a racket in an enclosed trailer.

Friendly chatter carried on the morning breeze. Without meaning to, she wandered in that direction, along the temporary fence, completely absorbed in her thoughts until she was only yards away from the cluster of caravans the troupe travelled in. She stopped and eavesdropped on the conversation.

"Sounds like it'd be a great job to have." She hadn't meant to speak her thoughts aloud, and it was too late to take them back.

One of the girls smiled and beckoned her closer. "We can get you a job here if you want."

Grace's mind spun. It was the last proposition she had expected that morning.

After the long trip home from Marble Bar, she'd rung the house phone, hoping her mother would pick up. Instead, her father had, and he'd mistaken the call, thinking she was her sister, Annette, when he'd agreed to collect her from the bus stop. When he'd arrived at the bus stop to find

Grace waiting, the look on his face was one of utter surprise, then remorse. There were no grand gestures or comforting hugs, only a muttered apology for the beating, which surprised Grace. He'd never apologised for any of his abuse before. She'd never heard the word sorry leave his mouth, ever. But Grace wasn't interested in apologies, and the truce didn't last.

She'd been glad to see her mother, Annette, and Robert, but Grace had changed from the naïve fourteen-year-old who had fled home close on eighteen months earlier. Now she did her own thing and lived independently and had worked at various stable jobs for a few months. She didn't need to answer to her parents anymore, but she *did* need a more permanent job.

With a rushed breath, she asked, "Can you?"

The teenage girl nodded and rose from the camping box where she sat. "Follow me."

⁅⚬❦⚬⁆

Grace straightened her smart black coat and gave the guests her best friendly smile as they arrived for another performance. The smell of sawdust and fairy floss tickled her nose, adding to the buzz of excitement that stirred inside. "Welcome to the circus." Grace took their tickets and showed them to their seat. "Are you excited to see the animals?" she asked a pair of twins bouncing on their toes, faces full of excitement. In the two months she'd been working with Sole Bros, each day had brought a new learning experience.

One of her first tasks had been learning to ride the elephant. The ringmaster taught her to sit and pose atop the enormous animal they called Rosie, in her fish-net stockings and sparkly leotards. Her heart had initially hammered at being so far off the ground, but Rosie was gentle and it hadn't taken long to bond with her.

In the past few weeks, she'd been training for the swinging ladder and descent rope acts. Her strength and persistence, coupled with her flexible body, made her very popular with the circus family. That night, she would perform it for the first time.

A slight shiver of nerves rattled through her limbs, and she rolled her shoulders to settle it. She had the confidence and the strength, and her circus family believed in her—something she'd never experienced before.

With her newfound family, they moved from town to town in a never-ending tour that brought colour, dazzle and excitement to communities that had experienced nothing of this magnitude. She loved being part of it. The management quickly took up her skills, and her love of animals shone through from day one. What added to her sense of belonging was being able to help take care of the animals. The palominos were her favourite, and she rode them whenever the circus had a day off.

As for her actual family, it didn't appear anyone missed her.

"Hey, Grace, time to change outfits." One of the other performers called out.

This call stirred her nerves again. Lost in thought, she'd forgotten her new act for a few minutes. But she knew the rules. Whenever she was afraid of anything, she would confront her fears head-on. She almost laughed at this as she made her way outside to her caravan. As long as she didn't fall off the swing rope and land in the fine sawdust sprinkled on the centre ring, she'd be fine.

She had a few minutes to compose herself and change into her dazzling orange leotard. She loved its silky texture against her skin, and the fish-net stockings that encased her legs made them look like they went on forever. Inside the small space they'd allotted her, she re-checked her hair and make-up that was done earlier. She would ride the elephants later in the program as she'd done at every other performance, but tonight she hoped to shine in her new act.

She tossed aside her black jacket and stripped down to her stockings before slipping into the leotard. Grace had to believe she could do this. Had to believe her athletic body had the strength to perform what she'd been training to do ever since joining the troupe. She crossed her fingers and said a silent prayer. It was something she rarely did but tonight was extra special.

⁌⁍

The trapeze act was first after the initial welcome by the ringmaster, and Grace took a deep breath as she waited in the wings. Even though her stretches were complete, her legs twitched, and she danced on the spot waiting the few extra seconds as her act was announced through the PA system. She closed her eyes, took one last calming breath and strode to the middle of the ring, where the swing dangled from one of the circus tent supports.

Her first move was holding the handle and swinging up in a hand-stand position with her legs twisted around the rope for support. To start with, she executed tricks with the rope hanging still. Then she swung the swing forward and backward. With the extra momentum, she'd do different tricks, doing everything possible not to let the handle fall from her hands. Whenever she had to let go of the handle, she wrapped her legs tightly around the ropes.

The single spotlight followed every move, almost blinding her, and the oohs and ahhs of the crowd grew with every swing until she performed the finale. It required a split second where she was neither holding the handle nor had the rope curled around her legs. But when her hands safely connected back to the handle, she let out a sigh of relief knowing she'd done okay on her first swing ladder act. Only then did she allow the excitement to filter to the end of her fingertips with a tingle.

Grace descended from the swing and bowed to all quarters of the crowd. Some members of the crowd stood and clapped enthusiastically. She offered them a small wave of thanks. The trumpet medley which signalled the entrance of the clowns blared, but her only concern was the next costume change and act. Pride swelled inside her chest, and her cheeks ached from smiling. She'd done it without a hitch.

Her mind was already on what she needed to do for her next appearance—the parade of animals. It was her favourite. In another fun-filled act, she entered the ring by riding atop Rosie. The cheeky monkeys would walk in on a lead. One even rode a bike. And finally, the graceful and majestic palominos would follow. Rosie needed no introduction. Its enormity and standing in the animal community spoke volumes. Small kids would sit with their mouths agape as she passed their seats.

That night, she would go to sleep revelling in her success. And tomorrow morning, she would get a precious sleep-in as they weren't moving to the next town until the day after. She gave one final bow, then turned and waved as she left the ring.

Chapter 10

Present Day

Erin typed the last sentence of her report, saved the work and switched off the computer. Dull, repetitive inputting of information was everything she dreamt of doing for a year. She smiled as she rose — reminded of some soreness near her butt from horsersiding — at how weird that sounded and how happy it made her and collected her bag. How stupid to wish for that? At her age, she should be living life to the fullest. Not shying away from the real issue niggling at the back of her mind.

Walking towards the building's exit, she admitted she'd never confronted this issue before. Never openly spoken about it to anyone except Grace. Not her parents and definitely not Nicholas.

When Erin had blurted out that she wasn't keen to finish her medical degree, Grace had questioned *her* about her family. It'd been easy opening up to Grace, even though she'd felt like a traitor to her family.

"All doctors, hey?" Grace had asked with raised eyebrows.

"Every single one." Erin had answered matter-of-factly.

"What about your mum's family?"

"Don't know anything about them."

"Maybe it's time you did some digging. It could help you find where you belong."

Grace was easy to talk to, and the weekly interviews didn't come fast enough. Monday was finally finished, leaving only Tuesday before Erin's next appointment with Grace on Wednesday. Erin was keen to learn more about why Tom thought Grace was a remarkable woman. Sure she had a multitude of trophies and ribbons, but she got the feeling there was more to his comment than her life achievements on display. The opportunity to ask her more was lost when Tom had hollered out that the horse was saddled and ready.

Ever since that conversation with Grace and her first encounter on a horse, she looked at the world from a different perspective. It'd taken a while to get her head around it, but now everything made sense. She didn't want to be responsible for taking on a person's health and well-being. She lacked the confidence. What was the point in finishing her medical degree if every day would only bring frustration, leaving her constantly uncomfortable?

Halfway across the car park to her Honda, she stopped, her heart racing frantically, her breaths quickening. What *did* she want to do?

She pressed her hand to her chest and took a deep breath in and out. With tentative steps again, she tried to address the problem she didn't know how to solve. It'd been whirling around her head, searching for an answer ever since she'd let slip her concerns to Grace.

She'd only driven down to Cairns that morning in time for work, having stayed the entire weekend with her grandparents and Lacey. She couldn't avoid her parents or Nicholas any longer. There'd be sour expressions and disappointed reminders. But all she thought about was her next interview with Grace on Wednesday and another offer of horseriding next weekend. Was there something seriously wrong with her priorities?

Only one way to find out. She settled in her seat, dumped her bag in the passenger footwell and started the car. The last of her confidence that she could work her way through this rocky patch was holding steady for now. How would she cope with facing her family and a boyfriend ... a boyfriend she was fast realising she might not love anymore? *Now, where did that come from?*

Erin puffed out a weary sigh. They moved in together six months ago after being a couple for three years. But something had jarred from the start of their lease and wouldn't leave her. Nothing had felt right once the subtle red flags to Nicholas' personality became more apparent. Once she understood she was being controlled rather than loved, her love for him had withered away. Would her resolve to stop her medical studies buckle at the slightest push?

Erin squared her shoulders and put the car in gear. She was an adult now; it was time to act like one.

Dinner at her parent's place. Always on a Monday night, always with a strictly medical theme. Her mother was too busy to cook, so she hired a chef and kitchen hand to prepare most of her meals. 'Life is too short to waste on menial, repetitive chores.'

Erin didn't bother going home first to shower and change and sent Nicholas a message to that effect. She'd worked as long as possible in front of her computer that afternoon and rubbed her tired eyes while stopped at traffic lights. She didn't want to give her mother too much time to pull her aside and remind her of their disappointment.

The drive had given Erin time to put her thoughts in order, and as she turned into her parent's street, there was clarity around the reasons she didn't want her life to follow the desired route her parents had hoped for. As for any missing link that might be hiding on her mother's side of the family, well—that night, she was going to change the table talk. She couldn't wait for the moment they all scowled at her audacity. *You can do this, girl.*

A second later, her heart sunk when she spotted Nicholas' car on the drive, and it looked like her brother James was there too. Great! She would cop it from all angles. She glanced at the time on the dash and chewed on her bottom lip as she parked. *Okay, so maybe I am a tad later than usual.*

When she stepped through the front door, voices filtered down the wide hallway from the living room. A glass of chilled white wine would be waiting for her on the drinks trolly. Except she wanted a beer. It'd been a long time between beers since she'd mingled with the outback university kids who'd welcomed her into their crowd. That nostalgic memory resurfaced regret at her poor attempt to stay in touch with them. They weren't the friends Nicholas wanted her to be around, though. She'd changed a lot about herself to ensure she moulded into Nicholas' ideal girlfriend. It was something else that irked her.

"Hi, everyone," Erin announced with as much enthusiasm as she could muster. With an empty tank to begin with, this was no easy feat.

The conversation came to an abrupt halt, all eyes turning to her. Then they all spoke at once.

"Why haven't you returned my messages?" Rosemary asked.

"Why didn't you honour the foundation with your presence?" Brian demanded.

"Sis, you are so in the bad books." Her brother James smirked back.

Only when Nicholas sidled up to her on the pretence he would kiss her, his fingers digging into her elbow where no one could see, did his whispered message send a shiver up her arm. "Nobody makes a fool of me and gets away with it." She bit her lip and produced a fake smile, while her heart thundered.

Her hand automatically went to her hip and pressed on the still sensitive bruise. Her other hand grabbed the glass of wine her brother held out. Anything to get some distance from Nicholas' grip. She gulped half of it before strengthening her resolve and wiping any trace of the forced smile off her face.

She considered herself a modern woman, aware of the many things to look out for in a controlling relationship. Not that long ago, she didn't think she had anything to worry about, but there was only so much more she would take.

"My apologies, everyone, for everything. If dinner is ready, we should make a start on it."

The conversation halted again. You could cut the air with a knife.

"I think you owe us an explanation, young lady," Brian insisted, standing from the lounge, whisky in hand. His questioning eyes bored into her.

Her instinct was to look away from the scrutiny, but instead, she held her father's gaze. "I will, but first, I have some questions I'd like answered. So why don't we eat, and I'll get started," Erin persisted and turned towards the door.

Behind her back, there was whispering from her mother and a curse from her father. Her bother said something along the lines of: "Shit's about to hit the fan."

Nicholas sidled up to her side and wrapped his arm around her shoulder. As they walked to the dining room at the back of the house, he pinched her hard right near her breast where his hand had been resting. It was a couple of seconds before he released it and laughed at a joke from James.

"Ouch," she hissed, resisting the urge to reach up and massage the spot or dig him in the ribs with her elbow. She clamped down on her jaw instead. There'd been a lot on her plate the last few months, many things circulating in her head. Much anxiety about where her life was leading and a tonne of insecurity about her capabilities. In an attempt to find the real Erin, she'd need to make changes.

There was no time like the present. She untangled Nicholas' arm, took a deep breath and strode to the opposite side of the table from where she usually sat. She may as well upset the entire balance of the night and ignored her brother's scowl when she plopped down in the seat he normally took. Nicholas glared at her from across the table. Flickers of distaste in his broody grey eyes.

Yep! Separating her life from Nicholas had just become priority number one. Idolised like another son, it wouldn't be easy. But she had a mantra replaying over and over.

Take it one day at a time ...

Their roast lamb with all the trimmings awaited them, sprawled from one end of the table to the other. Rosemary's pot warmers had been put to good use. When everyone was seated, an expectant hush fell over the room. Erin clenched her hands under the table, and she cleared her throat. "Mum, Dad, I'm sorry about not attending the function. As part of my research work, I had to keep a commitment on the weekend up on the Tablelands. I chose it over the foundation dinner." Not strictly correct, but she could live with that.

Rosemary dropped the pot lid; the noise rattled around the room. Brian slammed his now empty glass on the table.

"What about apologising to me?" Nicholas said with a tight expression. "You tell me an hour before we're due to arrive and give no valid reason?"

In her periphery, Brian nodded in agreement. She held Nicholas' gaze as she compiled a response, wanting to choose her words carefully. There'd be no taking them back once they were verbalised. She didn't owe him anything, especially an apology. It was he who should say sorry to her.

She bit her tongue at what she wanted to say and instead, in her most gracious tone, said, "Nicholas, you're right. I left it too late, and I apologise." Until she freed herself, she would be extra careful about what she promised—to anyone.

"Apology accepted." Nicholas said with a smirk.

Knowing he didn't mean it, she turned her attention to her father. "And Dad, I'm really sorry I didn't warn you. I know our family ranks high in the medical profession, but as I'm taking a year off from my studies, I'm going to step back from some functions to give myself a complete break."

Brian harrumphed. "Are you sure that's the best thing to do, careerwise?"

Erin studied her father — greying hair and extra lines and creases on his face — and remembered how much fun he used to be. Where did he go? She sighed and twirled her fork in her hand, the wrong thing to do going by her mother's frown. She put it down and said, "I'm sure, Dad, but thanks for asking."

Nobody had anything to say while Rosemary served the meat and vegetables. The delicious aroma of the meal reminded her of how many hours it'd been since she'd eaten lunch.

When her mother had nearly finished serving the food, her arm froze mid-air, causing a piece of lamb to fall onto the crisp white tablecloth. She turned to Erin. "What did you say before? Was there something else you wanted to talk about?"

Rosemary tutted annoyance when Erin forked the stray piece of meat. "Yes, I did. Thanks for remembering, but let's eat first."

Erin popped the meat in her mouth and chewed, the others staring at her odd behaviour. She squirmed under their gaze. Would she need to find her own way in the world, just as Grace had to after fleeing her abusive father?

Erin gave a small sigh and attempted to engage in the 'medical' conversation. No doubt *her* questions would be like a bomb going off, shattering the atmosphere. As she ate her meal and contributed a remark here and there, her mind wandered to Grace and how she was such a strong woman. Erin would go places if she mimicked her strength even a little. Running away from her problems was how she usually did it. Not anymore. She would bide her time for a few more minutes before making her demands known.

Swallowing her last mouthful of roast potato, her lips momentarily turned up. Grace's story of joining the circus sounded like something Erin could do right about now. Running from the circus *her* life was about to become was probably what a doctor should prescribe her. She didn't doubt it would get messy when she demanded to learn more about her mother's family, dropped out of medical school and ended her relationship with Nicholas.

She held back a frustrated sigh. A good scream was what she needed, but still, the circus life sounded like a great idea.

Chapter 11

16 ½ Years Old

Grace had tired of the circus life. The circus family was great, the horses her lifeblood, but the monotony of the repetitive nature nearly killed her. It'd taken her five months to realise all this.

Before the circus had reached the Nullarbor Plains she gave it away and found herself back in Kalamunda, working again with horses.

"This is *so* bloody stupid. How the heck am I expected to compete if I'm not allowed to?" Grace slammed the gate shut at the racing stables and stormed off towards the timber fence that circled the practice track. She ignored the common-sense advice her friend and co-worker, Sue, was trying to give her. Find a rodeo for women competitors. Right! Where? They didn't exist.

She perched her chin on the top railing and let the sweet Kalamunda air envelop her. She needed to cool down. It made her so mad when being female stopped her from doing what she loved: riding and competing.

Sue sidled up beside her, going one better than Grace by sitting astride the top rough-sawn timber rail. "The rules don't say you can't compete. They just say you can't compete against men."

"Yeah, I know the stinking rules. They've been rammed down my throat at every event I go to." Grace sighed heavily and slumped clumsily over the top rail. Her lunch break was almost over, and she was yet to decide whether she would bother hassling Sue to drive her to Parkerville, where the Peaceville Valley Rodeo was held. Two years older, Sue had a driver's licence and use of her family ute. A day out with Grace meant Sue could flirt with all the cute cowboys—and there were usually plenty. Sue had a particular reason for wanting to go to Peaceville. It involved one certain cowboy Sue had met recently.

"You know, if you were a boy, it wouldn't be a problem."

Grace didn't bother replying; instead, she mulled over life's injustices. *Sometimes I look like a boy when I'm dressed to ride.*

Grace jerked up straight. Her foot slipped from the hold on the bottom rail, and she landed on her backside on the grass with a thump. A loud resounding groan escaped her mouth before she started laughing uncontrollably.

She looked up to see a bewildered Sue, who had no idea what'd just entered her mind. *Ah ... yup, absolutely no idea.*

"Mind sharing the joke?" Sue asked. "And make it quick. We gotta get back to work."

Grace immediately curbed her laughter, the need to return to the stables becoming urgent. "I'm going to register a new person under the Australian Rough Riders Association." She rose from the grass and stood with her hands on her hips. "What's the name of your latest cowboy, Sue?"

"Ah ... you mean Bradley?"

"Yeah, nope, won't do. I don't look like a Bradley. I need to come up with a name for ARRA's newest member, and he's going to be all male."

"What do you mean?"

"Your idea, by the way, in case I land in jail over this."

"Grace, don't you dare do anything that will get me into trouble."

Grace chuckled. "You worry about driving me there; I'll sort out the rest. Now, what do you think of Deat Lucas? I get called Dino enough, but I hate that name."

Sue shrugged, not completely convinced about the whole plan by the look on her face.

"Relax, Sue. Deat will compete as a male at whichever rodeo I choose. I'll make sure no one knows me first before I register for events. Okay?"

"What? It's not that easy. Nothing ever is with you. You're a trail of trouble from the minute you wake up. I don't think you should do this."

"Aw, come on. Not my fault I can't sit still. Anyway, it's a totally dumb rule about women not competing. It's just as dangerous for men as it is for us."

"Yeah, but I'm going to be the one driving you to the hospital when something happens *and* ringing your family. Trust me, I'm always seeing accidents at these things."

"Okay, I give you permission to take me to the hospital and leave me there. You can ring my mum for me, and that's all."

"Christ, if anything were to happen to you, I'd be slayed alive."

"Sue, I can get away with it. I know it. They don't ask too many questions about age and stuff and let's face it, they're not going to argue over whether I'm a bloke when I nominate."

Sue ran a frustrated hand through her shoulder-length dark hair and squashed her Akubra back on. "Still don't like it."

"I can do this." Grace stared Sue down, daring her to defy her brand-new idea.

"Who are you going to tell?" Sue asked, "your family or your water skiing mates?"

"You mean Gary and the crew?"

"Well, aren't they who you socialise with on the weekends when you're not at some rodeo?"

"Yes, but—"

"And isn't Gary more than just a friend?"

"Nope, definitely not. Just a very good mate."

"Well, you have to tell someone," Sue spluttered, walking off towards the stables.

Grace followed, giving her question some thought. She wouldn't tell her parents. It wasn't worth the hassle. She wouldn't tell Annette, either. She was their golden girl. Grace didn't need to tarnish that image by having her keep a naughty secret. Nor would she tell her mates. "I'll tell Robert and swear him to secrecy." She said, following Sue's retreating back.

Robert loved competing on the rodeo scene too, and they could pretend they were cousins or something. He also had a driver's licence, and this way, she could make the most of the free lifts when Sue wasn't available. Robert would understand. They always got into scrapes. He'd appreciate this outlandish idea of hers. Shoot, he'd think it was a great lark. Why hadn't she thought of it sooner? She was constantly mistaken for a boy whenever she dressed in jeans and a cowboy shirt. Hell, she'd even cut her hair as short as possible to make it look more convincing.

She did a quick glance down at her chest before they reached the stables. For once, she was thankful to be relatively flat. There'd been no recent change, and she was okay with it. Getting away with the lie would be easy.

Its absurdity struck again. Sue frowned when she chuckled. "Thanks for helping; now we better finish the afternoon shift."

Sue groaned in reply. Grace had a few more hours of work at the racing stables before needing to get to her second job. It was at a nearby riding school, and it was her task to saddle and ready the horses for their lessons before the school kids arrived.

It was another dream job.

⟨∽⟩

"This will allow *Deat* to record some good times." Grace chuckled. The daring use of a male alias hadn't struck home yet. "They don't worry too much about divisions and skill at this age. I just love getting up on these animals and holding on."

Sue negotiated a sweeping bend in the road before replying. "I have to make sure I don't come up to you and call you Grace. I think it'll be easier if I ignore you. You got any problems with that?"

Grace lit up a cigarette for each of them and passed one over to Sue. "With your Brad in tow, I reckon you were going to snub me for most of the day anyway. By the way, what excuse are you going to use for having me around?" Grace blew out a ring of smoke and let it drift towards the window.

Sue took a drag on her cigarette. "You'll be a neighbour's son. An annoying one who somehow twisted my arm to take you here today." She revved the motor and moved a gear up.

Parkerville was a two-hour drive, and they were about three-quarters of the way there. They followed the one bitumen road leading out of town as the cool morning air nipped at Grace's face coming through the partly open window.

"Robert making a show today?" Sue asked.

"Nah, can't. Has to work."

"What's he think of your little scheme?"

Grace smiled wistfully, remembering the look of incredibility on Robert's face when she showed him the registration papers for ARRA and explained who Deat was. It had lasted about three seconds before he burst out laughing. Big belly laughs that had him rolling on the grass, unable to get it together for a couple of minutes.

"He said he had my back and couldn't wait to see Deat in action."

What he'd really said was: 'Dad'll flog you more than me.' It was their standard joke. Who would cop it the worse? But that joke had reached the end of its life. Her father no longer held any influence, and she'd been pleased she could rely on Robert to keep her secret.

Robert no longer lived at home either, but somehow the barbs they received from their father, on the odd occasion they were in the same place, still had the ability to spike. There would never be any pleasing that man and Grace didn't try.

With only five minutes until they arrived in Parkerville, Grace mulled over the events she wanted to enter. For her age, which she hadn't lied about, she'd have to show them her, or rather Deat's, skills to enable him to move through the different grades. But that was a few years off. Division two would allow him to ride a steer and a bronc, which was enough for starters.

She couldn't scrub the smile from her face. *Oh, yeah, bring it on.*
Adrenalin coursed through her veins, the same buzz she'd had the first time
she rode the poddy. She'd be near horses and steers and holding on for dear
life, and she wanted nothing more.

This new alias was the best decision she'd ever made. Climb on the
beast, do the time, get off. Simple as. Then lie low for the rest of the day.
There was no need to make lifelong friends. Deat didn't need this, and she
wouldn't risk getting exposed. For the first time in her life, she could show
her true skills without being devastated by the fact she was a woman. It was
a sport where the animals didn't care what sex you were, so why should
anybody else?

⸙

"Deat Lucas." The chute boss called her name and directed her to the
allotted chute. Her first event as Deat was to ride time on a steer.
Bigger than the one she'd ridden as a twelve-year-old. Steers were teenage
equivalents of the poddy calf—they were bulls with no nuts. She hoped it
didn't go crazy when she was on its back.

Climbing up into the chute, she wound the rope around her hand, the
smell of sisal strong on her palm. The sound of her heart clambering in
her chest blocked out all other noise. There was no turning back. Deat was
about to make his entrance into the world, and she was on the biggest high
ever.

She gave the required nod for the chute gate to open, and the steer tore
out, bucking wildly as it should. It was an exhilarating five seconds before
she hit the ground with a thud. A little dazed and seeing stars, there was no
pickup man nearby. From her periphery, the steer turned on her. Her eyes
flew open, and she tried to scurry backwards like a crab, digging her fingers
into the sand for grip. The steer snorted, took a step closer and stepped

on her calf muscle. She swallowed the gut-wrenching scream as the pickup man appeared and pulled her up from the ground.

"You okay, mate?"

She bit her lip. One sound, and they would guess she was a girl. Instead, she nodded, knowing she would have one helluva bruise to show for her efforts today.

"Medical tent for you. They can check you over."

She was certain nothing was broken. Relieved, she made a tough stance and asked to be put down once past the gate. She'd practised inflecting a bit of roughness to her voice, and the pickup man didn't notice anything different. She'd be hobbling around for a few days, and sadly, this would be her last event for the day.

Wincing, she made her way to the medical tent, debating whether to go in or not. It wouldn't stop her from coming again but being caught out would, so why bother.

Instead, she limped away, intent on finding some ice for her leg and tracking down Sue. Time to tell her they could go home whenever she was ready.

Chapter 12

Present Day

"Why did you go on and on? Couldn't you see your mother didn't want to talk about it?"

Erin wiped her toothbrush clean and turned to Nicholas, leaning against the door frame bare-chested and in his boxers. Usually, his toned abs would stir something deep inside, but not anymore. "I have a right to know about her family. It's part of who I am."

"Sounds like she was embarrassed about them."

"I disagree," she said, pulling her dressing gown tighter. "There's more to it than what she's saying. Yes, they argued about her moving so far away to attend medical school, but that can't be all. Once she secured the scholarship and didn't need their financial help, she gave them the flick. I need a better reason than that."

"Wouldn't you be embarrassed? She was striving to achieve more in her life than just becoming another outback station worker."

"Nicholas!" How had she put up with this irritating snobbishness? "Those people you dismiss are the backbone of this country. *These* outback station workers were her parents. Does it matter where they came from or what they did? They would've done their best to raise their family. She should've made more of an effort to stay in touch. My God, she has a brother and a sister. I have cousins I've never met."

"You're going to cause a rift with your parents if you don't give this up," he said tersely.

Erin bit her tongue and placed her hairbrush on the vanity. She wanted to roll her eyes at his statement but thought better of it. Instead, with nimble fingers, she secured her hair in a loose plait for sleeping, ground her jaw and willed herself not to retort. "You heard her yourself; she gave me some place names, and I know her maiden name."

"And a very clear warning to beware of how deep you scratch below the surface."

"Thirty years is a long time. Surely enough time has passed for her to mend this rift? They need me to find and reconnect them again."

"*If* you find anything. You're not much good at sticking to something." He stood away from the frame now and crossed his arms.

Erin's blood boiled. "Thanks for the vote of confidence," she muttered under her breath.

"What did you say?"

She stayed silent and didn't bother with her usual 'goodnight' either.

Nicholas followed and grabbed her right shoulder. "I want you to give this nonsense up and concentrate on getting back to your studies. You're so close, can't you see that?"

Erin tried to swat his hand away, but he squeezed harder, his fingers digging around her collarbone. When she twisted around, his vice-like grip released. When their eyes met, his glowered, he looked manic. For the first time, a shaft of fear speared through her. She was suddenly sweating in her gown. His behaviour wasn't normal. Her resolve to remove herself from this relationship took on a life of its own. She just had to approach it the right way. "One y-year, that's all I'm taking off from my studies. It'll be over before I know it."

"Make sure it doesn't go beyond that." He shoved her into the wall and stormed off to bed.

Erin gulped in air as she slid down the wall and hung her head between her knees. Her heartbeat throbbed as she rubbed her shoulder. By the morning, she would have another photo to take and more notes to add to her diary. How had she ended up in this situation at only twenty-five?

Erin fingered a small trophy Grace had passed to her. Mounted on top of a small marble slab was a miniature saddle with the year 1966 the only thing she could read on the plaque below. They sat in Grace's living room, and again Erin was dumbstruck by how Grace had managed to collect so many horse-related knickknacks. Today, they enjoyed lunch with two black horse-shaped salt and pepper shakers.

"I was twelve years old when I won it in a poddy-riding event."

Erin nodded. "Very impressive."

"They didn't want to give it to me because I was a girl. Hard to believe, isn't it?"

Erin put it down on the coffee table and raised the mug of strong tea to her lips. "These days, they would never get away with it. Too many anti-discrimination laws covering everything."

Grace chuckled. "You have no idea how difficult being a woman was in my day."

"Was it a rodeo up north here?" Erin asked.

"No, goodness no. I grew up in the outer Perth suburb of Kalamunda. I didn't move to Queensland until 1982. I was twenty-eight."

"Perth? Really?"

"Why's that?"

"I asked my mum about her family, and she said they were from Perth too."

"Perth is a big city. What was your mum's maiden name?"

"Brown."

Grace frowned. "A very common name, though I knew a Brown family close to where I lived. Do you have any other details?"

"I do, a few names and addresses. Mum wasn't very ... what would you say... forthcoming. In fact, I wouldn't be surprised if she gave me false information to lead me astray so I don't uncover her secrets. I don't have the information with me, though."

"Bring them with you next time, and I'll take a look. There's every chance I won't know them, but I have a good friend who spent years in the police force in Perth. He might be able to help us locate them."

"Oh, wow. Really? Thank you, I'll do that, but now I better keep working before our time runs out." Erin grinned as she placed her mug down and settled into the comfortable couch. "Let's go back to your complications. So, by this stage, they'd put the tracheostomy in place to keep you alive. What did that feel like?"

Grace groaned and pressed her hand against her throat. "They wouldn't let me drink water for seventy-three days. They were the longest days of my life. I could only suck on three teaspoons of crushed ice every day. I focused my entire bed-ridden life on getting a drink of water. The nurses didn't realise, but they used to rest their water bottles on the edge of their workstation, and I could see them from where I lay. I'd focus on them and work out ways of getting to them. I was so obsessed that it got to a stage where they had to handcuff me to the bed as I was constantly trying to pull out tubes and lines. If I didn't reach those water bottles, I was going to climb out the window and drink water from the garden hose."

Grace chuckled, but Erin shuddered. "Oh, you poor thing. I couldn't imagine not being able to drink when I wanted and not being able to talk and tell the nurses you were thirsty. Must have been so infuriating." Erin shuffled in her seat, reaching for her mug. She gulped most of it just in case something happened and it was the last time she could freely drink. Which was crazy, so she put it down, telling herself not to be so stupid. "What was it like being in an induced coma? Is it true you can hear things around you?"

Grace steadily rose and walked to a mantle shelf where she fingered a tall wooden horse statue. "I think it's a combination of hallucinations and hearing. I remember hearing my daughter arriving one day and playing some of my favourite music. I only remember Australian Crawl playing, but she confirmed later that it happened.

"Another friend of mine, a schoolteacher, came to visit me, and I remember her telling me how her day had been. I also recall having a weird conversation-type dream. One night, a nurse was telling me her back was sore. I told her to rest in my bed, and I'd sit up. I reassured her I'd wake her up in time to swap before the next shift. To me, it was a real conversation, but later I realised it didn't happen."

Grace meandered around the room, touching trinkets, moving picture frames, looking lost in thought. At one point, she picked up an old and battered Akubra and put it on her head. The smile that made its way across her face was huge.

Erin flicked over to another page in her notebook and pressed play on her recording device. "Once you were out of ICU, and they removed your tracheostomy tube, how did your rehab go?"

Grace returned the Akubra to the shelf before sinking into the lounge. "I had to learn how to swallow again. It felt like forever before I was allowed to drink water because I had to take this disgusting gelatinised water first. I was also carrying a colostomy bag on my side. That was worse."

"Why?"

"It leaked, it stunk, it … it made me feel less a human than anything I'd ever done before. With failed kidneys, I was also on dialysis. I was nose-diving quickly."

"You poor thing." Twice now, she'd said that. Was this the best reply she could come up with?

Grace nodded, lost in her thoughts again. Erin didn't rush her; she was happy to give her all the time she needed. This woman had gone to hell and back, but somehow, she seemed more together and content than Erin felt.

"A physio came every day to help me walk with a frame and—" She chuckled. "My God, I was so stubborn. One late night, I was so determined to walk again that I took myself to the toilet. The first time I attempted, I fell onto the floor beside the bed. On the second attempt about a week later, I made it to the toilet but then slipped and hit my head."

"I'm surprised they didn't chain you to bed," Erin said with a dash of humour in her voice. "But why didn't you press the assistance button?"

"I did, but on those two attempts, no one came. So, after a few minutes, I went on my own. The Gold Coast hospital is big, and I suppose they have limited staffing during the night."

"How many weeks did you say you spent in rehab?"

"Nearly six. I'd lost so much strength in my core muscles; it took that long to rebuild them. My specialist told me if I hadn't been as fit as I was before I went into the back operation, I wouldn't have survived any of this."

"How many months did you have to use a colostomy bag?" Erin snuck a glance at Grace's side. Her notes said she no longer used one.

"Fifteen long months. I didn't enjoy it one bit."

"Something remarkable must've happened for you to do away with it," Erin asked.

"It's a miracle, but at the time, I had to beg and—"

Two knocks on the doorway interrupted them. "Hi Grace, hi Erin."

Erin swivelled in the armchair towards the unexpected voice.

Tom stood at the entrance to the living room. His grin glowed warmly in the afternoon sun shining in through the window.

"Hello Tom, what brings you here?" Grace asked.

Erin couldn't pull her eyes from the way his work shirt looked good on him, or how his jeans fit snuggly. She was smiling like a clown; her breath hitched in her throat.

"I heard you had a visitor today." Tom gazed at her intently before continuing. "So thought I'd drop by and say hello. I have a cow up the road with birthing difficulties I have to see to. I know I'm interrupting, but—"

"Do you have time for a cuppa and a piece of slice?" Grace cut in. "I'm going to get very fat on Erin's great cooking by the time she's finished with me."

Erin managed to breathe again and chuckled.

"Not really, as delicious as it was last time," Tom said apologetically. "I thought I'd ask Erin if she wanted to give me a hand."

When he landed his full smile, dazzling and a little shy, in her direction, her limbs seemed to melt into a puddle on the chair. Why not? It would be interesting to see how a cow gave birth. Her hours were flexible, and she was allotted an hour to drive back to the coast. Since she was staying with her grandparents, she had that up her sleeve.

"It might end up being late, that's all," Tom added. "These things can be a bit unpredictable."

There was nowhere else she needed to be. Her grandparents would understand when she explained why she was late. She was her own person and could come and go whenever she pleased. That's what she loved about being with them, and she enjoyed their company too.

She looked at her unfinished notes resting haphazardly on her lap. They weren't done yet for the afternoon. "Ah ... I'm still working with Grace. I may not be able to."

Grace waved her excuse away. "There's always next week, or we could catch up over the weekend. I might have a rest now before Peter arrives home. I'm a bit weary. Why don't you give Tom a hand? As a med student, you'll know as much as he does. Except animals differ from humans. They're very therapeutic; it'll do you good."

Erin sat frozen in a quandary. She wasn't even close to learning why Tom thought Grace was remarkable. Add her feeling that Grace was pushing her onto the good-looking young vet. While she slowly nodded in agreement to the changed plans, she had to sternly remind herself she was still in a relationship. *Deal with that first, girl, and don't you dare cross the line until you have.*

Chapter 13

17 Years Old

Grace cruised into Sue's driveway, shifted the gearstick into neutral and pulled on the handbrake. She smiled in the dark car and let out a huge sigh of relief. Sue only lived a few suburbs away from Kalamunda, and as a new driver, she'd negotiated her way to Sue's place without too much difficulty. It gave her the same sense of satisfaction as riding well did. She slumped back into the seat and flashed her lights at the house.

She still couldn't believe Robert had loaned her his Holden Kingswood ute. The drive to the Busselton Rodeo was three hours. He had initially been coming until his boss needed him at work. She chuckled as she ran her hand through her messy morning hair. After a long list of dos and do nots, he'd finally relented and given in to her persistent nagging.

She'd attended many rodeos all over Western Australia with either Robert or Sue, and the adrenalin hadn't faded one bit. Deat made an appearance whenever she could get away with it.

Sue poked her face out the door and signalled that she needed five more minutes. They had time to spare, so Grace snuggled into the seat and closed her eyes. That day, she would compete as a woman. In the back of the ute was a bull rope she was keen to use for the steer riding competition. When she didn't have to pretend to be a male, she enjoyed showing off as a female. Today, she was just as excited that she had her driver's licence and would get three hours of open road driving.

Grace flicked her eyes wide when the passenger side door opened.

"Morning, Grace. Good Lord, this is early to be up." Sue shut the door, and in the hour before the sun rose, the sound echoed around the quiet neighbourhood.

"Thanks for coming."

"Yeah, yeah, I know. You need someone to take care of you if you get hurt."

Grace chuckled as she reversed out of the drive and onto the road.

"So, who are you today? Grace or Deat?"

"Grace today. I know some of the committee, so competing as Deat won't work. I don't know if they'll let me do any exhibition rides, but I'll see what I can wrangle."

"Bloody awful long way to go if they don't let you."

"They will. Or else!"

They laughed as Grace cranked up the radio and wound her window down.

"Ooh, I don't mind a bit of Carol King," Grace said as 'I Feel the Earth Move' blasted through the speakers.

Grace was sure anyone within a mile could hear them as they moved onto John Denver's 'Take Me Home, Country Roads' when it came on next. They continued to belt out the words to songs all the way to Busselton. Their singing was only interrupted with news segments telling them things like, 'Walt Disney Resort was opening in Florida', and 'Charles Manson and three of his followers received the death penalty'. The three-hour drive was over before they knew it.

Adrenaline kicked in, swirling inside her gut. They'd given Grace a steer and a chute number, and it was time to climb in. Her heart thumped in its usual way when she was about to ride. It was what she lived for on the weekends. Gave her purpose. Gave her a life. She dropped the rope down the side of the steer when the cowboy helping said, "You won't ride this one, you know."

Grace looked up and smirked. "What's your name, cowboy?"

"Jonny, and you're gonna get bucked off."

Grace straddled the beast and tied her hand into the rope. "How about we make a bet? If I make time, you give me that nice new cowboy hat you're wearing."

Jonny helped her tighten the rope. "Agreed."

The steer bucked beneath her. "So, we have a deal?"

"We sure do."

Grace checked the rope one more time and took a deep breath of dust-laden air. Stirred up by the hooves of the bucking steer beneath her, its strong, pungent smell was of animal sweat and dust. It stimulated all her senses in just the right way.

Helen Reddy's 'I am Woman' blared through the PA system as the crowd waited for the next ride. Oh, yes, she was all woman today, and she'd show these men, and Jonny, how good she was up against them. She breathed out, and with more confidence than she probably should have, she gave the nod and said, "Let him out."

The steer was good and made her earn her ride, but she stayed on for the full eight seconds like she knew she would. She'd never been so satisfied with a ride before and had scored a great-looking cowboy hat for her efforts. Today was better than she imagined.

Striding out of the arena and waving to the cheering crowd, she made a beeline for Jonny.

"Hey, Jonny, you own me one rather good-looking cowboy hat," she said, hands on hips.

He looked up from the steer he was trying to manoeuvre in the chute and quirked a brow. "You don't honestly think I'm going to give up my hat? Sorry, mate, but I like it too much."

"Hey, a bet's a bet, and I won it fair and square, so hand it over."

"Not on your life. It cost me a fortune," he said with a wry smile.

Grace took another step closer, almost close enough to reach up and steal the hat off his head. She gave him a pointed look. "What sort of fella makes a bet and then doesn't cough up when he loses?"

Jonny shrugged and turned back, helping the next competitor. Grace climbed the timber railings and continued to banter and light-heartedly interrogate Jonny about his poor sportsmanship. Still, he remained adamant he wasn't giving up his hat for anyone.

Only a few more events remained on the rodeo schedule, and Grace stayed sitting on the railing near Jonny as the last few competitors jumped and bucked around the arena.

"Who's heading for the bar?" another cowboy asked as the MC declared the rodeo was finished for another year. There was a roar of agreement from everyone in the surrounding yards, and Grace had every intention of joining them.

"Headed for the bar, Jonny?" she asked, jumping from the rail.

"Sure am, *with* my hat on."

Grace laughed at his determination. She never expected he'd hand the hat over, but it'd been fun trying.

She spotted Sue weaving through the crowd and heading in her direction and wondered how her day had been with Brad.

"You ready to leave?" Sue asked, yawning when she made it to Grace's side.

"Are you happy to stay another half an hour? I told some of the boys I'd meet them in the bar."

Sue shrugged and nodded. "Brad's already left as he has an early start in the morning."

"Great! Let's go." Grace draped her arm over Sue's shoulder, and they followed the crowd to the bar.

Grace loved the jokes and banter after a hard day's work on the rodeo circuit. Some of those boys were as tough as they came, but their spirit and fun drew them together. They were a closed group, and you'd never understand their bond unless you rode the bulls, steers and broncs. That's what Grace loved about it. It didn't matter who she was competing as.

Sure, they treated her differently depending on who she was on the day, but as a rule, Deat rarely hung around after the show and these cowboys had no idea she was both. Today, she would join in the camaraderie and be treated like a woman. Some days she didn't mind.

Grace ordered two lemonades and pushed one towards Sue. The ice tinkled inside the glass, and the fizzy, sugary drink found its spot as it slid down her throat. She lit up a cigarette to enjoy with her drink. The bar top was as short as it was long, with all the drinkers outside in the hot afternoon sun and the bar staff inside the cramped space allotted them.

Jonny sat only metres away when Grace called out, "Hey, Jonny! You gonna let me wear your hat, so I know what it feels like to own such quality?"

Jonny shook his head and rolled his eyes. It looked like it was the last thing he wanted to do, even though there was a crinkle of amusement at the corner of his mouth. She continued to badger him, telling all and sundry about his bet. It took another fifteen minutes, and with great reluctance and a lot of grumbling, Jonny conceded and passed over his brand-new hat. It fit like a glove.

Amidst all the laughter and talking, Grace ground out her cigarette in the ashtray and whispered to Sue, "Wait for me in the ute."

The way Sue's eyebrows rose had Grace smiling back. Sue wasn't stupid and knew Grace was up to something. Regardless, Sue finished her drink and left the bar area.

With Sue gone, Grace turned to Jonny. "Gotta go to the toilet. Won't be long."

Jonny stood and threatened to pull his hat off her head. "Leave the hat here while you go."

"Hey, two minutes. That's all I'll be. What harm could it be to wear it while I pee?"

"Bloody hell, alright, but I'm watching you."

Grace winked back. "All the way to the toilet and inside it?"

Jonny grumbled some more as she rose and walked through the crowd to the bush toilet behind the bar. Grace looked over her shoulder at the exact moment Jonny turned away to order more drinks. While he wasn't looking, Grace cut for the ute where Sue was waiting.

Grace jumped in, slammed the door and turned the key in the ignition. She flicked her gaze up. Jonny was zigzagging around the parked cars. At the sound of the engine revving, he burst into a run towards the ute.

"What the heck, Grace?" Sue spluttered, clicking her seatbelt into place.

"Hold on; we're getting out of here, now!"

Grace dropped the clutch. With the ground recently ploughed, the wheels failed to gain traction on the dirt, and the back of the ute fish-tailed dangerously. Jonny slapped his palm on the window and grabbed the door handle she'd been smart enough to lock.

Grace pressed her foot firmly on the accelerator. Jonny, who seemed to be getting dragged along beside the ute, yelled, "You bitch; you ran over my foot!"

With the window partially down, she yelled back, "Lucky the dirt is soft and you're a tough bronco rider." She found good traction on the gravel road and sped through the entry gates, a cloud of dust behind her and laughing so hard her cheeks hurt.

"Sweet Jesus, Grace, you're crazy!"

Grace smiled at Sue's stiff posture and hands gripping the edge of her seat. With Jonny barely visible through the dust, she lifted her foot off the accelerator. "It's exactly what Jonny deserved."

"How?" Sue demanded. "You could've hurt him."

"Aw, come on, Sue." Sue's body went limp with relief against the seat. "Even though they didn't let me compete for points, I rode a steer and made time. Jonny agreed to the bet; I didn't make him. He didn't think I'd win it, but I did. A deal is a deal. I won the hat fair and square." There was no way she'd be sidetracked from her great day.

Sue harrumphed, looked out the side window and didn't say another word.

She'd be okay in a few minutes. Grace just had to give her time to calm down. Her driving had been a bit wild and on edge. Luckily, nothing happened to either the ute or Jonny. She didn't want to explain the damage to Robert for something as dumb as running away with a cowboy's hat. It was *not* stealing in her books. God, no! It was a fair bet which she'd won.

Robert might rant and rave and threaten to flog her because of what could've happened to his ute, but that was as far as it'd go. Eventually, he would laugh over it. Robert always got her—because he was crazy too.

Grace wriggled her body and rolled her shoulders, settling in for the long drive. She didn't want to dwell on it anymore. She had a brand-new cowboy hat *and* no injuries to worry about—nothing to complain about there.

Instead, she recalled Helen Reddy's song playing when they let her out of the chute, and her chest filled with pride at her achievements today. She opened her lungs and let loose with a rendition of it.

Sue succumbed to her crazy ways and joined the chorus. Jonny was never mentioned again. The hat, though, well, that was a different story. Occasionally, on the three-hour drive home, she'd reach up and give it an affectionate touch. The felt was soft under her fingertips, and she daydreamed about wearing it to all the upcoming rodeos.

Chapter 14

Present Day

Erin parked her car near a shed and met Tom at the rear of his utility. "What can I carry for you?"

Tom grabbed a couple of medical supply cases and held them out to her. "You can take these two; they're not too heavy."

Tom's hand brushed against hers, and it tingled when she took the handle, almost dropping them again. That would've been embarrassing because they *were* light. *Get a grip!*

She waited for Tom to hoist the chains and rope lying on the tray back over his shoulder. "Follow me. I was here this morning, and it was looking routine, but this is a valuable cow, and the farmer doesn't want to lose both. It'll be bad enough if the calf dies."

"Thanks for thinking of me. It's not the same as humans but still a great experience."

"I thought so too," he threw back over his shoulder.

"How much time do you give them before you lend a hand?" Erin asked, quickening her strides to fall into step beside him.

"Depends on how much pain the mother is in. The farmer thinks this one is ready to have it pulled out."

In the enclosed yard, the legs of the calf protruded from the cow's rear. "This is a good sign. Nothing was showing this morning."

"Hi, Tom." The worried-looking farmer glanced up from looking at the cow as they arrived. "Time to give her a hand?"

"Yeah, I think so. I'll check her over, and then we'll get started." He let the chain and rope fall to the ground. "Joe, this is Erin. She's here to give us a hand if we need it."

After a handshake, they all turned to the Friesian lying on the hay-covered dirt. Erin looked into its pain-filled eyes, and her heart dropped. She immediately went and knelt beside the cow and began a light massage around her face while Tom did a physical check on its rear. She'd read a little on the Emmett Therapy used on horses and dogs but had absolutely no idea what she was doing. It was the need to do *something* that propelled her.

Joe and Tom readied the cow by tying her down, so she didn't go crazy as the calf was being removed and hurt it. Then they secured a rope around the protruding feet of the calf, with the other end tied to the back of a quad bike. When Tom nodded, Joe inched the bike in the opposite direction.

Every muscle tightened in the animal, yet her yowling changed and sounded less painful when it should've been increasing. She continued with the massaging when the cow didn't shy away.

After a couple of minutes, she glanced up towards the cow's rear and was surprised when the calf emerged only seconds later. Joe switched off the quad bike, and it was the sound of a bawling calf that rang sweetly around the enclosed pen.

"Good job, team," Tom said, removing his gloves.

"But I didn't do anything," Erin said, surprised at her inclusion.

"You kept the mother relaxed in those crucial last minutes, whatever you were doing."

Erin's chest expanded at the unexpected compliment. Honestly, she'd done nothing special.

Joe lifted the wet calf and positioned it closer to the mother so she could lick it. "I'll come and check every half hour to see whether the calf has tried to feed."

Erin rose and moved out of the way, allowing Joe to position the maize meal and water trough closer to the mother.

"Thanks for getting here when you did, Tom. Everything looks good now," Joe said.

"I'll come and do another check in the morning. Ring me if anything crops up overnight."

"Yeah, I'll be up and down all night. I should sleep in the shed," he joked.

Tom chuckled as he began packing up his gear, obviously not surprised at Joe's devotion to his valuable cow.

"Want me to take these out to the ute?" Erin asked, closing up the medical supply cases.

Tom looked up and nodded with a smile of thanks. Erin followed him outside and waited until he'd put the chains and rope in the back before placing the cases where he indicated.

"We finished sooner than I expected. Did you want to meet me for a swim at the lake? It's what everyone does here after a hot day," Tom asked as he tied down the cases with a strap.

A little tremor of excitement flowed through her. An afternoon swim was how she loved to end most of her weekend days. "I can go straight from here unless you have to go back to the surgery first."

"No, I just thought you might need to grab your swimmers first."

"I always have something in the car when I'm up here. Wouldn't you if you lived this close to the world's most beautiful lake?"

Tom laughed easily, and it lodged somewhere comfortably within her. It was only a swim, she reminded herself. She usually swam alone as no pets were allowed in the national park. *Don't make a big deal of it.*

"Okay, let's get cleaned up first. I have some hand soap here you can use," Tom suggested.

Erin emerged from the change rooms next to the lake and made her way to the concrete steps at the water's edge. She placed her bag and keys down on a grassy patch and searched for Tom. Not able to see him, she assumed he was already in the water.

She took a moment to fill her lungs with the pungent rainforest smell she loved. It helped ease her concerns about the number of bruises on her body and the lack of sleep she was getting. She needed every bit of help to get her through the tough times in the coming weeks. The thick rainforest surrounding the entire lake was like a cloak, protecting her from the outside world. If only she could stay in this place forever.

She dipped one toe in the water and gasped at its refreshing chilliness. It was always the same. Even as the sun blistered down, the water always felt like she was stepping into ice. There was only one way to face this, she'd learnt early on, so she took a deep breath and dived under the surface, pulling her arms through the water like a champion breaststroker.

It took a few moments for her body's temperature to adjust, and when it was perfect against her skin, she kicked her way up from the depths of the volcano-formed lake and emerged, gasping and grinning, her whole body enlivened.

Tom appeared beside her seconds later, causing her heart to thump inside her chest. She hadn't reacted to Nicholas in this way for a long time. A rapid heartbeat from fear was her usual reaction to Nicholas these days. She chewed on her bottom lip and worried about what lay ahead of her.

"Hey there." Tom's short, wavy hair was plastered around his forehead. The water darkened the usual golden-brown colour, but the afternoon sun emphasised his broad, tanned shoulders that rippled each time he moved. "Why the worried look on your face? No crocs in here," he said lightheartedly.

Was it that obvious? She attempted to transform her face with a smile and said, "Race you to the pontoon."

Tom picked up the challenge immediately, and by the time she'd taken her first freestyle stroke, it was apparent Tom was an excellent swimmer, and she had no hope of winning. She followed his powerful strokes with her own and tried to catch up to him, to no avail. She eased in to the pontoon, one hundred metres away, huffing and puffing in between bursts of laughter.

They dangled from the pontoon, holding onto the shiny steel bars. She used her other hand to push the hair off her face. When Tom reached out to help her, she stopped laughing, and so did he. His gaze was intense, searching, watching her closely. She was still trying to get air into her lungs. The exertion felt good, but she was a little out of nick.

"Can I ask you something?" he said, his chest heaving.

Erin was powerless to stop what was coming. She'd sensed the immediate attraction between them during her first riding lesson. Insane thoughts had looped through her head ever since. She wanted to explore it further, but only after dealing with Nicholas.

"Grace mentioned that you don't want to finish your medical degree."

Huh? That's what he wanted to ask?

"Why don't you swap over to vet science? You're a natural with animals. I saw it with Eve on the weekend, once you lost your initial fear, and today with Joe's cow."

Did this mean she had no affinity for humans? Her face dropped, and her hand performed figure eights on top of the water for something to do. She'd broached vet science once with her parents when she was on the verge of choosing her university options. She was howled at from their dizzying heights of wisdom and professionalism and had never been game enough to reconsider it. It wasn't like she had spent much time around animals at that stage of her life, so she had no idea whether it was a career choice she might enjoy.

"And then I'll ask if you're single."

She looked into his face, full of hope for today and the future, and attempted to slide back so they couldn't accidentally touch. His fingers rested only inches from her own on the bar.

Surrounding them, kids splashed and dive-bombed into the water, using the pontoon as their launch pad. Laughter and conversation filtered past her senses like they belonged somewhere else. Erin's world had shrunk to a mere square metre. Even less when Tom ignored what she thought was obvious and moved closer again.

"I'm so sorry, Tom." If she clamped on her jaw anymore, her teeth would bite through her bottom lip.

"Why should you be? You haven't done anything wrong."

She looked away. The way his gaze caressed her face, the kindness and the strength of everything he said hurt more. She had no right to it until she ended it with Nicholas.

His hand gently cupped her cheek. He turned her face towards his again. "Tell me."

Should she? Would she be able to look him in the eye after she told him? "I'm in a bad relationship which I have to break off."

He winced. "I'm sorry to hear that." When she raised an eyebrow, he grinned and admitted, "And a little relieved."

Erin took a deep breath and closed her eyes before letting it out slowly and gathering her thoughts. "It's not as simple as that."

"Yes, it is."

"It's not, Tom."

"Why?"

"I have to do it my way. Slowly. Please don't rush me on this."

His hand left the contour of her cheek and travelled down to her shoulder. Her body tremored with every touch of his skin until she winced when his fingers touched a raw spot. He frowned and leant in closer to inspect. The bruising was still visible even though she'd applied healing cream numerous times.

"What happened here?"

Erin slid out of his grip and kicked her legs to move away.

"Nothing, don't worry about it."

Tom floated closer and took another look at her shoulder. His jaw dropped and what looked like anger flashed across his eyes. "Bloody hell, Erin, it's him, isn't it?"

As he reached out to touch the bruise, Erin turned back and pushed away from the pontoon, paddling towards the steps on the opposite side of the platform. There was no escaping the look of horror on his face.

"That's why you have to take it slowly, isn't it?" Tom persisted from behind her.

Tears threatened as she climbed onto the pontoon that was positioned on the edge of the lake, and started back along the track to where she'd left her towel and keys. She hadn't gone more than ten metres when Tom's hand slid into hers, and he spun her around. "Listen to me, Erin, please. My family has gone through this with my sister. I know all the excuses. She came up with them for months while she hid the bruises."

Tears trickled down her cheeks. She couldn't look at him. "Let me deal with this on my own."

"Why? Talk to me about it so I understand what's going on."

"For your own sake, don't get involved." Why didn't he just go? She pulled her hand from his and sent him a determined look. "He won't give up easily, and I don't want to risk anyone else."

"Did you really just say that? There's no way I'll let you try and handle this alone." Tom slid his arm around her waist and squeezed her against his chest so other swimmers could pass them on the track. He looked down at her and swallowed. "There's something about you, Erin. Please tell me you felt something last weekend and today, and it wasn't just me."

Oh, it wasn't one-sided; her body moulded into his, and the goosebumps appeared up and down her skin, but she wasn't making any promises until she was done with Nicholas. "What if he makes our lives hell?" she whispered into his bare chest.

He shook his head as though frustrated. "I'm prepared to wait for the easy part." Droplets of water landed on her face. "Here"—he placed one hand over his heart—"something here tells me you're worth it. Talk to me, tell me what's happening. Please."

Like quicksand, her body was fast losing traction the longer her gaze remained locked with his. Could she trust Tom? Would it help or hinder the situation with Nicholas?

"I'll only go after him for a good thrashing if you ask nicely." He attempted a lopsided grin, but it slipped, and a worried frown replaced it.

His pleading touched a raw nerve of needing someone like Tom on her side. A deep, resigned sigh left his chest when he took a step back and dropped his forehead against hers.

"That's a lie. I can't keep that promise. I'll kill the bastard if he touches you again."

The little niggle of fear she'd managed to keep in a tight spot behind all of her reasoning suddenly blossomed, and her hand tightened around Tom's waist for reassurance. "Let's get our towels, and I'll tell you everything."

Chapter 15

18 Years Old

"I better get going, Mum. Thanks for dinner." Grace rose from the couch and took her empty plate and glass to the sink to rinse.

"Do you want a lift home?" her mum asked.

Grace lived a couple of streets away and was without wheels while her car had repairs done to the brakes. "Actually, no, I'm staying the night with Jackie. Remember her from school? She finishes work at ten, so I'll catch the bus to her flat," Grace called over her shoulder.

"Isn't it a bit late to be out and about?"

"You worry too much, Mum." On the way back from the kitchen, Grace gave her mum a hug, relieved her father had gone to bed. "Jackie has the day off tomorrow, so we can catch up all night if we want. It's been ages since we last got together. I'll finally get to meet her baby girl."

Her mother tutted at the recklessness of the teens. At eighteen, Grace had the world at her feet and loved every minute.

"Just take care, okay?"

"I will." She gave her mother another hug and left for the bus stop.

Grace glanced down at her watch and noted it was nine fifteen. She'd caught the initial bus near her parent's home and needed one more connection to arrive at Jackie's. She didn't know Jackie's suburb too well, only that her flat was close to a shopping centre. Grace's timetable showed the next bus was scheduled to arrive in a couple of minutes, so she sat and waited at the bus shelter. It was positioned directly behind the police station and was unusually quiet for a Sunday night. She lit up a cigarette to help pass the time.

Grace flicked her eyes up when what looked to be a greeny-coloured Corolla slowly rumbled past. The street light illuminated the car's interior to show a man wearing a black and white cravat around his neck. His unusual attire caught her attention. He braked suddenly and stared at her through his open window, tapping his thumbs on the steering wheel. Grace tensed at the steely look in his eyes and the sideways smirk on his lips. She sighed in relief and sunk further back into the shelter when he repeatedly revved the engine and drove away.

When the same man appeared on foot and approached her less than a minute later, she bit her lip to hold back a scream for help and dropped the remains of the cigarette. A medium-built man and probably in his late forties, Grace tried to calm herself by taking deep breaths. He was clean-shaven and well-dressed. Surely, he wasn't a weirdo.

Standing in front of her, and with a gruff voice, he said, "I know you."

Panic set in, but like every other time fear attempted to barge its way in, she faced it head-on. She stood and matched the man's height. "No, I don't think so."

"I know you," he insisted again.

In a sharper tone, she maintained her poise and repeated, "No, you don't."

He studied her with silent contemplation before turning away and disappearing into the darkness.

The connecting bus roared down the street, and with great relief, Grace didn't hesitate to climb aboard. The half-hour ride to Fremantle gave her the time to calm her nerves and get excited about catching up with Jackie. The opportunities to spend time together were few and far because of Jackie's nursing shift work. Add a new baby to the mix, and sometimes it was near impossible. Choosing to come out at such a late hour was a last resort option.

The bus pulled into the terminal at the shopping centre. Grace thanked the driver and hopped off. When it drove off, she spied the green Corolla parked in the car park next to a cluster of trollies.

Fear paralysed her for a few vital seconds, and she tried to wave down the disappearing bus, but its lights vanished around a corner. She scanned the rest of the car park for anyone else or anything that could help her. It was only her and the same cravat-wearing man who claimed to know her. Had he followed her? These weren't the actions of a sane man. *How dare he!* She pounded a fist against her thigh, her rousing anger increasing another notch. She wanted to protest, shout and tell him to get lost. And she desperately needed to pee. This was when her adrenalin kicked in, flight or fight. Nothing else penetrated. She gasped for air, struggling to breathe. If fear had a smell, she was covered in it. Smothering her like a heavy and musty blanket. Fighting this man wasn't an option, so flight it was.

With clammy fingers gripping her handbag, she surveyed the four-lane highway with a medium strip. She sprinted across the car park and two lanes, waiting for traffic to clear. The Corolla's engine revved as it did earlier. She dashed over the other lanes and down a side street running adjacent to the highway and ducked into the garden of the first block of flats.

She crouched low behind a row of shrubs. There was no hope of stilling her racing heart or making sense of what was happening. Who was this man, and what did he want with her? With increasing alarm, she spied the man driving slowly up and down the street four or five times, his head turning from one side to the other, searching. When the stoplight turned red near the shrub where she hid, she was sure he would hear her thumping heart.

She bit down on her lip, refusing to make a single sound or move a muscle as she seared the letters and numbers of his number plate into her memory. She remained cowering as the light turned green, and he sped off. When ten minutes passed and she didn't see him again, tension oozed out of her tired shoulders, and she plopped onto the grass and stretched her cramping legs.

Jackie lived close as this was the street address of her flat. Earlier, the bus driver had pointed out the direction she had to walk, confirming it wasn't that far. Grace rose. Regaining some semblance of confidence, she wrapped it around her securely. She was sure she'd find Jackie's place soon.

She swung her handbag over her shoulder and scampered down the street, tentatively looking at the street numbers on the buildings. Her spine stiffened when a car's brakes squeaked behind her and that familiar rev reverberated through the night. She gasped, terror overriding everything. Her feet were like concrete and wouldn't move.

Within seconds, he grabbed her upper arm, flinging her around. When her flight or fight instinct kicked in again, this time, it was to fight. Grace swung her handbag, the only weapon she had, and hit him on the side of the head with a thud. She thanked her lucky stars that she had a pair of runners and a myriad of other items weighing the bag down. For a moment, he seemed dazed, and his grip loosened; Grace yanked her arm free. Then she ran. She glanced over her shoulder and sprinted down the shared driveway, screaming for help. The man was hot on her heels, his footfalls a loud pounding on the concrete.

She veered down the side of the carport and into someone's backyard. A small fence divided the house from the neighbour, and it took Grace nothing to jump over it. She bolted for the next house which had a light illuminated in a back room. The pounding footsteps had stopped, and with another glance back, she couldn't see the man. She pounded on the back door of a house.

The door opened to reveal a man who looked to be in his thirties. "Please, let me in. There's a man chasing me."

The man didn't hesitate. "Quick, come in," he said, surveying the backyard over her shoulder and ushering her inside.

As the door closed behind her, she let out a shaky sigh of relief before realising her saviour wore only underwear, low-riding briefs to be exact. Was her nightmare about to get worse?

"Just excuse me. I'll go and dress," he said. "I'm Rob, by the way."

With her outstretched shaking hand and averted eyes, she said, "I'm Grace." And with his warm hand around hers, she felt safe. This man wasn't one of the bad ones.

"Make yourself comfortable in the lounge room"—he directed her towards a hallway—"and I'll make you a cup of coffee. You can tell me what happened. Sounds like you need to report it to the police."

Grace nodded, pulling her jacket around her still-shaking body. While she waited for this kind man to dress, she re-ran the numbers and letters of the number plate in her mind. The sooner she could write it down, the better.

⁂

"This is your friend's flat," Rob said, pulling to the curb and letting the car engine idle. It was only a few hundred metres down the street, but she was glad she didn't risk getting lost or accosted again.

"Thank you so much." Grace had told him everything over a warming cup of coffee.

"I don't know how you managed it, but memorising the number plate was the best thing you could've done. It'll play a big role in finding the perpetrator when you report it."

Relieved she'd done something right, she got out of the car and looked up and down the street for the green Corolla. It was nowhere to be seen, so she closed the car door, bent to the open window and thanked him again.

"No problems at all. Glad I could help. Take care and enjoy your time with your friend."

He drove off, and Grace sat in the stairwell near Jackie's door. Grace knew Jackie had to collect Paige from the babysitter after her shift, but every second until eleven o'clock, when Jackie and Paige arrived back, had felt like an eternity. Her pounding heart hadn't let up for one second.

"Shoot, Grace, have you seen a ghost?"

Jackie nursed a sleeping Paige against her chest and hugged Grace.

"Let's have a cuppa, and I'll tell you what happened."

"That bad, hey?"

Grace could only nod. She'd suffered enough stress for one night, and if she wasn't careful, she would spill everything out along with a lot of tears. Not her style at all.

An hour later, Grace rubbed at her tired eyes. Jackie had been a great shoulder to lean on and unburden the ordeal Grace had endured.

"I think you should report the incident and do it tonight while everything is fresh in your mind. He's out there prowling the streets right now. They might even spot his vehicle."

It made sense to do so, but with no phone connection in Jackie's flat, she had no choice but to walk back to the shopping centre to the closest phone box.

Any other night, it would've been a beautiful walk on a cool March evening, with plenty of street lighting. But that night, nearing midnight, Grace jogged back along the street and over the highway and thankfully reached the phone box without incident. After inserting sufficient coins, she rang the number for the central police station and spoke to an officer. Reassured that they would send an officer out to Jackie's house that night to discuss it, Grace was saying goodbye when the green Corolla suddenly came to a stop on the other side of the phone booth.

Terror seized her; she shouted, "Oh, my God, he's just stopped near me."

"Drop the phone and run," the officer commanded.

Grace did just that. She ran back over the divided road with the medium strip and didn't look back.

Her thumping heart brought with it every fear imaginable. What if he saw which ground-floor flat she'd run to? What if she put Jackie and Paige in danger? But Grace had no choice and pounded frantically on Jackie's door. When it opened, she rushed in and switched off the lights.

"Lock the laundry door and don't make a sound. He's after me again," Grace hissed in a trembling voice.

Jackie sat crouched on the floor with Paige in her arms, rocking back and forth. Grace silently moved to the kitchen and grabbed a carving knife. She tightened her hold around its handle as anger duelled with her terror. If something happened to Jackie because she'd led this psychopath to her doorstep, she'd never forgive herself. She would use the knife without hesitation.

Grace stood to the side of a window, obscured by the curtain. She could see quite well without the lights on because of the full moon outside. She looked out towards the main highway and gave thanks for the medium strip. It'd prevented the madman from getting to her *and* staying near his car. Unable to do both because of it, had effectively saved her life.

Grace gasped for a breath and froze. Walking around the flat and trying to peer inside past the curtains was the same man. Her hand tightened around the handle of the knife. She didn't dare say a word or move an inch. She was too far to the side to see her, but she wasn't taking any chances. Any movement of the curtain and he'd be immediately alerted.

It felt like an eternity to Grace, but probably only ten minutes before she was confident enough to collapse to the floor and relieve the shaking in her legs.

"What do we do?" Jackie slid closer to her after placing a sleeping Paige on a rug.

Grace kept her voice to a whisper. "I don't know if he's gone or not. We just wait until the police come. They told me they would."

It took an agonising hour for the detectives to show up. Grace was beyond tired when they took her statement, a description of the man and his car and the number plate details. When the police left and she curled up on Jackie's cracked-leather lounge under a small crochet rug, sleep eluded her. She tossed and turned, the frightful thoughts of what could've happened running rampant. Added to that was the fear for Jackie's safety. She'd led that psychopath right to her doorstep, and in the morning, she would press Jackie to find a new place to live.

Eventually, she must've snoozed because Grace woke to another knock on the front door. "It's the police," a male voice sounded behind the door. With her heart still hammering inside her chest, she checked the security latch before slightly opening the door. She sagged against the wall with relief at the sight of the two detectives.

"Good morning. Are you Grace?" one of the officers asked.

Grace rubbed her sleepy eyes and nodded.

"If it's okay with you," the other asked, "can we show you some photos? We'd like you to identify the man."

Grace didn't hesitate, slid the security chain off and stepped back to open the door fully. "Come in. This is my friend's flat; she and her baby are still asleep. You won't need to wake her as she didn't see anything." Grace pressed one hand to her churning stomach, recalling how frightened Jackie had been. The last thing she wanted was to wake her up. She would've had a disturbed sleep too.

"No, that won't be necessary," the detective said, opening a manilla folder and pulling out a wad of photos.

"Would you like a cup of tea or coffee?" Grace asked as the detective lined up the pictures on the kitchen table, ensuring the names were covered.

"No thank you. We'll do this quickly and leave you to enjoy the day," the second detective said as he pulled out a notepad and pen from his top pocket and wrote something down. "When you're ready, can you look closely at each image and tell me if the man who harassed you last night is displayed."

Grace tentatively stepped towards the table and ran her eyes over the dozen images. Without any hesitation, she pointed to one of the mug shots. "That's him. Without a doubt."

"Thanks, it ties in with the number plate you gave us. Except for a number and letter in the wrong order, it matches his perfectly."

She was relieved she'd remembered most of the number plate details despite the circumstances. "Do you know of this man?" Grace asked, slipping into a chair after her legs nearly gave way. The trauma from the previous night wasn't even close to leaving yet. If it ever would.

"We sure do but haven't been able to pin anything on him before. We suspect him of raping some girls and murdering a couple of others on separate occasions down by the beach suburbs. The rape victims identified him, but we had nothing concrete until you gave us the number plate. With his registration details and address now on hand, we have detectives on their way to arrest him. We wanted your positive match to assure us we had the right man."

Grace's jaw dropped. Not only did she save her own life with her quick thinking, but she also saved the lives of future victims from this predator. She'd seen his dogged determination to stalk a girl. If her actions took him off the streets and put him behind bars for life, then she'd achieved something great. Still, she couldn't hold back the swift anger that swept her chest. It was too late for those unlucky few who had already lost their lives.

"He has a taste for a certain type of girl."

"Sorry, what was that?" Grace directed her tired mind back to the detective.

"The description of all of his victims is tall, thin and blonde."

She'd never cursed her looks in the past. She enjoyed having an appearance that allowed her to dress up and be girly when needed and compete as Deat and get away with it. But to think her looks qualified her as a potential victim in the eyes of a rapist and murderer sent a shudder along her skin.

She was saved this time but would be aware of the dangers from now on. For now, she'd relax and try and get more sleep. Then she and Jackie could enjoy their Sunday off and catch up on all the gossip. One more predator was off the streets, and good riddance to him. This was good news and enough for her heart to stop hammering inside her chest.

The world was already a better place.

Chapter 16

Present Day

"Can you just sign the damn thing? You know I'm running late, and it's been sitting on the kitchen bench for a week."

Erin took a deep breath and released it slowly. This was it. Her anxiety-filled days had led to this, and it was time to confront him. She tried to ignore his irate mood. He didn't know it yet, but it was about to get a lot worse. "Nic, I um … won't be signing it." She shoved the papers away.

"It's Nicholas, or have you forgotten?" He menacingly towered over her, his finger harshly tapping the kitchen table where she sat.

Oh, she hadn't forgotten a thing. She'd spent three years making sure she remembered everything required of her.

Nicholas thrust the lease renewal documents under her nose again. "What the hell has gotten into you?"

"I'm not renewing it. I'm sorry." It was never going to be easy. She'd debated the wisdom of leaving a note, but Tom had suggested she say it in person and record the conversation. She now wished she hadn't been so hasty in refusing Tom's offer to be nearby. At least she had her phone set to record every word.

"Why not? Where will you live?"

"I'm sorry, Nicholas. I know this will be hard for you to accept, but I'm leaving you. Our relationship isn't working. Where I live won't be your concern anymore."

"Huh, you leave me? You haven't got the guts to do it, and even if you did, how would you survive without my income? You" — he poked her in the chest — "need me." A moment passed before he continued his tirade. "And what do you mean 'our relationship isn't working'? What planet are you on? Are we going to talk about it?"

Even though her instinct was to shy away from his intimidating presence, Erin didn't flinch. This next bit was crucial, but she had to stick to the plan. "You want to talk about it? Sure. How about we talk about the fact that you always tell me how to act, dress, what to eat and drink, even which events to attend. *We* never talk, Nicholas. *You* tell me what to do, but you never let me speak. You never listen to what I have to say or what I want, and you never have. You're demanding and controlling, so it'd be a waste of time introducing 'talking' now."

"I won't let you leave." He hissed each word between drawn lips.

Erin tried to swallow the lump of fear caught in her throat. Composure, she had to maintain her composure. This argument was coming for a while. It was one of the reasons she'd put off the inevitable. Their relationship had run its course and had to end. Now.

She looked up and locked gazes with Nicholas, summoning all her strength. "Can you please stop hovering over me? Either sit down or take a few steps back. You're making me feel uncomfortable."

Like a petulant child, he took two exaggerated steps backwards. "Happy now?"

"Thank you." She fingered the edge of the lease document, smoothing down the pages. "Surely you can see it's not working. You've told me that finishing my medical degree is non-negotiable. It's not your decision to make, and I've decided I won't be going back to finish it. We just aren't on the same page anymore. It's better this way, Nicholas." That had been Tom's suggestion. Be nice about it, don't get angry and play it calm.

"Do your parents know any of this?" His hands clenched and unclenched by his side, and that maniacal look came over his face.

She licked her lips and took a gulp of water from the glass on the table. Before she spoke, she cleared her throat. "Nicholas, I don't need to answer to them. I'm an adult now and very capable of making my own decisions."

"Bullshit." He grabbed the back of the chair next to her and slung it aside, the crash causing Erin to flinch. With a smug look, he hissed, "They'll disown you, and you'll have no one."

She knotted her fingers on her lap to stop them from shaking. He looked ready to explode; her heart felt ready to explode. She said a silent prayer and, with a determined voice, said, "Having no one is better than having a family who doesn't support what I want. And having no one is better than being physically and emotionally abused by you."

"You ungrateful bitch." The slap across her cheek resonated around the kitchen and shook her to her core. Her hand flew up to touch the scorching spot as she shoved her chair back. She took a quick look around the kitchen and realised with a sinking sensation that Nicholas had cornered her. This wasn't how it was supposed to happen. Tom had said being calm was the best way, and she had remained calm for the entire conversation. Calm and truthful. But Nicholas had completely turned on her. His true nature bubbling to the surface.

"After everything I've done for you." He lunged at her, propelling the round table against the wall. It crashed, leaving a hole in the chipboard. "The mentoring, tutoring and guidance," he growled through clenched teeth. "The money I've wasted on you—"

"Like hell!" The shock of the vicious hit sent a piercing pain to her temple, and she stepped back from his reach but came up against the kitchen sink. With trembling hands and a level voice, she said, "You haven't spent a single cent on me, and I've paid half of everything for his place."

"You lying bitch," he roared.

Calm went out the window, and anger showed its face. She owed him nothing. Feeling along the bench for a weapon, all her hand found was the soggy sponge. She slid further along, trying to put more distance between them. "Touch me again, and I promise you'll regret it. I have every bruise photographed and recorded in my cloud storage and my mother's inbox right about now."

He advanced on her, grabbing her arm. "You have this all planned, don't you?" With a slow, torturous twist, he pushed her arm behind her back. She grimaced until the pain bordered on unbearable. Then with all her weight behind it, she elbowed his groin. Nicholas groaned and stumbled back, cursing as he doubled over.

In his moment of weakness, she dodged the upturned table and chairs and raced for the front door, yanking it open. Once outside, she gulped air into her deprived lungs. Through the screen door, she could just make out Nicholas staggering towards the doorway. She was safe where she was, for now. He wouldn't touch her when she was in view of their neighbours. Her car was parked, waiting for her in the driveway. It was packed, and her handbag and keys waited in it.

Nicholas pushed the screen door open and stood in the doorway. Pure hatred rolled off him in waves; that quicksand sensation of fear threatened to overwhelm her again. She took a step back until she was nearly standing in the garden bed. Her parents still needed an explanation, and she needed to see whose side they were on. But before she left, she had to make sure Nicholas understood she carried all the evidence of his abusive ways.

"I'm not finished with you yet," he said, the harsh tone matching the fierceness on his face.

Her body tensed further, but she straightened and pushed her shoulders back. "Neither am I, *Nic*. Not only do I have every bruise photographed and dated, but I also have this afternoon's episode voice recorded." She waved her phone in the air. "You go your hardest because when you come after me, I'll sure as hell come after you with everything I've got. I promise you that." Where was this braveness coming from? Her legs shook, her heart thundered, and all she wanted to do was run to her waiting car.

"You'll never pin anything on me." He took a step outside, having managed some semblance of recovery. His ramrod shoulders were proof that pretending to remain aloof was killing him. He probably wanted his hands around her neck.

"Play it your way. If you don't leave me alone, every time I hear you have a new girlfriend, I will send her the images and today's recording. She's going to know the real you before it's too late."

"You bitch." His hands clenched tighter by his side. His face turned redder by the second.

"Stay away from me, Nicholas, because if you don't, the photos and recordings might end up in places that'll hurt you more ... like your work."

He advanced another step, and the screen door slammed shut behind him. She put a hand out to stop him from taking another one. "But I swear, if I ever hear of you abusing another woman, I won't sit back quietly. That I promise you."

She debated whether she should turn away from Nicholas or shuffle back, keeping him in her view. The question was answered when the neighbour drove up his driveway, giving her the easy getaway she'd longed for. The man waved at them from his car, and Erin put on a stilted smile and made for hers.

Her hands shook as she opened the car door. A glance in Nicholas' direction and his searing gaze hadn't left her. She ignored him, locked the car and reversed out of the driveway and away from the monster.

The next stop was her parent's home, and with tears streaming down her face, she pulled over to end the recording and send a copy to her mother. As their daughter, she hoped she wouldn't have to explain anything. She'd have to wait and see. The medical degree would take a bit of negotiating, but she wasn't backing down.

As she drove down the street, the sting in her cheek reminded her of the nasty blow. She reached up and gingerly touched it. The blossoming bruise should be explanation enough for her parents.

To Erin's relief, her parents supported her decision to leave Nicholas. They met her in their driveway with outstretched arms when she pulled in and shut off the engine. Her mother's eyes were full of tears, and her father looked like he was about to murder someone. They'd hugged her intensely and whispered soothing words before helping her inside and settling her on the lounge with an icepack pressed on her cheek.

They were horrified by the photos and recording, and Brian had driven her to the police station that afternoon to make a full statement. What they didn't support was her decision to quit her medical degree. She didn't utter a single word about the vet science option because she hadn't decided. Once she was settled back in her old bedroom, she refused to discuss it with them, making it very clear where she stood.

They were giving her the rest of the year to decide, so she'd keep her mouth shut. Let them live in hope if they wanted it that way. Her mind was already made up.

Brian and James had rescued her remaining furniture from the townhouse, and she'd settled the account with the real estate agent with no further drama.

Her father's reassurance that Nicholas wouldn't come anywhere near her again had been the balm she needed. She had to believe it or go insane. She didn't doubt her father's contacts in the medical field were enough of a threat for Nicholas to stay away. Either that or have his career destroyed.

After a week of recovery with her parents in Cairns, it was the tonic she needed waking up in the hinterland to Lacey nuzzling her nose into her face. She'd been avoiding Lacey and her grandparents since the split, but the drive to the country and the embrace from her grandparents were the extra sustenance she'd needed to move on.

As for Tom, she sent him a message explaining what'd happened, asking him not to reply. She wasn't rushing into anything new until she had plenty of time to heal.

In the kitchen, her grandmother hugged her tight, the same comforting hug she gave when she was a child. "Did you sleep well?"

"Yes, thanks, Grandma." Erin brushed the flour off her hands and checked the butter melting on the cooktop. She had worked a few hours that morning using her laptop in the small bedroom her grandparents had converted for her use.

"Do you want me to start melting the chocolate?"

"Sure."

Her grandmother had fretted over the news Rosemary had shared about Nicholas. On the other hand, they must've instructed her to keep the pressure up to convince Erin to return to her medical studies. Her grandfather had harped on it for a bit, but Erin got the feeling they were getting tired of trying to change her mind. Their quiet encouragement had been the only thing to get Erin through the past six years.

Her grandmother's comment the previous night: "You do what's right for you, dear," had confirmed for Erin that they had her best interests at heart. She'd slept soundly for a change.

With her morning work schedule over, Erin donned her hand-sewn apron, which lived behind Grandma's pantry door, and made a batch of double-choc brownies. They were to die for if you were a chocolate lover, which she was. Grace had a sweet tooth too.

With some yellowing still visible on her cheek, she'd applied a light covering of make-up. Grace didn't need to know about her problems. She missed last week's interview citing illness as an excuse. Cancelling another week just wasn't an option. She enjoyed Grace's company and was beginning to understand why Tom had said she was a remarkable woman.

She also had the notes on her mother's family with her. What were the chances Grace, or her policeman friend, could trace them? It probably wouldn't make any difference to her life, but what the heck; she'd added the slip of paper to her briefcase.

She dipped a spoon into the brownie mixture for a taste check. "Yum, Grandma. Want some?"

Her grandmother didn't argue, stepping forward with her mouth wide open like a baby bird being fed by its mother. Erin had found another sweet tooth soulmate, and they giggled over the naughtiness of it. "I better get this in the oven if I'm going to make it in time."

"I'll make us some toasted cheese jaffles for lunch," Grandma said, wiping her finger around the top of the bowl and then sucking the chocolate gooiness from it.

"Perfect, I'll start cleaning the mess in your kitchen!"

Erin and her grandmother worked quietly in unison until Erin turned up the volume on her grandmother's portable radio. It was playing a Lewis Capaldi song about losing the love of your life. Such a sad story and one she'd shed tears over when watching the original music clip.

It was enough to stir up odd feelings. She'd never shed a tear in the week since leaving Nicholas. Her feelings for him were never that strong, apparently. But a tiny part of her wondered if Tom was the sort of man she would shed a tear over were she to lose him one day.

When the song ended, she turned the volume down and hugged her grandmother, planting a kiss on her forehead. "Thanks for everything, Gran."

"Everything will turn out right. You've got a good head on your shoulders. You wait and see."

Unexpected tears blurred her vision, and she blinked them back. "I hope so, Gran."

Chapter 17

19 Years Old

Grace splashed water on her face and gasped at the iciness before patting it dry with a towel. Deciding to enjoy an extra twenty minutes of sleep meant rushing a couple of pieces of toast if she didn't want to arrive late at the stables. She looked outside into the pitch-black morning and hugged her thick coat closer to her chest. The autumn air was unusually nippy, and she would have an unsavoury word or two to say when winter arrived.

She pulled out the last two slices of bread, making a point to remember to buy more food that afternoon, and popped them into the toaster. She managed okay if you called living in a tiny caravan where the wind whistled through the windows that didn't quite close properly, living. Money was scarce, but she got by. As long as she worked with horses, there was nothing to bitch about.

Gobbling the toast with only butter as she had no jam or Vegemite, she raced outside and grabbed her bike. She wanted to save on fuel this week, and pedalling from the van park to the stables would warm her up. She'd be sweating by the five-mile mark, which was a good thing on a morning like this.

Once at the stables, she leant her bike against the hay bales, hung her backpack inside the door and rushed to her favourite horse. It was a Hanoverian warm-blooded breed, and she was doing an amazing job of breaking her in, a skill she was fast learning. Now it was time for her morning run, and nothing excited Grace more than being on horseback at speed.

"Hello, beautiful girl." She scratched the horse behind its ear and was rewarded with a resounding whinny.

"You'll have to stop talking to that girl so much. You'll have people worried about you."

Grace spun around and smiled. "Morning, Bob." He was another of the trainers at the racing stables, and they understood each other when it came to horses. As for talking to them, it was easier than talking to humans. Others didn't understand how a horse responded. By the shake of its head or how it nuzzled your hand.

"Anything on this weekend?" Bob asked.

Bob was in his fifties and a great mentor to her for the time she'd worked at these stables. They usually chatted together while they completed their chores. She straightened the blanket on the horse's back before hefting the saddle into place. "My brother and I are off to the Northam Rodeo."

"That's a coupla hundred miles up north, isn't it?"

"Yeah. We might leave Saturday arvo and get a good night's sleep in, ready for the action on Sunday."

"How many broken bones will you come home with?"

Grace chuckled as she fitted the bridle and put the bit in the horse's mouth. She hugged her horse before donning her helmet and strapping it on. "What's a few broken bones when you're having the time of your life?"

When Bob smiled, everything in the world looked right. The only thing she hadn't shared with Bob, or anyone at the stable, was that over the past couple of years, she had continued competing as Deat at every opportunity. Sue and Robert were her only co-conspirators. Deat hadn't won any major awards, but he (or she) was making good times in many events and keeping her injuries to a minimum.

Those who knew of her passion assumed she competed as a female. Sometimes she did if the rodeo was close to home and people knew her. The Northam Rodeo was far enough away that she wouldn't be caught out. In fact, she was getting to know some of the boys really well. It was a great lark, and she loved how she got away with it. As long as she never ran into Jonny again and he insisted on taking his hat back.

Leading her horse outside for its warm-up, she glanced at her breasts. Even with her thick coat on, there wasn't the slightest raised bump. Oh, well. She smiled into the dark. It made her job easier. All she had to do was crop her hair short before any rodeo and she was set to ride as Deat.

As for her voice, she looked young enough not to have broken it yet. Deat wouldn't last forever, but she was having the best time with every ride she got away with. When Deat got too old for her to compete, well ... she would cross that bridge when she came to it. She was also thankful her parents didn't watch her. Her father couldn't be bothered, and her mother used the excuse it made her nervous. It suited Grace perfectly.

She slipped her foot in the stirrup and straddled the mare. With a rub on her neck, she said, "You ready for some fun?"

"You talking to me, Grace?" Bob asked from his mount beside her.

"Sorry, Bob, I'm talking to my girl again. Easy trot to start with?"

"Ah ... so now you're talking to me, I assume?"

Grace's laughter tinkled in the crisp early morning. She let Bob lead on the warm-up, passing other horses being exercised on the track. It'd be a tough workout for both rider and horse, but it would leave her well satisfied for the rest of the day's chores.

⁂

Grace pumped the air with her fist. She ran a dust-covered hand across her brow before straightening her riding cap. She'd done eight seconds twice that morning, and her jaunty stride probably looked girly as she left by the exit gate to the arena.

The first event had been a steer ride and the second one a bronc. Not a single touch down, and she loved every minute. Surely her points were up there with the best in her age bracket? But it was time to douse the excitement and get back to acting like a boy. Keeping the smile off her face was proving to be a problem, and the last thing she wanted was to arouse anyone's suspicions.

Removing a water bottle from her day pack, she took a long swig from it. It was time to search for Robert and have lunch together. First, she needed to find a toilet, urgently. Normally, she could hold it in for hours.

The muscles around her chest clenched for a split second. She had a problem. One she hadn't encountered before. She couldn't enter the female toilets looking like a male. Which then lent a problem if she went to the men's toilets. She'd never entered men's toilets and was as nervous as hell. *Bugger!* She was uncertain of what to do but then grinned. Time to find a shrub and do her business behind it. After all, they were out in the bush—no harm in squatting behind a shrub.

She left the crowded arena and made for the other side of the parked trucks. There were a few shrubs and trees but not a lot to choose from. She checked left and right, making sure no one was around. When she found the space empty, she pulled her jeans down and squatted, her mind going blank with relief. She was close enough to the shrub to smell the strong lemon scent coming off its leaves. She inhaled, clearing some of the dust clogging up her airways.

"Bloody hell, you're not a bloke; you're a bloody sheila."

Grace jumped at the voice, fishing her jeans from around her ankles. She hadn't finished her business, but she hastily rose and pulled them back up. She recognised one of the stock contractors. Competing as Deat, he'd been friendly and funny, but going by the frown on his face, no jokes were about to happen.

"You've been competing as a bloody bloke and had us all, by the looks of it."

There was no denying his accusation. Squatting had given it away. She shrugged as he turned away and stomped over to Dave, the chute boss.

At a loss with what to do next, she meandered back towards her day pack and gear. She understood things would change immediately, and there was no use getting worked up about it. They couldn't hurt her, and they wouldn't jail her, she figured, so go with the flow and accept it. But that's what stuck in her throat and made her so mad.

She looked up when Dave arrived.

He didn't mince words. "What the bloody hell is your name?"

Grace squared her shoulders, ready to put up a fight. "Grace Lucas."

"And who the hell is Deat Lucas?"

"Same person."

"Bloody hell, Grace, women are not allowed to compete against men. Are you trying to make trouble for me?"

This was when she ground her teeth. "No, damn it, I'm not. I just want to be allowed to compete. Find me a bloody rodeo where I can."

Dave shook his head, but an answer was hard to come by. Competing females were few and far between, and it wasn't fun competing alone.

"I'm sorry, mate, but you'll get us into a stack of trouble if they find out what's been going on. I'll need to put out the word to keep an eye out for you and make sure this doesn't happen again."

Oh, great. Now she was blacklisted. They had stripped away all the fun from her in that one sentence. The adrenalin rush she experienced every time she climbed on a bucking animal torn from her—nothing to live for.

"I'll check with the other blokes, but you can do exhibition rides. It doesn't involve points, and you won't be part of the competition."

It was her competitive nature that drove her every time. "But I want to compete. Don't you get it? It's no fun when you can't." She would give it one last shot, even if it killed her. "Nothing has to change. Let Deat keep competing. It's not like I'm going to dob you in."

"Not on my bloody watch, Grace. Sorry. I'll be spreading the news far and wide."

With that, Dave turned away, not an ounce of friendliness in his posture. A female had tricked him and plenty of other chute bosses, which probably hurt the most for them. *Bloody arrogant bastard*, she wanted to yell to his retreating back.

Exposed! Finally. It wasn't the way she wanted it to end, but despite the anger coursing through her veins for being stopped from doing something she loved, she had it in her to produce a sad lopsided smile. She'd gotten away with it for a good couple of years and would keep fighting for women's presence in rodeos. She'd talk about it at every exhibition ride and wouldn't stop until they gagged her.

For now, she still had business to finish and damn them to hell, she would find the women's toilets and use them. Put on her best girly smile and stride straight in.

With a touch of sadness that Deat had died an unnecessary premature death, she wished him well in his other life and purposefully strode away.

Chapter 18

Present Day

Erin wasn't surprised when she spotted Tom's work utility beside Grace's stables. She wouldn't call it an annoyance, but she opened and closed the gate with great trepidation.

Like the last time, three horses emerged from the paddocks surrounding the house. One of them was Eve, and all were vying for the brownies she held as she got out of the car. Their enormous size still terrified her, and she tried to mimic Tom's behaviour to encourage them to wander off.

All to no avail. The threat of those hooves squashing her feet remained a real thing.

"Oh, I give up," she said as she shouldered her way towards the knee-high fence near the house, her knuckles turning white from gripping the sweets' container.

"Need a hand?"

Erin stopped in her tracks and turned around. She hadn't seen Tom emerge from the stable. His gaze snared hers with a probing look, sending her pulse racing. They stood facing each other, the three horses weaving in and out with no intention of leaving. She didn't know what to say. She'd thanked him for his help when she messaged a week ago, but she was still drowning and struggling to breathe. This was too much, too soon.

He made his way closer, giving each horse a friendly pat until he stood mere inches away. "It's okay, Erin. I understand. I'm not here to harass you. Just wanted to check if you were okay. I promise to leave you alone until you're ready. If you're never ready—" He shrugged, letting the words hang. "I won't annoy you. It's up to you."

Relief swamped her, and she smiled slightly. Had anxiety been written all over her face when she'd turned around? Hearing Tom's words were what she needed. She could breathe again and not feel pressured.

Maybe it was how her cheek lifted when she smiled. Or maybe it was the slant of the sun that made him reach out and touch her cheek. She gasped at the gentleness. Then he turned her face for a closer inspection. She hadn't said a word about the slap, but he'd noticed. His mouth compressed into a straight line, and his jaw tightened.

"Christ. Why didn't you tell me?"

Her smile disappeared. "There's nothing you can do. It won't happen again."

He dropped his hand and thumped his thigh. "If that bastard ever comes near you again, I'll—"

"Stop, please." She reached for his hand and squeezed it. "It's over. I just need a bit of space and—"

Eve's tail flicked across her face and tickled her nose. In fact, she kept flicking her tail, and no amount of tapping her on the rump would get her to move. "Oh, please, Eve, go away." Erin tried to step around the horse, but Eve and its tail followed. When Erin couldn't take it anymore, and all Tom did was chuckle under his breath, Erin laughed, sending her unique sound into the air. Tom stared back in a trance. It was the perfect distraction to break the tension between them.

Erin stopped laughing, losing herself in the way his gentle gaze drank her in.

Tom broke the connection and tugged Eve's mane to get her moving. "And what?"

His question confused Erin. *And what?* "Oh," she said with a lopsided grin. *I'm going crazy.* She held the container of brownies up. "I made a few extras. Have you got time for a break?"

Relief rushed through her when a grin a mile wide broke out across his face. She didn't want to upset Tom. He was her normal, her light at the end of the tunnel. For now, though, she needed space and wanted him to understand that.

"I'm guessing a lot of chocolate and sugar. Right?" he asked, peeking into the Tupperware container.

Erin nodded, and her smile matched his infectious one. Being able to cook for someone who so obviously enjoyed eating was the best buzz she'd experienced in a long time. She hadn't expected to see him that afternoon and had baked for Grace and Peter's benefit. But being around a man who oozed rugged strength was making her light-headed. She was likely to say lots of crazy stuff when she was in this condition, and inviting him to afternoon tea was just the start.

"Okay, you've twisted my arm. I'm nearly finished here anyway. Give me five, and I'll be inside. You put the kettle on. Grace is feeling good today, so she'll chew your ear off if you let her."

She was about to take off when he said, "Hey, Erin?" She turned back.

"You're not so scared of these big monsters anymore, are you?"

"Yes, I am," she huffed back.

"Nah, like putty in your hands. Go on, tap one on the rump."

Erin did just that, and the horse wandered off as though she'd lost interest in the entire affair. Her eyes widened.

"Told you."

She laughed again, surprising herself with how good it felt. She would take any endorphins to help recover from the split with Nicholas. It was nobody's fault she had more reasons to laugh when she was around Tom.

"Up for more riding lessons this weekend?" he called.

Erin sobered, pulling her shoulders back. The need to keep her distance from Tom and not rush things was still there. The unease must've shown on her face because he walked back and gently rested his hand on the outside of her shoulder.

"Only riding lessons. Nothing else—for now."

Her heart fluttered with the promise of something when she'd asked for nothing. This wanting felt good. Definitely more addictive than the double-choc brownies they were about to eat.

"The dream is a new kidney, but that's a bit down the track," Grace said, wiping a brownie crumb from the corner of her mouth.

Erin nodded and rose from the table to help clear the cups and saucers. Tom had snuck in three slices and gulped down a mug of hot tea before work commitments had him leaving in a hurry. With the promise of horseriding lessons on the weekend, she tried to ignore the disappointment of his departure. His sunny smile warmed the air around her, and with him gone, a little bit of cloud cover had moved in. It nagged her conscience. *Leave it alone, girl,* she wanted to shout. Rushing into something new was not on the agenda.

"You settle yourself in the living room, Grace. I'll clear this, and then I want to go back to where we left off. You mentioned something about begging."

Erin collected the serving plate and spoons, comfortable in Grace's home. It was the sort of place where she fit in with ease. Only her grandmother's place of late had given her the same vibe.

Back in the living room, Erin organised her writing things on her lap and turned the recording device on when she remembered the slip of paper in her briefcase. "Oh, Grace, I have those names and places for my mother's family." She scrounged around in the case until she found it. Here." She passed it over to Grace.

Grace put her glasses on and stared at the sheet. "Rosemary Brown, daughter of Larry Brown?" She looked up; her face showed surprise before turning to a frown. "I once knew a Larry Brown. Surely he's not the same person?"

Erin shrugged. She wasn't expecting miracles, and with the surname of Brown, there could be dozens of Larrys. "I'll leave it with you. If the names and places match, we'll take it from there."

Grace seemed satisfied with this and rested the slip of paper by her side. She closed her eyes, and Erin gave her a few moments. "Are you okay, Grace?"

Her eyes flicked open. "I sure am. I've just got some pain. Hopefully, it'll pass in a few minutes. I'm sorry about this, Erin; I was doing so well this morning."

Was the sugar from the brownies too much? Grace had eaten her fair share, and Erin internally debated the wisdom of baking every time she came. "Is it the baking I do? Should I bring something healthier?"

Grace grimaced. "Don't you dare, young lady. If I can't enjoy a sweet treat now and then, what's the point in living? Anyway, you're pretty darn good at it, and I know for a fact both Peter and Tom have been enjoying it too." She sat up straighter and looked directly at Erin. "I don't want to pry, but I can see a bruise on your cheek."

The air whooshed out of Erin's lungs, and she froze. Was it that obvious?

"It's okay, Erin," Grace reassured her. "One day, I'll tell you about my second marriage with an abusive husband. My only advice is to get away from it as fast as you can."

Erin bit her bottom lip and murmured, "I have. Only last week."

"Good girl."

"I certainly won't be rushing into anything new."

Grace chuckled. "I know exactly what you mean. I put Peter off for a good couple of years, and damn the man; he wouldn't give up. But that's another story for another day."

Something warmed inside Erin's chest. She and Grace had so much in common, and knowing there were many more stories that Grace wanted to share with her gave her a sense of purpose and hope. "I'd love to hear it. I'm also dying to know why Tom thinks you're such a remarkable woman. He told me to ask you?"

This seemed to perk Grace up, and she smiled wistfully. "Looking back, it was crazy, but it gave me the best adrenalin rush a person could ask for. I used to do rough-riding."

Erin flinched. "As in rodeos and stuff?"

Grace choked with laughter. "Yes! It was out of this world and it gave me a thousand reasons to end up in hospital. Still, it didn't stop me from doing it. It's part of the reason my stomach is such a mess and why I had to beg and beg my specialist to reverse the colostomy."

"Why was he so reluctant?"

"Because of my stomach adhesions. I've had about thirteen operations over the years, and it's in a pretty bad way."

"What sort of operations are we talking about?"

Grace listed some of them. "Appendicitis, ectopic pregnancy, gall bladder, tubes tied, removal of adhesions. They did my back surgery through my stomach, and then they had to go back in and fix the infection. Trust me, the list goes on and on."

"Wow, that is a lot."

"That's why he didn't want to go in another time to reverse the colostomy, but I wouldn't stop begging."

"Obviously he relented and sent you in under the knife again."

Grace smiled smugly. "He sure did. Apparently, after eight and a half hours of surgery, my blood pressure dropped so low it shocked my body and should've killed me. Then it kick-started my kidney function."

"Hence the reason they want this report?" Erin said, scribbling on the notepad.

"Exactly. Doesn't happen often. I'd somehow regained seven percent of my kidney function. That was enough for me to do away with dialysis as long as I'm careful with what I eat and drink."

Erin looked up. "What should I avoid when I bake?"

"Avoid nuts if you can, and I'll be fine."

"Okay, I'll remember that."

Grace looked across at her with a serious expression. "I get the feeling cooking is therapeutic for you. For me, it was always horses. From as far back as I remember, the thought of being close to a horse got me through. You've got to do something you love or you go crazy. For me—" She smiled again and looked lost in her thoughts. "As crazy and dangerous as rough-riding is, I loved it—and it kept me going."

Grace winced, and her hand pressed into her thigh.

Erin sat forward and shuffled the papers to the floor. "What's wrong?"

"Trust me, Erin, any"—Grace grimaced as she massaged her leg—"number of things could be wrong with me. I don't know how I'm still alive."

"Can I help?" She hadn't done four years of medical training for nothing, and Grace brought out her compassion. She rose and knelt before Grace.

"If Peter doesn't rub my legs every day, they ache and I get cramps. It's not as intense as it used to be, but sometimes rubbing is the only thing that helps ease the pain."

"Do you have any baby oil?"

"No, but there's cream in the bedroom, on the bedside table."

Erin was back within the minute and found Grace lying on the couch, her head propped up with a cushion.

"Thanks, Erin. I hope you don't mind."

"Not at all." With generous amounts of cream, she rubbed up and down Grace's legs, using her knuckles to gently massage her calves and hamstrings. She noted several scars and deep wounds and tried to imagine this sick but robust woman atop a bucking animal. It was hard to visualise, but it told a lifetime of adventure and daring that was foreign to Erin. Her legs had barely a scratch to show for her life so far.

"Thanks, Erin, that feels so much better," Grace said, propping herself up on her elbows. "Sorry about this, but I think I should rest some more now."

Erin didn't mind. She would go back to her grandparent's property and put in a few more hours before calling it a day. Then she'd take some time out and have a good think about her future. Things like where she should live, what work she should do and whether she should switch her degree and start after mid-term.

"Do you want a hand getting to the bedroom?"

"Thanks, I'd appreciate that. Peter will be back soon, so you can leave when you like."

With Grace settled back in her bed, Erin opened the window and poured Grace a glass of water. "I'll see you next week, Grace. I hope you have a good week."

"I'm determined to go to the lake tomorrow for another swim. It'll put me out for a couple of days, but it's worth it."

Erin shook her head but smiled. There was no stopping this woman.

When Erin turned to leave, a framed photo of Grace caught her eye. She was neatly dressed in a red riding coat, immaculately groomed and sitting with a perfect posture astride a grey horse. Erin remembered her determination to point out a ribbon, trophy or framed photo and ask Grace about it. If anything, it would take her mind off the pain in her legs.

Erin picked it up and had a closer look. "Are you dressed for the Olympics in this photo?" It wouldn't surprise Erin if Grace *had* competed in the Olympics. Actually, nothing would surprise Erin anymore.

Grace chuckled and put her hand out for it. "Good Lord, no. It was taken during my clerk of the course days."

"Your what? It sounds more official than the Olympics."

Grace indicated the chair again, and Erin complied. There was nowhere urgent to be, and she made herself comfortable.

"It's a job, Erin, and I was the first woman employed by Far North Queensland Amateur Racing to be the clerk of the course. Over several years, starting as far back as 1987 when I first arrived, I worked at the Innisfail Turf Club, Tolga Turf Club and the Cairns Amateur Races, where this photo was taken."

"I'm going to be absolutely honest, Grace. I have no idea what a clerk of the course is."

"Well, you'll learn something new today, then." Her grin was fast. "It's the job held for the official rider on a horse at racing meets. The clerk of the course takes the horses from the saddling enclosure around to the barriers. They help jockeys who have trouble getting their horses to the barriers and catch any runaway horses. They also lead the winning horse to the winner's circle."

"Oh. That makes sense now. I've seen them on TV when the Melbourne Cup is run."

"I would've loved to have done a big race meet but settled for the Cairns Amateurs. It's the biggest regional horse meet in the country, so I was excited about doing it. You'd be surprised how many miles you do in two days of racing. When you have six to seven races each day, and by the time you take the horses to the barriers and then the winner's circle, it all adds up."

Grace handed back the framed photo, and Erin took another good look at it. "Why so dressed up and official looking?"

"It's a big occasion. On one day we'd wear white jodhpurs and on the other, black. Always with a red jacket and a nice lace shirt underneath. We also turned out our horses in immaculate condition with their manes plaited with a red ribbon with white spots on them. That's me on Grey Aztec. He looked a picture, don't you think?"

Erin nodded. The overall impression was perfect poise, polished and professional.

"Grey Aztec was a champion, and I practically begged the owner to have him after his racing days."

"I suppose I've never wondered about what happened to horses after their racing days were over," Erin said, fingering the frame on her lap.

"I was at an earlier Cairns Amateurs with a young and skilled girl, Shiree Walmsley. She was sharing the duties with me, and after the last race when we were unsaddling, this voice yelled out, 'Great job, Grace'. It was Tomas Hedley. I'd been told by the jockey he was the owner of Grey Aztec. I jumped off, asking Shiree to hold my horse, and ran to the member's area where Tomas was and asked him what he would do with Grey Aztec when he finished racing. 'Why do you want to know?' he'd asked. I told him I'd love to use him for a course and show horse. I'd fallen in love with the horse, and right or wrong, I wanted him.

"Tomas hesitated for a moment and then said, 'He has a few more starts in him before I retire him, okay? Then he's yours.' I couldn't believe my luck and was totally thrilled. Two months later, I got a phone call from Tomas saying he was finished with Grey Aztec and I could pick him up. It wasn't the only horse Tomas gave me over the years, but he knew I looked after them like babies and cared for them. I gave Grey Aztec a spell of about eight months where I cared daily for him, giving him lots of love and affection, which I must say he lapped up. Then I did some shows with him that season and had him ready for the Cairns Amateurs in that photo."

Erin rose and placed the photo on the shelf next to a bronze horse statue. "Well, I think you both look stunning."

Grace chuckled. "The funny thing is, on that day, I was called into the steward's room for a pre-race meeting, and the chief steward said, 'I believe you have Grey Aztec here. Do you think you can hold him?' I said, 'Yes, sir. I believe I have him prepared. But what happens if I lose control?' Grey Aztec was known to win races by six to eight lengths. The steward replied, 'Then stick to the outside fence and don't interfere with the race.' I was amused by the thought the clerk of the course horse could beat the field home."

"So, scare me." Erin laughed delightfully. "What happened?"

Grace laughed too. "Of course, we did what we were supposed to do, and once the horses had come around the course for the last stretch, I gave Grey Aztec some forward distance and came home at a gallop. The crowd cheered as I flew up the straight, and I know Grey Aztec loved having that run."

Erin leant back against the dresser and folded her arms. "How many years did you do this stuff for?"

"Thirteen. My last Cairns Amateur wasn't so professional. Peter and I had moved to the Gold Coast for a few years, so I had to fly up and borrow a horse to do my clerk of the course duties. On this final year, I'd gone to the track the day before for a quiet ride with the borrowed horse, and it completely lost it. It reared so high it fell back on me and broke my shoulder."

"Oh, no!" Erin's hand clasped over her mouth.

"Yeah, so I couldn't ride, but I did what was necessary on foot. I was still dressed in the proper attire, and I spent a lot of time walking that weekend with my arm in a sling and a great deal of pain."

Erin cocked her head. "Has anyone ever told you you're crazy?"

Grace chuckled, her eyes dancing with amusement. "Plenty of times."

Erin moved away from the dresser and smiled. "Okay, this time I'm going for real, and you can have that rest."

"Thanks, Erin. Thanks for listening to this crazy old lady."

"You're very inspiring." Erin reached over and squeezed Grace's hand. "I hope I can claim to be a little bit crazy by the time I get to your age."

"Oh, before you go"—Grace picked up a folded newspaper from her bedside table—"there's an advert here for the local vet surgery. They're looking for a vet nurse."

Erin studied Grace's face. She embodied daring, guts, determination and boldness—and the constant need to put her near Tom. Erin faced her square on, hands on hips. "Grace, you're not meddling, are you?"

A mischievous smile crossed her face. "He's a good soul. I've seen him work with horses. If he's that gentle and kind to animals, he'll *never* hurt you."

Erin chewed her bottom lip, determined to take things slowly, despite her body betraying her every time she was near Tom.

"Drop into the vet surgery on your way home. Where is the harm in doing that?"

Whenever she was near Tom, her body awakened and her resolve weakened. If she took this job, she'd encounter him every day. How could she take things slow and steady when there was no distance between them?

Erin took a long, hard look at Grace. A woman who refused to take things slow and steady. She lived by the rules of adrenalin rushes and risks. Grace didn't say anything further as she left, but the look on her face expressed a thousand words—*get out there and live your life to the fullest while you still can.*

Chapter 19

19 years old

"Still upset about it, aren't you?"

Grace nodded as she sat beside Gary, now a local police officer and still one of her best mates. The park bench was a well-shaded spot in Kalamunda, and she'd suggested it when Gary told her he had an hour break for lunch.

"It makes me so mad. Deat and I were having a great time. Why'd I have to pee behind a bush that day and get caught with my pants down?"

Gary chuckled as he squashed a few more mouthfuls of his sandwich into his mouth.

Grace smiled at her friend and was ready for a sarcastic comeback. Instead, he was too busy chewing to give her a hard time, and she let it rest. But only for that day. Being with Gary wouldn't be normal if one or the other, but usually both, didn't fling around a sarcastic comment or three.

She sat back and nudged her shoulder against Gary's.

"You okay?" Gary asked.

A miserable sigh escaped, and Gary turned to face her before pulling a slice of tomato from his sandwich and eating it. He nodded, waiting for her to continue.

"Some days, I'm so downright dispirited about losing Deat. I'm not allowed to compete at all anymore. Exhibition rides or nothing."

The biggest loss, she realised, was the way it clamped down on her sense of freedom. That's what competing as Deat had given her. Being female restricted that and upset her more than anything.

"If I wasn't your friend, I'd have arrested you for identity fraud," he joked.

"Hey, I didn't pinch anyone's identity. I just made up one."

"The same thing."

She'd only confessed to Gary a couple of weeks ago, not long after Deat's sudden death. Gary's reaction was priceless. He'd ranted about how risky and illegal it was pretending to be someone else. He'd even taken out his notebook and written it all down.

"Are you finished now?" she'd asked him back then.

Gary had leant against his cop car and folded his arms. "Yeah, I suppose I am." Then with a sheepish smile, he added, "Want to come out with the gang tonight?"

And that was that. The end of her criminal life and never to be broached again. But not before she took control of his notebook and tore out the pages. She ripped them to shreds and let the breeze carry them away.

She looked across to Gary as he slurped down chocolate-flavoured milk. His extra-large shirt was stretched across his chest, its buttons threatening to pop. Gary would never change, and she allowed a small smile to touch the edges of her mouth. She let him finish his lunch in peace and watched the eucalyptus branches swaying gently in the light breeze, relishing the cool air against her skin. Their familiar scent tickled her nose and reminded her of days gone by. Kids kicked a football on the other side of the council-kept park and across the street, locals did their grocery shopping in the mall.

Her new car was parked nearby. It was a second-hand MGB in British racing green, and she couldn't still the flutter of excitement in her chest every time she looked at it. She'd never worked so hard at saving in her life. With the sky a picture-perfect blue, it was the perfect day to open the convertible on the drive over. Nothing beat the exhilaration of air rushing past her face and through her hair.

She turned back to Gary as he finished his lunch, her smile never far away when she was with him.

"How did they ever let you in the police force?"

Gary smirked, probably giving himself a few moments to come up with some smart-arsed comeback. They'd become best mates when the first words spilled from each other's mouths, a few years ago when she'd snuck into a party pretending to be eighteen.

Gary used a serviette to wipe his mouth and hands. "Because they know I'm great with all sorts. I can communicate with them. It's the magic word these days."

"I've never seen you serious before, and that mouth of yours should be quarantined sometimes."

"Yeah, but it's only with you when the worst comes out of it."

Grace laughed. They said the nastiest things to each other and still came out the other side laughing.

"Anyway, doing anything this weekend? Want to come for a water ski?"

"Gary, have you got up yet?"

"Ouch, that hurts. Of course, I have. I got up on doubles only last week, as a matter of fact."

"What did they need? An ocean liner to get you up?"

"Hey, you watch it. Just because you're all legs until you get to your bum, we both know it's all bloody cheek after that."

Grace slapped him on the arm playfully, and Gary retaliated by poking her in the ribs. He was a big man but had a bigger heart. She only had a few close friends growing up, and she respected Gary's friendship over the past couple of years. It didn't matter where her jobs took her; she could always count on Gary whenever she was closer to home.

Her definition of home was still Kalamunda. Occasionally, she dropped in to say hello to her parents, but the atmosphere had remained toxic. Her parents argued more and more, and Grace refused to be used as bait. She worked and lived her own life.

She got by. They all did.

Kalamunda wouldn't be home for too much longer. Grace had secured a new job as the shearer's cook with a team of shearers working in and around Yerecoin, the sheep and wheat belt north of Perth. It began in a few weeks.

After the monotony of the circus life, her wanderlust had spread to various jobs. She'd start early in the morning with breaking in horses, track riding and riding rough horses for those who couldn't control them. For some reason, she had a knack for it and developed a connection with those problem horses.

As the day progressed, she did modelling work, waitressing and discotheque dancing in nightclubs. All her bills were paid, and she got along just fine.

"Actually, I can't. Robert's coming with me to the Peaceville Valley Rodeo. I don't want to miss it as it might be a while before there's another chance, and it's one of my favourite rodeos."

"Still trying to live that dream, are you? Hoping you can change their minds and they'll let you ride *and* compete."

Grace grimaced. The thrill never dampened and refused to go away. "I'll keep bitching about it until the cows come home." She leant back against the park bench and lifted her knees to her chest. "Hey, did I show you the newspaper article they wrote about me when I did some exhibition rides at the Riverland Corral?"

"Like about six times."

Grace mock-punched his shoulder. "No, I haven't."

"You told me about it. *A lot.*"

Gary tilted his face and rested his index finger on his cheek. "Um ... let me see. You broke a finger and tore a muscle in your leg. You rode a big steer and a big black horse. You 'made time' on both rides, and you're a woman. And yeah, all the men hate it when you ride because you show them how much better you are."

Grace burst out laughing. Gary had it spot on. It had been a mild sunny day late last December when she rode at the Riverland Corral. Her riding had been impressive, even if she came away with some injuries.

A female competitor always infuriated the male competitors, but she'd be damned if she stopped to keep them happy. This new job as a shearer's cook might keep her away from the circuit for longer than she'd like, but she didn't have a choice. The money paid well, and she was ready for a new adventure.

"So, how about getting together the following weekend? The water will still be good."

Grace rose and stretched her arms above her head. It was time to return to work. "Thanks, Gary. I'd love to. Is that cute chick you've been chasing coming too?"

Gary slumped messily over the park bench. "I don't think she's ever going to notice me."

"If she doesn't make a move soon, I will." Grace chuckled and patted him on the shoulder.

His wobbling emotions swiftly changed to a huge smile beaming across his face. "You're not so bad a chick, Grace, but not my type. I'd go nuts with worry every time you climbed on top of those crazy animals. I think I'll find myself some nice, sweet girl who loves to crochet."

"Except she'd be as boring as hell."

"Well, if the alternative is someone like you, no, thank you. You'll only come skiing next time if you don't have a broken this or that or a sprained whatsit." Gary shook his head but kept the merriment alive in his eyes. "Thank God we're only friends."

Gary rose from the park bench and belched into his hand.

"You say some of the nicest things you know," she said sarcastically. Deep down, though, she loved the banter between them. She'd never considered Gary as anything more than a friend. Her need to spread her wings and seek life and adventure could never leave her tied to someone like Gary. But to have an ear and a mate in him was something she subconsciously had been seeking all her life. She'd found it and wouldn't give it up. She flung her arms around his shoulders and pulled him in close. "Don't be so dramatic. I won't break anything, and I'll see you on the water next weekend."

"We'll see." He had trouble hiding a blush. "I better return to the station, or they'll send out a search party for me."

"You should be easy to find."

"Hey, watch your tongue, or I'll have no choice but to arrest you."

They both laughed. Gary had parked his patrol car beside her MGB, and they walked in that direction, Gary whistling and her feeling good about the world. There was still so much for her to discover and do, and she worried she'd never fit it all in.

For now, excitement thrummed through her as she envisioned her new adventure. She'd loved her only shearing experience at Marble Bar. Putting her hand up to be the cook was one way of getting her foot in the door. She wanted to learn how to classify wool. It had interested her at Marble Bar, and somehow, she would wheedle her way into the shearer's shed in between cooking the meals.

Chapter 20

Present Day

Erin shut herself into her bedroom-cum-office and worked on Grace's report all afternoon. The closer it got to five pm, the harder she pounded the keys on her laptop. At four thirty, she saved the file and slammed the laptop closed.

After a rushed explanation to her grandmother, she drove back into town. The vet surgery was on the outskirts of Malanda. A small town with its beating heart beside the iconic Malanda Falls. It amazed Erin that an expanse of rainforest on the edge of town hid a waterfall and swimming spot—all within walking distance of the compact business centre.

Unease, mixed with nerves, had her driving slightly over the speed limit. She pressed her foot on the brake and took a deep breath to calm down. A job up here meant living on the Tablelands. Her grandparents had offered for her to stay with them as long as she liked, but should she? Employed by a vet surgery while studying vet science made sense. *Jeez.* Her boat had never been rocked this much in her life. There were so many options to consider, so many decisions to make, and she hadn't even been offered the job yet. Was she getting ahead of herself?

In ten minutes, she had her Honda parked and made her way to the surgery's entrance. The *next* ten minutes could change the course of her life.

When she entered, a receptionist wearing a name tag with Jennifer looked up from her computer screen and greeted her warmly and with the obligatory, 'How can I help you?'

"I'd like to apply for the vet nurse position advertised in the paper. Do you have an application form I can complete?"

A man with a stethoscope around his neck joined Jennifer and rifled through some paperwork on the desk.

"Don, do you know anything about the ad in this week's paper? A vet nurse job?" Jennifer asked.

Don flicked a cursory glance at Erin. She squirmed but tried to maintain her professional poise and friendly smile.

Don straightened before reaching for a tray on a shelf. He picked up an envelope and passed it over. "Do you have any experience ah ..."

"It's Erin," she said, extending her hand.

"Nice to meet you, Erin," he said, shaking her hand. "Sorry to be so direct, but we've lost a couple of good staff. One pregnant and one leaving town."

"I'm a fourth-year med student, but I'll be changing to vet science mid-term. I can't give you full-time hours, but I'll manage what I can with my studies. That's all I can offer." Erin's heart pumped inside her chest. She'd done it, made a commitment by speaking it out loud, and God help her, it felt good.

Don and Jennifer stared at her with looks of disbelief.

"Really?" Don said.

Erin shrugged. "Yes. Is there a problem? I've got a resume and all the uni documents, plus some referees. It's all in here." She pulled an A4 envelope from her handbag and handed it to Don.

"Can you start next week?" Don asked, sliding the papers from the envelope and running his eyes over her resume. He turned the page, studied her results and mumbled: oh, wow, excellent, hmmm, great and finally, yes. "You sound like just the person we need."

What? She released the breath she didn't realise she was holding. The few minutes Don had taken to read through her credentials were painstaking. Now it was time to question her rash move. A quick shuffle in her head, and her only commitment was to finish the report on Grace. She could work on it after hours and have it completed within a matter of weeks. As for somewhere to live—sorted for now. So, what was holding her back? Nothing! She could do this. For the first time in a long time, it was like stepping out into the sunshine after a long and dreary winter.

A smile gathered strength on her face, and she nodded enthusiastically. "You know what? I think I can manage that."

"Good. All the application forms are in the envelope. Fill in the details and drop them back here ASAP. I've got to go now, but ring Jennifer if you have any questions. Thanks, Erin, and welcome to the team."

Erin glanced at the time on her phone. It had taken five minutes for her life to turn towards a path she hadn't envisaged before meeting Grace and Tom. She looked up when a familiar blur stumbled past the corner of her eye.

"Hey, Tom. Come and meet our new vet nurse." Jennifer stood and tidied the brochure stand on the corner of the counter. He hadn't seen her yet. When he stepped into the reception area, the initial shock of the news had his jaw dropping.

"Erin?"

"Hey, do you pair know each other?" asked Jennifer with a curious look.

He waved away Jennifer's declaration, obviously distracted by her presence. "We met at Grace Luppi's property. I've been helping with a bit of horseriding on the weekends."

"Sweet. You can help her find her feet here too—and maybe be a mentor for her vet science studies she's switching over to."

A rush of air left Erin's lungs as her gaze locked with Tom's. She'd only committed minutes ago. Not expecting to confront Tom so soon, a blush seared her neck and cheeks. She had to find her tongue fast and leave. "Um … thanks, Jennifer. I'll drop this in tomorrow." She waved the application form. "Ah … bye, Tom."

She jogged to her Honda and doubled over, gasping for breath. Any onlooker would've thought she'd run a marathon.

"Hey, Erin, wait up."

She stalled with her hand on the door handle. She gulped in more air, closed her eyes and said a silent prayer before turning, but nothing could stop the rush of heat speeding through her when Tom reached her side and rested his hand on hers.

"I'm finished here in a few minutes. Did you want to go for a 'celebratory' swim at the falls? It's just down the road."

She knew where it was but had never stopped there before. Her choice of swimming place had always been the lake. But to go there with Tom? It was everything her damn traitorous body wanted, and the exact opposite of what her brain was telling her was a good idea.

Somehow, she managed a nod.

⌒⌘⌒

"It's never busy at this time of day," Tom said, directing her in front as they walked towards the falls along the narrow concrete path. Picnic tables dotted the way with public toilets tucked into the side of the small cleared patch of rainforest. Someone had etched the flood water level showing 1967 on one of the covered picnic shades, showing how high the water had once risen. Erin shivered. It was hard to imagine a torrent of water anywhere near that high.

She was barely keeping her nerves at bay. Being alone with Tom while on the rebound was amazing and far too risky, and the constant knowing he was staring at her back, body and backside was leaving her mouth dry and her heart beating erratically. There was a simmering, crackling tension, a conversation that neither wanted to start.

"Did you know that years ago, they turned the falls into the local swimming pool?" Tom asked, breaking the silence.

Erin peered down at the falls. On either side of the falling water, the locals had concreted the banks. It was easy to picture the place being used as a rudimentary pool.

"But be warned, the water is freezing. It flows through the dense rainforest, and not a spec of sun touches it until it reaches the top of the falls."

Erin shivered again, and goosebumps broke out when Tom's hand squeezed her shoulder.

She ducked underneath his hand and walked off towards the toilet block. "Give me a minute to change."

She didn't look back to check his expression. As she moved toward the toilets, she found the space to breathe again. The pounding against her ribs echoed in her ears, and she clenched her swimming bag tighter to her chest, needing to silence it. She had the urge to scream into the tangle of rainforest. Nothing could happen with Tom. She was still in pieces and freshly headed in a new direction. The last thing she needed was a workplace romance.

Too soon for her scattered thoughts and feelings, she was descending the last few steps into the water. Tom was waist high and slapping the water playfully. She put one tentative toe in and shrieked. Any other thoughts fled. This was impossible. There was no way she was taking another step in. Feeling every vestige of heat zapped from her body, nothing else existed. Just her and the cold water surrounding that one little toe.

"Come on. Let's swim to the falls. It's not very deep. You can stand up under it, it's that shallow. It'll be the best massage you've had in your life."

She shivered and hugged herself. "I can't do it. It's too cold."

"Oh, come on, where's your courage?"

She shied away from the water he flicked her way, along with his disarming smile and those dimples. "Who cares about courage?"

"Drop quickly. Get wet all at once and see how good it feels."

"I can't," Erin wailed. It seemed too impossible a mission. "I can't do it."

"Yes, you can," Tom insisted. "If you can look for a new job and change the direction your life's been going in, if you can change your mind after four years of a med degree and do something you actually might enjoy, damn it, Erin, that's courage. You can do this."

"I can't," she argued while her legs slowly, painfully sank into the water. Her last outraged squeal before her face dropped below water level was enough for Tom to laugh outright. But damn it, he was right. Within seconds her body temperature had adjusted, and they were slow crawling the forty metres to where the water cascaded over the dark black rocks.

"Stop here; there's a rock close by," Tom shouted over the noise of falling water.

Erin's skin burned when Tom touched her, despite the cold water, and directed her to stand upright on a rock rising from the bottom of the river underneath the flowing water.

"Now lean back. The rocks aren't too sharp."

She did as he suggested, and Tom did the same thing beside her. The water cascaded over the black rocks, hitting her in the back in the most relaxing way. She looked towards the other end of the pool, where they'd first stepped in, enjoying the massage over her body. You wouldn't do this in the wet season as the power of the water would push you away, but today it felt perfect. Tom took her hand and kissed her palm before letting it go. One simple gesture awakened every nerve ending in her body and relaxed every muscle as she lay back against the rocks.

She wanted to stay there forever enjoying the natural beauty, but Tom had other ideas. He tugged on her hand, and they slipped back into the water and swam to the steps.

Back on the concreted bank, the late afternoon breeze had chilled, and it seeped into her wet skin, causing her teeth to chatter.

"Quick, get that towel around you." Tom grabbed it from where she'd left it earlier, wrapping it around her shoulders and rubbing his hands up and down her arms like you'd do when a child got out of the bath. Once she was relatively dry, they huddled next to each other on the warm concrete bank.

"I think we'll have a stack of fun working together." Tom smiled hopefully, which warmed her better than the damp towel was doing.

Heat radiated where their bodies touched, from shoulders right down to their thighs. Strong legs, muscular arms. Her breath hitched. "I think you're right."

Then Erin's heartbeat went from steady to frantic when Tom reached across and tucked a strand of hair behind her ear, cupping her chin and gently turning her head to meet his eyes which were soft and full of longing. Thank goodness she was sitting as her legs turned to jelly with the delicate kiss he pressed to her lips. The scratch of his two-day growth pulled at her core as he grazed his lips to the corner of her mouth, cheek, temple, and finished back where he started. Her eyes flashed open when he pulled back. *Don't stop.*

He exhaled sharply, throwing a pained grin her way. "I know, I know. That's not slow. I just couldn't ... I *can* do slow. Totally."

Erin took in his pained expression before laughter spilled out, temporarily dispersing some of the electricity between them. Visibly relieved, Tom joined in.

Tom shuffled over leaving a metre of awkward space between them.

"Thank you," Erin said softly, "for trying to take it slow and — for the kiss."

Tom glanced at her, surprised. "Erin, I'm obviously not trying hard enough." He shook his head, amused, and indicated they should make for the car park. "As for the kiss, well — I better let you go home before I try again."

Chapter 21

21 years old

Grace embraced Gary tightly on the front steps of her mother's house before showing him inside. He followed her into the kitchen. "No uniform, so I assume you're off duty? Have you got time for a cuppa?"

"Yeah. I've got a couple of hours before my next shift," he said, leaning against the kitchen counter.

She bustled around the kitchen, flicking on the kettle and gathering cups, sugar, milk and the biscuit tin. Neither of them said anything, which was unusual where Gary was concerned. It had been a good eighteen months since they'd seen each other. Almost another lifetime ago, and she'd appreciate unburdening onto her friend's shoulder.

"I heard about the miscarriage," he said, breaking the uneasy silence.

Grace winced as she dropped the tea bags into the cups, blinking back unexpected tears. She couldn't look her friend in the eye, unsure how to explain what had gone wrong in her life since they'd last caught up. News travelled fast in this corner of the world. The memory of that day was still painful, and if she dwelled on it for too long, it eventually got to her.

"How's it going, living back with your parents?"

Grace poured the hot water into the pot, giving the tea leaves a few moments to infuse. Most days it wasn't going too well. She sighed heavily. "I had nowhere else to go."

"How's the little fellow?"

Grace turned to Gary, holding the steaming mugs and smiled at his question. He was yet to meet her seven-month-old baby, Colin. She handed a mug to Gary. "He's amazing. I love him so much already."

He grunted as she led him to the front patio. "More than that loser of a husband who couldn't keep someone as beautiful and amazing as you?"

"Oh, Gary, I can't put all the blame on Norm. I was half the problem too."

"What? Let me guess, you worked just as many hours and took care of Colin as well?"

Grace eyed her best friend as they settled on the outdoor chairs. Some woman would be very lucky one day when they snared him.

"He was just never around. I was alone for so much of the time I may as well have not been married."

"Your marriage barely lasted *one* year. I get that you were pregnant before you married him, but couldn't he have made a bloody effort?"

"He was too much of a mummy's boy. He preferred to spend his days with her." She blew into her steaming tea. "Look, we weren't compatible."

"He was compatible enough to get you pregnant again."

"Yeah, just my luck I fell pregnant again when Colin was only five months. No way was I ready for that again."

"How are you feeling now?"

She'd arrived at her parent's doorstep with a tiny baby and two months pregnant. "I'd been feeling okay. I didn't think I was under that much stress. It was more stressful when I bled on the new carpet. The only thing I could think of was Dad would kill me because they would never get the stain out."

She grimaced at the absurdity of it.

"For God's sakes, you were losing a baby, and all you thought about was staining the carpet?" Gary pointed out.

"I know, stupid, right? Except you never lose the fear of what your father is capable of."

"Is he different now? You know, now you've been married and have a baby?"

"Sort of, but I still don't trust him."

"Where are they now?"

"Out visiting."

"Is Colin asleep?"

"Yeah, he's due to wake soon, then you can meet my little man." Grace nursed her cup against her chest and embraced the maternal feelings she never knew existed. From the first moment she clapped eyes on her newborn son, she'd loved him with an intensity she couldn't have imagined previously. "He's so worth it, Gary. I'd go through ten marriages just to have a beautiful child, like Colin, each time."

"Grace, please. One bad marriage is enough."

"Yeah, you're right. I'm a single mum to one now, and it could easily have been two if I didn't miscarry."

Gary sighed into his cup of tea. "You know, something didn't quite strike me as normal from as far back as your wedding day."

"What do you mean?" This was news to Grace. Looking back, she realised how rushed the wedding was — not realising she was pregnant until nearly four months — but believed she'd found the love of her life. Why would she have doubted back then that it wouldn't last?

"Well, heck, when the groom can't even make it to the church before the bride, you've gotta wonder."

Grace chuckled, recalling the awkward moment when she'd been waiting outside the church with her attendants. The priest had been running late too, and unaware the groom hadn't arrived, had suggested she start walking down the aisle. They'd done so, only to realise that Norm and his groomsmen were nowhere to be seen.

"They were caught up in footy-final traffic," she recalled.

"More like drinking too much because of the footy final."

She shrugged. Old news now. Leaving Norm hadn't been as hard as she expected. Money had been tight, but Grace was prepared to work and parent, even if it meant she ended each day exhausted.

"You back working?"

"Yeah, Mum's been great. I think having Colin around has given her a new purpose in life. She helps while I go to work." Fitting back into her old routine of working a few jobs had been easier than expected. Old bosses remembered her, so her work ethic couldn't be all that bad.

"What sort of things are you doing? Still with horses?"

"You bet. Breaking them in and training. My second job is working for a company that organises venues for bands and accesses models for clothing companies. I've also been doing some barmaid work and dancing at the Sheraton."

Gary raised his eyebrows and smirked. "I feel like I should be surprised, but now I think about it, of course you'd be a great dancer."

"Thanks, mate. So, did you snare that girl you've been chasing?" she asked with a wry smile.

"Actually, she's coming along just fine."

"Good for you. That makes me happy. It's so good to see you again. Stuck out in the middle of nowhere, I missed your company. I sure could do with a water ski again."

"A few of the old gang are getting together in a couple of weeks. So, there's your chance."

"You're on. I'll be there."

Colin's cry made its way to the patio, and Grace leapt to her feet. "I'll be back in a sec. I'll change his nappy and bring him out."

She raced into her bedroom, scooped him out of the cot and nuzzled him against her chest, swaying from side to side, cooing quietly, soothing his anguished cries.

⁘

"Here you go, Gary. Meet my special little man," she said, handing over a freshly changed Colin.

Nestled in the crook of Gary's elbow and against his bulky frame, Colin looked like a miniature doll. The look suited Gary, even though his face told the story of a man who had no idea what to do with the tiny creature.

She ran her hand over Colin's mop of brown hair sticking up like a mohawk. "I'll fix up a bottle for him. He won't stay placid for too long."

Gary rose and followed her into the kitchen, holding Colin like a piece of fine china. "You're not leaving me out here if he's about to start crying again."

Grace laughed. "Chicken." They made their way to the kitchen where she began heating the milk on the stove.

"I'm going to start on the rodeo circuit again as soon as I can."

"Are you crazy, woman? You've got a little boy to take care of." Gary manoeuvred Colin to his shoulder and started patting his padded bottom.

"He may as well learn early that his mother is a wild one," she said, testing the milk's temperature on the inside of her wrist. "Mum has offered to babysit and help with Colin, so there's no reason I can't fit it in. And by the way, you're right at home with him; maybe I could call on you for babysitting duties too."

Gary shook his head vehemently; not sure if it was for the rodeo or the babysitting.

"Come here, little man." Grace prised Colin back when he let out a screeching cry. "Take a seat." She pointed to another one around the kitchen table and sat opposite, tying a cloth bib at Colin's neck. The second the bottle was in Colin's mouth, a delightful slurping sound settled in the room. "But Mum reckons I need a break first. She suggested I take a holiday."

"I agree with your mum, you've had one heck of a year. Where you headed?" The chair beneath Gary squeaked as he stretched his legs and settled with his arms crossed.

"I've saved enough to fly to London. I'm hoping to pick up some part-time work while I go, hoping to stretch it out to six months. After a bit of Britain and Europe, I'll make my way to the USA. I've met a cute US Air Force pilot recently. He's been dropping into the bar where I work.

I'm going to surprise him in Seattle. Mum has agreed to take care of Colin for me."

"Well, that doesn't surprise me. If you had ten men chasing you, I wouldn't be shocked. I don't want to sound creepy or anything, Grace, but you're some beauty."

Grace looked up from feeding Colin and saw the sincerity on Gary's face. She'd never been able to rely on her intellect because of the difficulties she experienced, like reading. It was a condition she understood better as an adult and one she would pursue when the opportunity arose. But she knew she was good to look at, and it had come in handy more than once. Being able to model and dance at the Sheraton helped pay the bills. If she had to use her body to her advantage, she would do it.

"When do you leave?"

"Next month. But I'll miss this little fella. I'm not sure I should be leaving him behind but mum insists she's more than happy to take care of him, and it'll give me time to recover from the miscarriage."

"He sure is worth missing. But you'll come back refreshed and—"

"And ready for the rodeo circuit. It's been ages since I've ridden in anything, and I miss it. I'm going to kick some butt about women being allowed to compete. I'm so over it."

She was more determined than ever these days. She'd experienced firsthand how hard a married woman had to work if money was short in the household. It also reminded her of the unfairness of how the raising of the children was left to the women. Her mother had been a stay-at-home mum, and now Grace could appreciate how much of herself she gave up to do so. Not that her mother would see it this way. It was how it was done in her mother's era, but society was changing. Women were expected to work and contribute financially. Going out to work didn't bother Grace because staying home all day stifled her sense of adventure and threatened to choke the very life out of her. With her mother more than willing to babysit Colin, Grace would continue to work and financially support herself and Colin, and fit in this once in a lifetime holiday opportunity.

"I don't mind if a woman has to work and do the mothering thing, but what I really hate is how we're treated when it comes to competing in a sport where men think females aren't capable."

"Christ, I'm already scared for all those wimpy male competitors you're going up against," said Gary.

Grace harrumphed. "If a woman can work, have children and take care of them, then they can bloody well ride in a rodeo *and* compete if they chose to." Colin squawked as the bottle slipped from his mouth. "Except I can only do exhibition rides, remember. My name is blacklisted. They don't want to be outdone by a woman, that's for sure."

They both laughed. Hell, it was good to have Gary close again. She could let go of all her inhibitions and talk freely. Life was good around him.

For now, she had an exciting holiday to look forward to, thanks to her mum. Was it too long to be away from Colin? Her heart contracted at the thought of leaving him behind. They'd been together every day of his short life, but a break would help to refresh her both mentally and physically. The past year had taken its toll on her body and mind. "It'll be over in a flash."

Gary rose to rinse his cup. "What will be?"

"My holiday. Before I know it, it'll be over."

"Yeah, holidays are like that. But I'll see you on the water in a couple of weeks?"

"Sure will."

"Bring your little man. I'm sure everyone will want to meet him. I'll even give it a go nursing him while you ski."

"Done deal." She raised Colin to her shoulder and rubbed his back until he let out a milky burp. "And thanks, Gary. You mean everything to me. Better than any husband."

He chuckled before reaching down to place a kiss on Colin's cheek. "I can't wait to see this little man grow up."

"I hope so."

"Okay, I better go now, or I'll end up on the missing person's list."

Grace wrapped an arm around the broad bulk of his shoulder from her sitting position and squeezed tight. "Thanks, Gary."

And she meant it. A friend as precious as Gary was worth ten husbands. As long as she didn't begin a trend of discarding husbands, she'd be fine. She promised to work extra hard on her next marriage.

Chapter 22

Grace had chewed through her spending money faster than planned. She had done all the touristy stuff in London before finding her way to Athens and joining a dance troupe.

"There's something off about this contract." Grace and a couple of girls from Australia and London huddled around a small table at an outdoor café. They were enjoying a well-deserved coffee and a smoke. The mild autumn sun spread its warmth over her back and infused her body with energy. The nights were late by the time they finished with the dance show, and this was a pleasant way to recharge before it started all over again.

"What do you mean?" one of them asked.

The dance troupe earned commissions on the drinks they sold before the show. The term they used, she'd learnt, was hustler.

Unable to drink alcohol, it should've been a hard job to do, but she got by. She'd learnt the hard way a few years before that a single drop of alcohol would send her body into toxic shock and she would end up in hospital. Still, no doctor could tell her what was wrong, so she stayed away from it all together.

Without being vain, she took advantage of her good looks and innocent face and easily hustled prospective customers. Parting with their money on drinks was easier than what it'd taken to clean water troughs in the hot Marble Bar sun, and she was slowly but surely refilling her empty well of funds. Before returning home, she still had to make her way to the US and surprise Justin, her handsome Air Force pilot.

Except, Grace couldn't let go of this hunch she had about the contract. "A couple of nights ago, I kept selling champagne to an Iranian Englishman. We had a great conversation, but one thing he told me is women don't dance in Iran like we do here."

"Well, why are they sending our troupe over there?" asked another of the dancers.

Grace mulled over this for a moment. "I know, right? Something feels off."

The troupe manager had told them to be ready to leave the next day for a two-week stay in Iran. Her fellow dancers didn't seem to think it was too out of the ordinary, but something kept niggling its way around Grace's head. She might've been none the wiser if she'd never met the Iranian Englishman, but she had, and the situation unnerved her.

The night they'd met, he'd finally caught her out after the seventh glass of champagne. He'd suspected something when Grace wasn't one little bit tipsy and said as much. The staff were trained to pour coloured tea into her glass so she didn't get drunk or sick. Despite being conned into buying so much champagne, he'd been a true gentleman. Her conversation with him, though, had planted a seed of doubt about this contract they were meant to sign.

"Don't sign it, girls. I'm going to pay a visit to the Australian Consulate this afternoon and ask about it."

They half listened to Grace as they giggled and swapped travel stories. While she'd come overseas alone, finding travel companions who didn't mind her company had been easy. Even before arriving in Athens, desperately short of cash, she'd had some memorable encounters.

Crossing the English Channel had been interesting enough. She smiled into her coffee as the chatter continued around her. It'd been a rough crossing the entire way, but she'd spied a good-looking guy checking her out. They'd clicked despite her seasickness and, as a joke, had swapped jackets, only to get separated, complete with her money and passport in the pocket of the jacket he wore.

A language barrier to deal with and a frantic dash, and she had her passport and money back. She wouldn't do that again.

Other interesting people came her way as she travelled to Athens. She fondly remembered the mouse-like girl who'd shared a train carriage with her in Switzerland. She was shocked to learn that this quietly spoken, English-speaking young girl, not much younger than herself, would take watches from Switzerland, sell them in Greece and forward the monies to the Israeli army.

Grace was fast learning that the world consisted of many different individuals. Like some fancy cocktail, they swirled together in an exciting mix of cultures and ideas. She was far from the quiet Perth suburbs or the sweltering outback towns that dotted Western Australia.

For now, she had this dilemma. She'd always learnt to go with her gut instinct. This contract wouldn't leave her alone. Compared to other women, Grace was paranoid. She always felt responsible for saving her own skin, probably because her upbringing had demanded more vigilance than most. Now she was having difficulty deciding whether her anxiety was reasonable or an overreaction.

Added to that was her desperation to return to Colin. She missed him like crazy and would constantly worry about her safety until she was home. Ringing her mother too often wasn't an option, but on the few occasions she had, her mother had assured her Colin was fine and doing well. Grace just had to make sure she returned home in one piece.

With a couple of hours before she was due back to start her next shift, she stood and scraped her chair back. She was on a mission, and until she resolved her concerns, she wouldn't settle.

Grace hugged her dance troupe friends and took one last look at the room she'd called home for the past two months in Athens. They'd all thanked her for saving their lives. Yeah, the contract had not been all it seemed.

'Human trafficking' was what the consulate had advised her. An intricate scheme to lure young women to foreign countries and do ... She didn't want to think about what she or her friend's fates would have been if they'd willingly gone to Iran. She was fast learning how nasty humans could be, and it made her skin itch.

Today, she was getting a lift to the airport and boarding a plane to Seattle. Justin would be a familiar face after being away from home for so long, and his letters to Australia had held the possibility of romance. She craved some close companionship, and what better way to kick it off than with a surprise visit.

Grace had starved her jetlag with a good night's sleep in a lumpy bed at a cheap backpacker hostel. With a new day ahead of her, she wouldn't plan any accommodation options until she surprised Justin. She unfolded the address she kept in a pouch around her neck and straightened it on her knee as the bus jerked to a stop. Getting to Justin's house required a couple of bus changes but nothing she couldn't handle, and she was content to watch the Seattle streetscape pass by.

She smiled, remembering the jokes and laughter she and Justin had shared in the afternoons she'd worked at the local pub. Still stinging from the failure of her first marriage, Grace wasn't going to run headlong into something new. But they'd connected easily, often joked and laughed plenty. Perth was a long way from the streets of Seattle, but she couldn't stop the excitement thrumming through her veins at the prospect of seeing him again.

She doubted anything would come of it. She didn't picture herself living away from Australia, and Justin had yet to meet Colin. Having a child always complicated matters, and she wouldn't let any man come between her and Colin.

Her back slouched and filled with pity for Norm. His reasons for not being interested in his son always baffled her. She also worried Colin would miss out on things without a father figure. She would marry one day again. To whom, she'd have to wait and see. Justin, well, she didn't think he'd be the best option, but a bit of fun after her disastrous first marriage wouldn't hurt.

"Just go down to the corner and turn left," the bus driver called out helpfully as she descended the steps of the bus.

"Thanks, mate."

After the fifteen-hour flight in a cramped economy class seat, a good stretch was what she needed. She wasn't used to such inactivity, and she had a nostalgic moment when she wished for a horse and a solid canter across a paddock.

Instead, she wrapped her coat tighter as the lazy autumn breeze whispered and wheedled around her. She breathed deeply the crisp, frigid air and watched a cloud of fog leave her mouth as she blew it out. It was a Sunday, and she assumed the streets didn't quite teem with their usual weekday traffic. Would she find Justin home? Did he share a house with other workmates or friends? She didn't know too much about his private life. That hadn't seemed important on those stolen afternoons down by the river after her work shift.

All letters between them had been directed to and from the base where he was stationed, but he'd once told her his home address which she'd memorised and then later written down.

She stood on the footpath in front of the house and noted the lovely lace curtains in the windows and the neat garden behind the white picket fence. Maybe he lived with his family? Would his mother greet her?

The latch on the gate squeaked when she lifted it. Suddenly feeling nervous instead of buoyed by the coming reunion, she took a deep breath, pushed the gate open and walked up the path to the door. A large brass ring was fixed to the front of a solid timber door, and she tapped it a couple of times. The sound of footsteps emerged on the other side, and her breath caught.

A beautiful woman swung the door open, her shiny black hair resting on her shoulders; her mouth carried the glimpse of a smile as if she'd been laughing at something or someone.

Grace baulked, the air rushing out of her lungs. Was this Justin's sister? Or ...

"Can I help you?"

Even her voice came across as sweet, and an ugly thought refused to be pushed away. Thinking fast on her feet, because there was no way she would hurt anyone, she said, "Ah ... I'm from Western Australia, and my brother asked me to look up a friend of his if I passed through Seattle. Would this be where Justin lives?"

The lady's smile spread further. "It sure is. I'm his wife, and he often mentions the friends he's made in Australia. It sounds like such an exciting place. He's promised to take me there one day."

And there it was. Her heart sank to the bottom of the ocean. The lie Justin was living. She willed her face to remain in a friendly smile—the need to swear struggled to stay confined.

"Justin doesn't usually work on a Sunday, but they had an emergency and were all called to the base, and he won't be home until tomorrow. Can you come back then? For lunch or dinner?"

Grace thanked her lucky stars. Doing her darnedest not to grimace, she waved away the wife's concerns about missing out on seeing Justin. There was no way she was hanging around for his return. She couldn't guarantee what she'd do if she was within hitting range of his face. The bastard!

"That's a shame; I'll be out of Seattle this afternoon. Maybe you could just pass on a hello from my brother. Tell him Robert's sister Grace dropped by to say hello on his behalf."

After some inconsequential small talk about kangaroos and koalas, she thanked the wife and headed back to the bus stop. Finding out Justin was a married man left a horrible taste in her mouth. She loathed men like that. Lying, cheating bastards. He wouldn't be game enough to show up anywhere close to where she was, and Perth wasn't that big a place. She felt sorry for his wife. She looked nice enough; why couldn't he be satisfied with her? How many other women had he conned into a fake relationship?

She could only shake her head. They had not progressed too far past the friendship stage. He'd hinted a couple of times at taking things further, but she'd been steadfast in taking things slowly. The miscarriage was still a very fresh memory, and falling pregnant wasn't something she wanted with a man who fleetingly visited.

Being so far away from home, family and friends, she understood how loneliness sometimes took over and made you consider things you wouldn't normally do. She had to admit she'd considered a fling with Justin on this visit. It was her reason for extending her holiday and making the surprise trip. How complicated matters might've turned out if she'd been unlucky to end up pregnant with a man from the other side of the world *and* already married.

At the bus stop, she considered how lucky she was to have come away from this experience unscathed. This was twice now she'd walked away from potential danger, still intact.

What sort of life would she experience if she'd been forced into slavery in Iran? She shuddered every time she thought of the consequences of landing in Iran and possibly never getting out. The thought of never seeing Colin again opened up a hole the size of a crater in her chest, and her hand subconsciously came up and rubbed against her heart. Was someone watching over her? Did that God, the one her mother never spoke about, really exist?

When the next bus arrived, she shook off the disappointment of finding Justin married and embraced the sudden luck that walked by her side. As she climbed the steps, she gave the bus driver a warm smile and mumbled a quiet thank you to the heavens. Where to next? She certainly wasn't going to allow one lousy bastard to spoil what was left of her holiday.

Chapter 23

The plane touched down with a couple of bumps and a loud rush of air as the pilot applied the brakes. The sparseness surrounding the Perth airport and the small number of planes on the tarmac were the first things to penetrate her jetlagged mind. After the chaotic but somehow orderly scenes of some of the airports she'd passed through, Perth came across as a backyard operation. Heathrow, Los Angeles and even Sydney, to name some of the world's busiest airports, had you wondering how they coordinated it all without planes flying into each other.

She'd arrived home with ten cents to her name. Not enough to call her mum from Sydney to check if someone would be waiting for her. Grace was banking on her mother keeping tabs on her flight itinerary.

As the plane taxied and did all the things it had to before they disembarked, Grace's heart beat a little faster. She desperately missed Colin and was afraid he wouldn't recognise her. Would he prefer the arms of his grandmother?

Grace grimaced and squeezed her eyes tight to stop the tears threatening, forcing her mind away from the worrying thought. She was still getting over the shock and disappointment of learning about Justin's marriage. If Colin didn't willingly come to her, it might finally make her cry. So far, she'd abstained from such nonsense, declaring Justin wasn't worth crying over. But hell, his lies had hurt more than she'd expected.

Regardless, she'd finished her holiday travelling through Vancouver, Alaska and back to Canada's Quebec, scraping through with barely enough money.

There was one more scare when she'd hitched a lift with a truck driver to Vancouver. The memory of it came back to haunt her. The second she'd hoisted herself up into the truck and closed the door, she knew it was the wrong decision. The looks the man kept giving her had her thinking of jumping clear of the truck at the next stop. Her mind had swirled with memories of the other time she'd been stalked like prey, and his first words confirmed her worst fears.

"Ain't a girl like you kinda frightin' about travelling through the States alone? Ain't you afraid someone might hurt or rape you?"

Grace had shown true grit in the face of danger. And she *was* in danger. How she came up with her response still astounded her. She replied, "Hell no! You don't think I'd be stupid enough to hitch a ride without knowing self-defence and carrying a weapon, do you?"

She'd unzipped her backpack, rummaging inside as though checking for said weapon. After turning a satisfied smile in his direction, the driver never uttered another word. Her backpack never left her lap the entire drive, and her arm remained tightly around it. At the next truck stop, she duly thanked him and got out fast. She wouldn't accept a ride from a stranger again in a hurry.

The incident had amplified her desire to go home. Even now, just thinking about it made her heart race at what could've been. Twisted with the nightmarish memories of the night she'd been stalked on her way to Fremantle, her usually calm nature in the face of adversity had altered from the trauma. She'd played a significant role in getting the owner of the green Corolla securely behind bars, and this knowledge had somehow helped her from losing her nerve.

The 'fasten seatbelt' sign flickered off, and the cabin steward announced they could leave the aircraft. Others around her rose and collected their hand luggage. It was time to disembark, and hopefully, someone was waiting for her.

She spotted her mother in the crowd waving to her and swallowed back tears. She wasn't holding Colin, but then again, she hadn't expected Colin to be there. It meant another couple of hours before she could lose herself in his baby smell she'd longed for every day since leaving.

She wrapped her arms around her smiling mother, surprised because they'd never been an affectionate family in the past. "Mum, it's so good to be home."

Her mother's reply was to squeeze tighter.

"Where's Colin?" Stupid question, but she couldn't help herself.

"Let's get you home so you can see him. Robert's waiting in the car park."

She hooked her arm with her mother's and made for the luggage carousel. "Dad didn't drive you in?" She wasn't sure why this hurt so much. He'd never been bothered with her in the past, so why would he change now? She just wished she could accept it and move on. She kept promising herself she would.

"I don't live with your father anymore."

Grace stopped mid-step and spun around to face her mother. "What?"

"You heard." There was a certain assertiveness in her mother's voice. "It was coming for a long time. In fact, I don't know why it didn't happen a lot sooner."

Grace studied her mother with fresh eyes. Even the need to hold Colin was pushed to the back for a minute. Her father had been a cruel and controlling bastard for as long as she could remember. She always assumed his anger was directed at herself and Robert. Never once had she considered his abuse might've been directed at their mother. "Mum, are ... are you okay?"

This was huge. Her mother's role had always been as a home keeper. She'd never held a paying job before. How would she manage?

"I've been staying with your aunty and uncle for the past few weeks. Now that you're home, we'll find ourselves a small place. They're happy for all three of us to stay with them, but I don't want to impose on them for too long."

Guilt assailed her for leaving Colin in her care while her mother was suffering through such a difficult time. Then fear grappled at her chest. Did her father resent Colin being in the house because he belonged to her?

She turned cold as a question burned inside her. "Mum, did Dad hurt Colin?" She had to know. If he had so much as laid a finger on him, she'd confront him immediately.

"No, nothing like that. I promise." Her mum squeezed her arm for reassurance.

Grace was lost for words, unsure of what sort of comfort her mother needed. The clanking of the carousel signalled the arrival of luggage, and all she could do was stare at it dumbfounded. Her jetlagged mind struggled to make sense of the chaos. She needed a good night's sleep, and then she had to find work immediately. That wouldn't be a problem, but could they afford the rent on a place big enough? With Robert and her sisters already living independent lives, it would be her responsibility to take care of her mother — and she would do it gladly.

"Stop worrying, Grace."

Huh? Grace broke out of her tired trance.

"Robert helped me find a place. It's small but big enough for us, and the rent is reasonable. We can move in whenever we're ready. I also have a cleaning job which I started last month. Your aunty has been taking care of Colin while I work, so I've put a little bit aside."

Already? She spotted her tired-looking suitcase and lunged for it before it trundled past her. She hoisted her smaller hand luggage over and shoulder and turned to her mother. "Thanks, Mum. I'll find a job straight away. We can do this."

Her mum managed a small grateful smile for the first time since her arrival. "I know. You're a strong and independent woman. Very stubborn, but I think every woman needs to be to get through life."

Was it just her tiredness or had her mother been replaced with someone new? "Thanks for taking care of Colin. It means a lot."

Her mother took hold of her backpack, so Grace only had to carry the suitcase. As they made their way towards the car park, she added,

"I couldn't imagine a life without him. He's so precious, Grace, and absolutely perfect. Every day, I showed him photos of you and explained it was his mummy. He says Mama and is walking on wobbly legs everywhere. I'm so glad you're home now."

Grace choked back her tears. She *was* exhausted, which was exacerbating all her emotions. They formed one tight ball in the centre of her chest. For now, she wanted to wrap her arms around her little man and hold him close to her heart. Then, after a good night's sleep, she would go out and take the first job on offer. She had to take responsibility for her son and give her mother space to find herself. She wouldn't make millions and didn't need much. Just enough to feed and clothe her little family. She was more than ready for the next stage of her life.

When she spotted Robert lounging against his car, she dashed towards him and gave him an awkward hug. Another surprising moment for their family. "Hey, Rob, where's the next rodeo?"

When he recovered, his laughter spread around her. "Yeah, the circuit's been a bit quiet without my crazy sister to upset things."

Grace mock-punched his arm as he lifted her suitcase and put it in the boot. She'd missed being close to animals and couldn't wait to climb on a horse, ride a steer or a bronc and get a mouthful of dust.

Taking a big gulp of dry Perth air, she held it in for a few moments before letting go one small breath at a time. She was home, and there was nothing better than breathing clean air. God, how she loved this part of the world. For all she'd seen and experienced, there was nothing like coming back home.

She'd learnt a lot in her travels and would never take what she had here for granted. In their sparsely populated country, a person had space to breathe and live. She couldn't imagine choosing to live in a crowded city where she wasn't able to keep a horse.

"Get in you lot, or are we going to stand around here all day?" Robert chided.

Grace rolled her eyes at him. Some things never changed, and she laughed with heartfelt gratitude. He'd always been the big brother who looked out for her, sometimes taking the brunt of their father's anger when she'd been as mischievous. She owed him something.

She plonked herself on the back seat, allowing her mother to sit in the front, rested her head against the window and released an enormous sigh of relief. She was home, safe and sound, and even Robert's car smelt familiar, causing a wad of emotion to build in her chest.

While Robert negotiated the traffic out of the car park, she closed her eyes. Her sense of adventure would always be there, searching for any outlet. She wasn't born to be shoved in a corner and forgotten about. Filled with wanderlust, she could satisfy that yearning just as easily in this spacious country.

She'd gone into the big wide world and taken a look. But now it was time to knuckle down, be a good mother and earn money for her family. Hard work had never scared her before, so there was no reason for it to start now. With the support of her mother and family, she could do this *and* raise her son.

Chapter 24

"Is this you in the newspaper?"

Grace straightened from the car she was cleaning and craned her neck. *Hm. Him again.* "Depends on which one you're talking about."

"How come you didn't tell me last night you do this sort of thing?"

One blind dinner date, and no, she hadn't mentioned it. It wasn't something you told a person who only talked about themselves. "Why are you here, Phil?"

"Transferring my terrific car salesman skills to this car yard."

It was going to be a long day.

Phil waved the rolled-up newspaper under her nose. "It says you're Western Australia's only female bronco rider?"

Grace ignored him and crouched to clean the mags on the wheels. "I'm not WA's only female bronco rider." There weren't too many other women, but that wasn't the point. The previous night, she'd barely got a word in. Yeah, he sold cars and played AFL. She got all that *and* in great detail.

"It says it here."

She twisted around and glared at Phil. "Don't believe everything you read."

He unrolled the newspaper, looking hopeful she might look at it. It wouldn't work. She'd read it earlier that morning. Turning away, she went back to polishing the wheel. Her first job when she arrived back from overseas was as a car cleaner. She'd stuck to it for about six weeks until she convinced the boss to employ her to sell new cars on commission.

On quiet days, she still liked to do the cleaning. It satisfied her to see a car go from messy to shiny beneath her hands. She didn't mind the work. It kept her busy outside of her horse training and dancing at the Sheraton Downunder. Yep, life was hectic, but she was doing okay.

"'Grace Lucas, rider, skydiver and part-time model, is a tough lady who won't let the rodeo men ride roughshod over her,'" he read.

Grace inwardly groaned. When was he going to give up? "Phil, I know what it says. I've read it." If he continued to read right until the last bit, she would fling the wet sponge at him.

"'She's been to rodeos where the riders have threatened mass walkouts if she competed.'"

"Don't you have a job to do?" Grace flung over her shoulder as she walked around to the other side of the car.

Phil glanced around the car yard and smiled. "I'll be onto the first customer as soon as they enter the yard."

Grace groaned again. Arrogant. This was the vibe she'd gotten from their blind date.

"'Some of these rodeo guys are just ignorant, Grace says. I can ride equal to or better than any of them. But they still kick up a stink if I compete.'"

"Phil, that's enough." She didn't need him to read the article word for word.

He followed her around to the same side of the car where she was cleaning.

"But this is unbelievable. Who would be crazy enough to climb on a bucking horse or bull? I can't believe you didn't say anything. You said something about training horses and dancing but nothing about this." He tapped the article with more force than was needed. "Are you embarrassed because it's not something a woman should do?"

Grace bristled. She straightened and rolled her badly bruised shoulder. The slight concussion on the weekend had them all worried, but at least there weren't any serious injuries.

"'Grace is waiting for the breaks, so she can form a Girl Rough Riders Association in WA to break into the male-dominated rodeo ring.'" He wasn't letting up with the story as he leant against the clean car. "Why would you want to do that?" he asked with a cranky tone.

"Why not?" She didn't have to explain herself to this man. One blind date didn't mean anything.

He shook his head. "I wouldn't want any girlfriend of mine involved in this sport. Look here"—he was still trying to shove the paper under her nose—"you even say it yourself, and I quote, "'I wouldn't say I'm tough. I burst into tears if I'm not allowed to ride.'"

Her hand squeezed around the sponge, and water dribbled over her foot. "I did not say that! Don't believe everything you read. I do *not* burst into bloody tears if I'm not allowed to ride. Trust me, I'm more likely to swear. At least they got the last bit right where they say I'm determined and stubborn, because if I believe in something, I'll work for it."

Grace dropped the sponge in the bucket and stood with her hands on her hips. She faced Phil with a tough, determined stance, the exact thing the newspaper article was talking about. "And women should be allowed to compete in rodeos, and I won't stop until it happens." She stooped back to her bucket, determined to ignore Phil for the rest of the day. "Now get to work. Go and sweep the bloody showroom if you have nothing else better to do."

❦

"Mum, I'm pregnant." Grace wrapped her arms around Colin and tried to keep him still, but he didn't want a bar of it and wriggled free, dashing outside to play with his dog.

"Will you marry him?"

"He proposed yesterday when I told him the news."

"Well, that's great, isn't it? He seems okay with Colin, and you can settle down."

Grace nodded at her mother's no-nonsense solution, but something wavered inside her chest. Phil had been wooing her for nearly four years. It'd been fun along the way, she could admit that, but lately, she'd noticed things she didn't like.

It was no secret he hated the rodeo circuit and never came near one, let alone supported her passion. He couldn't stand horses either, and this hurt her in more ways than she cared to consider. On the other hand, she couldn't find any interest in the AFL game. She tried but watching a bunch of men chasing a ball that didn't bounce properly seemed a waste of time. It was only fair that she didn't hold it against him when they failed to recognise each other's interests.

"How far are you?"

Grace thrust her unsettling thoughts to the side. "I'm six weeks along. We're planning a wedding in two weeks' time."

Her mother rose from the couch and went into the kitchen to put the kettle on. Grace followed as her mother continued, "It's so soon, but it's a good idea. People will say the baby came early."

Grace grimaced. There was still some of the Dominican nun in her mother, and she would hate the gossip.

"But do you think he'll make a good husband, Mum?"

Her mother took a couple of teacups out of the cupboard and set them on the table. "Grace, you don't have a choice. You're pregnant, and the child's father wants to marry you. Why would you ask that question? He's an attractive man and has a job. What else do you need?"

Grace sat at the table and mulled over her mother's words. She was right; she didn't have a choice. To bring a second child into the world as a single mother wouldn't look good. But she couldn't help going back to their very first date and the impression he'd given. She remembered thinking he was arrogant, and that had stuck with her, so how the heck had he weaselled his way into her affections? Sex had been great, and she'd tried her hardest to avoid getting pregnant, but not hard enough.

"Everything will work out just fine." Her mother squeezed her hand. "Here, drink this."

Grace reached for the teacup and sipped the hot, sweet drink. After her first disastrous marriage, she'd promised to try extra hard on her second. A baby was on its way, and she had to admit it was the only thing keeping her going.

She steered away from thinking she might've walked away from Phil if she wasn't pregnant. He was starting to say the weirdest things and showed extreme jealousy whenever she spent time away from him. It was one thing not to like her rodeo outings, but without her animals, what was the point in living? When would he see that?

She sighed into her cup and took another sip. Her mother was right. She had no choice. With a baby on the way, she *had* to make it work.

Chapter 25

"I was rushed to ICU about five times last year." Grace continued her chatter while Erin resisted the urge to sprawl her tired body over Grace's comfy couch. After an entire week of work, a nap on a Saturday afternoon with a belly full of banana cake sounded like a good idea.

"When you don't have a proper functioning kidney, anything can happen."

They'd spent half an hour detailing more of the medical treatments Grace had undertaken since getting sick, and there wasn't too much left to cover. Grace's ability to remember things astounded Erin, who on some days could barely recall what she'd done last Tuesday.

She smiled to herself and rolled her shoulders. Regardless of how tired she was, she was a lot more relaxed these days. "What things are you doing to monitor your condition?" A yawn emerged, but she smothered it, not wanting to look bored or tired in front of Grace. She idolised this woman and the daredevil way she'd lived her life.

"I know when I feel faint and my body is shutting down. With a fortnightly blood test, I can self-administer medication when my haemoglobin readings are too low. I must be careful, though. If my red blood cell count gets too high, I risk my blood pressure becoming a problem."

They were getting closer to the end of the report and fitting it in with her full-time work had proven to be more difficult than she'd expected. "You had no intention of giving up, did you?"

Grace took another leisurely drink of tea before placing it on the coffee table beside her. "There's a reason I'm not ready to hang my hat up yet. I haven't told you about losing Colin, have I?"

Erin looked up from her scrawl. "Who's Colin?"

"My son."

Erin sat up straighter. Over the past weeks of interviewing and spending time with Grace, she had a sense of coming to know this woman and her life. How had not a single word come out about her son? She'd briefly met her daughter and son-in-law and their two children the weekend before but never had Colin been mentioned.

"How old was he when he ... died?" Erin asked, her words barely a whisper.

"Only thirty-two." Grace's eyes misted; she turned to focus on something outside the window.

Erin gave her space and a few minutes to gather her thoughts. Grace was an amazing storyteller and would tell it her way. A lone tear trickled down her cheek when she met Erin's eyes. This strong woman rarely had time for tears, but her son's death was doing it.

"Was it recent?"

Grace dabbed her eyes with a tissue she found in a pocket of her jeans. "Twelve years ago, but you know what hurts about him dying so young?"

Erin's brow furrowed. What sort of life experiences did she have to answer that?

"He had a dream, and he ran out of time to fulfil it. His dream was to canoe solo around Australia, but his body failed him. He battled long and hard to fight the leukaemia, but in the end, his body rejected everything the doctors had done to save him."

Erin looked around the living room. There wasn't a single photo of Colin anywhere, which was strange. Grace was so vocal about how important her family and friends were; whatever happened to Colin? Of course, she had no right to ask, but her friendship with Grace exceeded all her expectations, and the words flowed from her mouth before she could censor them. "You don't keep a photo of him in your home?"

A stricken look must have crossed her face because Grace smiled sadly. "It's okay, Erin. One day I burst into tears and couldn't move from this very chair for the rest of the day. It was like I was in a trance. Every photo of Colin twisted my despair deeper, and I was spiralling further out of control. All day I reasoned with my head. If I couldn't see him, it wouldn't hurt me as much. So the first thing I did when I could stand was to take all his photos down and hide them. I didn't miraculously recover, but it helped. It was the start of a slow and torturous journey of healing. I had to believe I could keep him inside here"—she rested her hand against her breast—"and have him close anyway. Without any photos, it lessened the chance of triggering another episode. Trust me, Erin, you talk yourself into believing anything. One day when the fog clears, you look back and wonder what the hell it was all about. But if it helped me get through, who cared what stupid stuff I did."

Erin squirmed and asked tentatively, "Can I see a photo of him?"

Grace rose from the couch and walked to a sideboard. She opened a cupboard door and rummaged around, returning with three framed photos. She handed them over, and Erin looked at a teenager's face with a cheeky grin, Colin at a rodeo about to compete, and the final one was of Colin dressed in a defence force uniform. A smiling young man with the world at his feet.

Something tugged inside Erin's chest. She'd never experienced pain, hardship and loss like this woman had. Looking at the photos again, she ran her finger through the thin layer of dust. "I'll be back in a sec," she said to Grace. She stood and took the photos to the bathroom, found a clean hand towel in the linen cupboard and wet one corner of it. With infinite patience, she wiped the three frames clean and then dried them. When she returned to the living room, she squatted in front of Grace and asked, "Can you manage to see them for one afternoon? You had such a beautiful son; I'm so sorry for your loss."

Settled back in her chair, Grace stared at Erin for the longest moment, like she was debating the biggest decision of her life, and maybe she was. "Maybe it's time they came out again."

Erin squeezed Grace's knee before standing and arranging them on a shelf, manoeuvring them around the horse trinkets and trophies. Her heart thumped inside her chest. Was she pushing Grace too far? Who was she to dictate when Grace should put the photos back?

"It's okay, love. I'm tougher than you think. I should be able to handle seeing my son's beautiful face again. It might do me some good for a change."

Erin released a nervous sigh of relief. Grace had a knack for knowing what was going through her mind. Was there anything Grace wasn't good at?

"For years, I suffered a lot of guilt over Colin."

"How?" Erin wanted to look at the photos from different angles and walked around Grace's living room, looking back at them and how she'd positioned them amongst the horse mementoes.

"I always wondered if stress in young kids could bring on an illness or disease."

Erin stopped in her tracks. "What do you mean?"

"Until his eighth birthday, Colin was exposed to a lot of abuse in our family. I think I already mentioned I had an abusive second marriage?"

Erin nodded.

"You don't realise how bad it is and its effect on the kids until you escape the toxic environment and see things differently. What if all the stress Colin experienced as a young boy brought on the leukaemia?"

Erin's medical studies begged to differ, but she didn't want to interrupt.

"It's too late now, I realise. We were blessed to have him for the time we did, and thank you for putting the photos back out. I should've done it years ago. He deserves all this and so much more." Grace took a shuddering breath and whispered, "His death also broke my mother's heart. She and Colin were very close, and it was in my mother's arms that he died. She gave up so much of herself to help me; I can't thank her enough. Even moving away to the other side of the country, she continued to play an important role in our lives, and after Colin finished his schooling, he would visit her often."

Grace paused and wiped her nose, and Erin guessed the memories were piling up and wanted to spill. "You know, we did something to help Colin fulfil his dream."

Erin tilted her head, not sure what was about to come.

"We have a bottle floating somewhere in the ocean. Inside it, we put Colin's essence. Some of his ashes, his memorial service booklet, a badge of hope from the Cancer Council and a guardian angel." She swallowed before she could continue. "I have to keep living. I want at least one person to find it and keep that bottle's journey going, so we can fulfil Colin's dream."

"Oh my God, that is so beautiful." Erin choked back a sob at the desperate measures a mother would take to keep her son's dream alive.

"We only had him for thirty-two short years. So you, my dear Erin, have to live life to the fullest because you never know when it'll be taken away from you."

Something flipped inside Erin's stomach. She got the feeling Grace was conveying a special message to her. "Thank you for making me see that."

"No worries," Grace said, closing her eyes.

Erin let Grace rest for a few moments in relative peace. She didn't doubt Grace's mind was occupied with thoughts of Colin, so she turned her thoughts to her own life and the changes wrought over it recently.

It'd been nearly four weeks since starting her new vet nurse job, and in a couple of weeks, she would begin the grind of studying again. She and Tom had managed to keep their distance for most of that time, but it didn't stop her heart hammering whenever she was close to him. It also didn't stop her from questioning why she wanted to keep this distance. *Live life to the fullest.*

This coming weekend was another celebration. With family and friends surrounding her, Grace was going to ride Eve again after a year of being too sick to do so. A barbecue was organised, and those near and dear were invited to come, watch and share. That was the way Grace did things.

Secretly, she was excited about the barbecue because it meant being around Tom in a social environment. They'd managed some more riding lessons but always with someone else there. New junior vets one day, Grace and Peter another time.

With her project on Grace almost complete, Erin didn't have any other reason to spend time on the property, and it was a loss she was already feeling.

The phone rang, its shrill sound interrupting Erin's thoughts. One handset rested on the coffee table beside Grace. When Grace sat up and took the call, Erin strolled towards the kitchen, intending to go outside to give her some privacy.

The homestead-styled home had three steps leading down, and she sat on the top one, looking out into the vivid greenness she was fast coming to associate with the Tablelands.

She rested her elbows on her thighs and her chin in the cradle of her palms, prepared to question where her life was going. She inhaled the freshness of the green lawn and let it surround her peacefully. At least she could think straight these days. With Nicholas fast becoming a distant, distasteful memory and her parents reluctantly accepting her change to veterinary science, she'd never felt so alive—and eager. Only a small niggle continued to invade her head space. Had she rid herself entirely of Nicholas? A small part of her feared that one day he would intrude on her life and make trouble for her.

She grimaced. If only she weren't so tired from the long hours she worked during the day and the hours she put in on the laptop at night. But still, her change of course had revitalised rather than daunted her. Her life was back on track, and her feelings for Tom had held steady.

The screen door squeaked on its hinges behind her. She twisted around as Grace stepped onto the patio and sat on the chunky timber bench.

"Oh, am I glad you're still here," Grace said.

Erin smiled. "I wouldn't leave without saying goodbye."

"No, I didn't think you would, and lucky for you. That was my friend Gary, the retired policeman, and boy, does he have news for us."

"He does?" Erin turned fully to face Grace, then stood. There was a lightness in her chest. "What is it?" she rushed.

"If Gary has the right family, and he's ninety-nine per cent sure he does, then I knew your great-grandmother, Liz, very well. I also know your grandfather. Liz has since passed on, but Larry is alive and well. I lost contact with them a long time ago, but you know what—?"

Erin gulped and grabbed for the patio post before sliding down it and plonking her butt back on the steps. The words refused to come out. *My grandfather is still alive?*

"Liz got me on my very first poddy. She's the person responsible for allowing me to achieve what I have in my life."

Erin stumbled up from the top step and plopped beside Grace on the spacious timber seat. "Really? She started all this?"

"I know, right. Who would've thought? Larry was like a big brother to me when I had a hard time at home in my teens. Gary gave me a contact number. Let's hope it's the right Larry. I'll make a phone call later, and if it is, I'll surprise him."

"This is too easy. I thought finding my lost family without my mother's help would take years if I found them at all."

Grace patted her hand. "Some things are meant to be. Don't question it too much. I'll tell your grandfather I've met you and that you're keen to meet. What do you say?"

Erin nodded, lost for words. Her stomach roiled, nerves twisting themselves into knots. What if the news she learnt made it worse for her? Finally on track with *her* life, did she want to know what had caused the rift between her mother and grandparents? And what would her mother say about it now?

She thought about it for a full five seconds more and then decided that yes, she wanted to know. She was sick of hiding behind conformity, of doing what everyone else wanted. To hell with that. She was a part of this unknown family, and an invisible link just stretched and tightened its hold on her.

It was time to find out!

Chapter 26

Nearly 25 Years Old

Grace tensed, placing a protective hand over her bulging eight-month belly. The front door slammed, her body ramrod straight as she tried to ignore the noise Phil made.

Something hit the wall in the kitchen. Probably his fist. Every fibre of her body was attentive to his movements. He'd been okay for a few days. No blow-ups, no yelling, no arguments.

"I knew it. I bloody knew it." His angry words spilled out into the hallway only seconds before he barged into the bedroom. With him came the pungent fumes of alcohol. She'd long given up reasoning about how often he went out drinking at night.

What was it this time? What accusation would he let fly that night, giving him a reason to hit her? The bedside clock in her peripheral vision mocked her. At three in the morning, she should've been in a deep sleep, exactly where her exhausted body needed to be.

He pulled on his hair, half his work shirt hanging out of his trousers. "You're carrying someone else's bastard. Aren't you?"

Reasoning with him wouldn't help. Wearily, she sat up and leant against the bedhead. Her sleep was erratic these days with the baby moving constantly. Moving was getting harder, and she had to protect her baby at all costs. She wrapped her arm around her belly and looked at Phil with what she hoped were pleading eyes.

"Please, Phil, you know I've never been with anyone else since I met you. Who's told you this rot?"

"It's true. I know it. All those rodeos you went to with all those cowboys; Christ, it could've been any one of them. You were pretty bloody quick to say yes when it was time to find some sucker to look after you both and the other bastard boy."

Relief for a second swept through her. Colin, her precious Colin. Thank God he'd stayed the night with her mother. He'd heard way too much for a five-year-old. But this tired argument, which she'd tried to put up with, was sounding old. She didn't have the strength to keep fighting, not with a baby due in only weeks, but now and then, pure rage roared through her.

He kept ranting and raving, hovering at the end of the bed, going over the same ground as if waiting for her to agree that, yes, the baby wasn't his. But it *was* his, and he'd bloody well be the father to it if she had her say in the matter.

Awkwardly rising from the bed, she pulled her purple nightie down over her bulging belly and prepared to spew forth the hate building up since their marriage six months ago. How had their relationship deteriorated so fast? She would pay for this, but sometimes her stubbornness reared its head, and she'd go to hell first before she did meek.

"Shut up, will you! Just shut the fuck up," she yelled. He did and stepped around the corner of the bed and loomed over her menacingly. His face was the colour of sunburn. "When I married you, you bastard," she spat, "you at least had a job. You don't even play AFL anymore. You're a loser and a heavily drinking one at that. You're the father of this child, and so help me God, I'll make sure you're held accountable for it."

The slap came fast. Her hand flew to the stinging on her cheek. There were stars and then she blacked out for a second. Physically, he was so much stronger than she was, especially with a belly full of alcohol. She'd never tried to hit him back. She would only come away broken and regret it more. This way, she could hide the bruises under her winter clothing.

Then his hand gripped tight around her forearm, and he yanked her off the bed, dragging her along the carpeted floor. If she fought this, he'd pull her arm out of her socket. He could inflict more damage on her and the baby than riding a steer or bronc could. She gritted her teeth and tried to steady her breathing. He'd come to his senses eventually. He always did. Always sorry. For how long, though, she never knew.

He swept the front door open and dragged her outside, the screen door crashing into her leg, and heaved her onto the patio before releasing her arm. The slam of the door in her face heralded the ugly truth. The lock clicked and the security chain rattled into place. No amount of knocking would convince him to let her back in.

She lay panting on the honeycomb mat, its rubber edges digging into her skin. Her flimsy nightie was no match for the freezing August winter. She began to shiver uncontrollably, and she tried to roll over and sit up but was struggling to breathe.

She wracked her brain for a course of action before hypothermia set in. Her elderly neighbour, Bonnie, across the road, would help her. Bonnie knew what was going on behind closed doors. She'd offered her cups of tea when the bruises had been at their worst. She hadn't come outright and said anything but the few things she had, gave enough away. Grace was reluctant to wake her up at this time of the night. At her age, she'd have a heart attack if Grace knocked on her door.

Instead, she rolled onto all fours, sucked in a few deep breaths and eventually, on shaky legs, stood. She stumbled across the street and down the footpath to the park where she took Colin to play on the swings and slippery slide. Street lights emitted a blurry light, shrouded in a fuzzy mist. It cast her shadow in an eerie manner that did nothing to alarm Grace. The fact she was a semi-naked, pregnant woman walking alone in the wee hours of the morning meant nothing. She had nothing left inside. No capacity to acknowledge threats, pain or fear. Just numbness. She'd been here before after a beating from her father.

With numb feet and a throbbing head, she leant against a phone booth, her baby taking that moment to remind her of the life she carried. Tears streamed down her face. What sort of life could she offer this child? What kind of family was Grace bringing it into?

The door to the booth swung inwards from her weight, and she welcomed the warmer air inside. She took the phone off the hook and dialled the number she'd memorised only months earlier—a free call for those in need.

"This is Lifeline. How can I help you?"

"My husband locked me out of our house. I'm eight months pregnant, and I ... I don't want to live anymore ..."

Grace cried a bucket of tears as she spoke to the stranger on the other end of the phone. There was no one else she could talk to about it. She couldn't confide in her mother, and she didn't want to burden Gary. It wasn't a subject her other friends or family were interested in. In the end, there was little this gentle counsellor could do for her other than give her the address of a women's shelter and suggest some other charities that could help. With the baby nearly due, she'd stopped working a few weeks ago. She had no source of income, and neither did her monster of a husband.

She spent the rest of the night sitting in the phone booth, frozen from the cold, convincing herself she had no choice but to go back to Phil.

As the first shades of dawn became visible over the horizon, a voice through the glass of the booth broke the eerie silence. "Are you okay, honey?"

Grace could barely move her body but twisted around to see who was asking. The kind face of a middle-aged woman looked her over. Grace bowed her head as her teeth continued to chatter. There was nothing of her left. Her tears may have dried up, but she didn't doubt her eyes were still bloodshot from all the crying and lack of sleep.

"Here, let me help you out," the woman said, opening the door and slipping her parker off and draping it over Grace's shoulders.

The woman turned to beckon a man, her husband Grace presumed, and they gently lifted her under the arms and almost carried her to their car. "Do you live nearby?"

Grace nodded.

"Let's warm you up with a hot drink. What do you say, lovie?"

Grace would've gone to the ends of the earth with this kind, loving couple. She'd take what she could before she had to face the contempt of her husband.

The realisation had come to her an hour before the sun had begun its ascent. She had to make the best of a bad situation. Through the numbness that had chilled her from the outside in, something hardened inside her chest. She would get through this, raise her children and be the best mother possible. She believed in karma, and Phil's day would one day come. She would never let him get beneath her skin again, and she'd fight him with every ounce of strength she had.

There was goodness out there in the world. Some days it was more visible than others. This gentle couple had taken her into their home, dressed her warmly, insisted she have a warm breakfast and hot drink, and then drove her home.

She would never forget their kindness.

Chapter 27

28 Years Old

Grace gasped at the sudden searing pain shooting across her abdomen. She'd been feeling off for about six weeks and suspected she might be pregnant again. Her breasts were sore, and she was experiencing early morning nausea and had occasional spotting.

"Colin, Natalie, come here." Fear ramped up in her chest. Her two beautiful children appeared before her. At eight years old, Colin had seen and experienced too much for a boy his age and picked up on the urgency in her voice.

"Mummy, what's wrong?"

Grace clutched at her belly. She hated exposing her amazing little boy to so much, but with the memory of her second miscarriage eighteen months ago still fresh in her mind, she summoned all her strength. She needed to get to the hospital.

As Phil had started another new job, her mother was her only other choice. The only other person Phil had allowed her to have contact with without his jealousy rearing its ugly head. She'd long relegated her friends to a past that could've been a century ago.

Her life revolved around her children and the one other thing she truly owned—a ratty horse purchased cheaply but had managed to bring back to a remarkable condition after a few years. She credited that horse with keeping her sane. How she'd convinced Phil to let her buy it, she'd never know. It had been a weak moment for Phil, one he hadn't let her forget since.

"Colin, go put some of your clothes and toys in a bag. And do the same for Natalie."

Toothbrushes and the like they already had at their grandmother's place. A few basics were all they needed.

"What's wrong, Mummy?" Colin asked again.

"Come here, honey." While Natalie played with a toy horse, Colin came into her welcoming embrace. "Darling, Mummy has a sore tummy. I'm going to ring Nan and ask her to come here and drive me to the hospital. You can sleep over at Nan's for a couple of days."

A smile wreathed his adorable face. His Nan was someone he trusted and loved and staying over always put him at ease. She wanted to bawl at the relief on his little face. Her little boy would do anything to escape the constant anger and tension that surrounded Phil and invaded their family home.

"Okay, Mummy," he said.

"Go put some things in a bag for you and your sister like Mummy asked."

He squeezed her around her hips, his little arms barely touching at the back, and Grace melted at his touch. She loved her children so much. They were the only thing keeping her going. That and her determination to be the best mother in a bad situation. And not much had changed in the nearly three years since Natalie's birth.

Grace telephoned her mother. Once her mother confirmed she could leave immediately, she sat down as another bout of pain had her doubled over in the chair, leaving her dizzy. This pain differed from her other miscarriages, and alarm swept throughout her body. Nothing could happen to her. Her children needed her.

Colin chatted to Natalie, asking what things she wanted packed. He was such a great little organiser, and she worked her hardest to stem the tears wanting to fall down her cheeks. The last time she'd cried in front of Colin was two years ago, and she vowed never to show her fear or sadness in front of him again.

It had been a morning when Phil had smacked her repeatedly as he left for a drinking session at the pub. He still spent most of his earnings on alcohol. He couldn't see that the children needed things like new clothes and food. What he especially resented was the extra feed her horse sometimes needed—the extra bale of hay, horse medication. That day, she'd done everything to keep her promised vow, but it was getting harder. With her battered body in so much pain, she'd burst out crying and slid down the laundry wall.

Colin found her in the foetal position on the laundry floor, and the memory was etched in her mind forever.

"Mummy, why don't we leave?" Colin had asked in a frightened voice.

Such profound words for a six-year-old. Was she failing her children? "We can't, Colin. We have nowhere to go and no money." She'd told him in between her gushing tears and hiccups.

"I'll get a job, Mummy. I'll help you."

His words caused her to bawl for most of the day.

When another pain sliced through her abdomen, she winced. She needed to pack a bag for herself. She had a sinking feeling she would be staying overnight in hospital. Something wasn't right. Despair grabbed at her chest. The loss of a possible life always left her worse off. She'd already coped through two miscarriages. The last one had left her feeling like a failure. Like it was her fault.

Since her marriage, she hadn't been near a rodeo, but Phil was always quick to remind her that her previous injuries were probably to blame. Hence her reluctance to tell him about her suspicions about being pregnant again.

Phil stood by her hospital bed freshly dressed, his strong aftershave making her nose twitch. "I'm just on my way out with the crew."

He'd done this nearly every night for the duration of her stay.

Grace remained mute. There were no words anymore. Her children were safe with their grandmother, and Grace was being taken care of in the hospital. She had no idea who his crew or friends were. Ex-footballers, workmates, she didn't care.

Ten days ago, she'd only just made it in time for the nursing staff to catch the beginning of her ectopic pregnancy rupture. Severe bleeding had threatened her life. Grace clearly remembered her out-of-body experience when her heart stopped for a few minutes and the sensation of floating up and off the bed. The nurse had tried to rouse her by tapping her on the face and telling her, "You gotta want to come back."

All Phil was concerned about on his occasional visits was getting out of the hospital as fast as possible. He didn't like them, wasn't comfortable there. There wasn't an ounce of affection to come her way. She might've been raised in a home where affection was scarce, but she would've appreciated some. With no wife and children in his way, it looked to Grace like he'd gained some new freedom.

Her chest muscles tightened that little bit more. Had she ever hated a person so much? Determination flowed strongly through her veins. She *would* get better and then leave him. She'd tried her hardest and was doing her best to keep her promised vow, but she couldn't do it anymore.

Grace looked at her shrinking body with despair. Her weight had dropped to fifty kilograms, and concern wormed its way around her. She looked like a skeleton. Her hips and collarbones protruded, her cheeks were sunken and she had permanent dark rims under her eyes. She turned away from the mirror and delved into the overnight bag she'd packed over two weeks ago.

It was time to leave the hospital, and already she'd wasted two days waiting for Phil to come and discharge her. The nursing staff wouldn't let her go home without someone to assist her, but she grew stronger each day. The new determination to take back her life had lodged itself in her chest and wasn't going anywhere.

Dressed as best as she could with her dress hanging loosely off her body, she took her overnight bag, determined to leave that night. Phil hadn't shown up, and his promises to take her home soon sounded hollow each time.

"Grace, Grace, you can't leave on your own," a nurse called, scurrying after her as Grace ambled down the hospital corridor. She'd already argued with the nursing staff and didn't have the energy to argue anymore. She kept walking, blocking out the concern coming from the young nurse.

Outside, a couple of taxis waited in a queue. She reached the first one, and the driver hastily grabbed her bag, then her elbow and guided her to the back seat. Did she look that sick? She'd been unwell a lot during her life, but nothing had diminished her body like this experience.

She gave the taxi driver her address and relaxed back into the seat with an exhausted sigh. It was time for her to heal and regain her strength. She could do that from home. She didn't need to be in a hospital. Her children and horse could help her heal faster, and she desperately missed them all.

"Will you be okay, Miss?" The driver looked dubiously at the darkened house as he pulled into the curb and offered to carry her bag to the front door. It would be a blessing to have a quiet house without her husband. Phil could stay out all night; she wouldn't care.

Grace nodded. "Thank you. I'll be right from here."

When the taxi drove away, she scrambled around in her bag for the house keys. Her breath hitched when the key wouldn't turn or budge the lock. Surely he wouldn't have changed them. Her heart started an erratic beating. With lethargic movements, she walked around to the back door and tried that lock.

A suspicious dread worked its way around her body. Back at the front door, she used the paltry streetlight to better look at the lock and the shiny new plate.

"The bastard." She swore some more, her flagging strength suddenly buoyed by her new determination. No changed locks would stop her from entering her home. She swiped at the tears threatening to come and steadily made her way around the house. In the dark, she checked every window and screen until she found one she could use.

It didn't matter how weak she was, she used what little strength she had to climb in through the screened window that got her into a back bedroom.

Staggering to her bed, she collapsed and pulled her knees to her chest. This time she couldn't hold back the tears. She clutched her pillow to her face as she bawled and bawled and cried out, "Mum, Mum, please, someone help me," over and over until she rocked herself into an exhausted sleep.

Chapter 28

The smile on Colin's face was hard to ignore. He didn't need help like his little sister did, and he held the reins like a grown-up.

"Look, Mum," he said, applying some gentle pressure on the horse's girth.

Grace hadn't once taken her eyes off her radiant son. And that's what broke her the most inside. They'd spent the afternoon with her horse, Command, on the nearby property where the owner let her keep it for free. He had a fenced-in paddock with a water trough and was happy for a horse to keep the grass down. Away from the tension-filled house where Phil was liable to blow up, Colin could be himself. That alone meant the world to Grace.

How had she allowed this to happen to her little boy? She remembered her childhood and how it had always been lived watchful of her father's temper. She didn't want that for her children. Natalie was still young, but Grace had seen her little body tense whenever Phil bellowed through the house.

It was over six weeks since her near-death experience, and Grace had thought much about her future. After Phil discovered her in the locked house, the tension between them worsened. She must've appeared near enough skin and bone because he was yet to raise his hand at her, and she didn't have the strength to fight or argue. He ignored her and spent a lot of his time away from the house, which suited her perfectly. Money was tight, as he wasn't sharing his wages, but somehow, she managed with help from her mother.

Was this how she wanted to live the rest of her life? What happened to the kid with wanderlust? What happened to the woman who loved the rodeo circuit and her determination to be allowed to ride a bull? Where had she gone?

It was a constant battle getting through each day. Her health was slowly improving, but she was having trouble gaining back the weight lost. Needing to put on a brave face for her children killed her desire to eat. It was fake. Her life was a sham. Should she keep at it for the kid's sake? But doing so was killing the life in her children. Every day they were subjected to the verbal abuse from Phil, and the hidden physical abuse that left her defeated would only make it harder to save them.

Grace had finally capitulated and phoned Jackie, who was on her way that very day.

Natalie tugged at her jeans. "Mummy, my turn?"

Grace smiled at her eager daughter. "Of course, darling." She waved Colin back in, and he cantered to where they stood. When Colin slid off the tatty and worn saddle, Grace took a moment to hold the horse and rub her cheek against it, relishing the smell and tickling sensation the hair gave her nose. She wanted to drink in every moment with her companion. She knew what was coming. The slowly forming idea wasn't going anywhere, and it'd break her heart when the time came to make the decision, but it was inevitable. She'd nurtured this horse from the beginning, and its shiny skin and good health were because of her hard work.

She drank in his smell one last time and blinked back the tears. Command snorted back, telling her he loved the attention. She'd always been able to communicate with her horses. It was like they spoke in their own special language.

"Mummy, help me up," Natalie said, trying to hook her foot into the stirrup and failing, landing on her backside. "Ouch."

Grace gave Command one more hug before lifting Natalie from the ground and swinging her onto the saddle. "There you go. Remember how I showed you to hold the reins?"

At three years old, Natalie was too young to ride on her own, so Grace led her around the paddock. Nonetheless, it brought an enormous smile to her little girl's face. Her daughter made it impossible for Grace to regret marrying Phil entirely. Natalie was worth all the pain and suffering. But for how much longer could she tolerate it?

⁙

"Come on, girlfriend, we're going on a road trip."

Grace couldn't stop the wide grin spreading across her face. "Where to?"

"Kalgoorlie."

Her smile slipped. "That's a long drive."

"Yeah, I know, but I have a friend who's loaned us a house to stay in. Got your bag packed?"

"I'm ready. I didn't pack much as I thought you were taking me back to your place. The kids are ready, though. They can't wait to spend some time with Mum."

"Kalgoorlie is going to be much better than my pokey flat. I know this sounds extreme, but I think you need to be as far away as possible from here for a bit. I've settled Paige. She's happily hanging out with Mum and Dad, so it's just us girls, like old times."

Gratitude spread around Grace's weary body. Why had she let Phil keep her away from her friends? "Thanks, Jackie." Grace embraced her with a firm hug. Good friends were hard to find, and she was relieved she'd reconnected with Jackie when she most needed one.

She didn't miss how Jackie took a good, long look at her, though. She'd seen her reflection in the mirror, and it'd scared the hell out of her. Jackie didn't say a word, but the way her mouth remained a straight line when she thought Grace wasn't looking, said enough.

Grace relaxed back and sighed. She wrapped her hands around the cold bottle of ginger beer and relished the fizzy and spicy drink. It'd been years since she'd drank one, and she would enjoy it.

Jackie insisted Grace rest with her feet up while she prepared lunch. The drive the day before had been long and draining. Grace couldn't believe she'd slept through most of it. It was what she needed but not what she'd planned. She followed it up with another incredible sleep that night, leaving her feeling refreshed.

"When did it start?" Jackie asked, cutting up food to go on a platter.

Grace didn't have to ask what she was referring to. With some experience in domestic violence through her work as a nurse, Jackie had advised her that talking to someone who could help was the first step to solving the problem. Why hadn't she sought help sooner?

"Not long after I fell pregnant with Natalie."

Jackie exhaled a long breath. She motioned for Grace to get up and come to the table for lunch.

They picked at the fruit, cheese, crackers and cold meats from the platter while Grace unburdened all the sordid details of her failed marriage. With each telling of how varied and constant Phil's jealousy and physical abuse had become, the weight of something heavy lifted from her shoulders. She'd never been able to talk to anyone about it, and being brave enough to leave the day before with Jackie had been a monumental step forward.

When she ran out of words to say and finished her drink, Jackie offered her another. Grace shook her head. Her undernourished body could only cope with so much, and she was pleasantly full.

With elbows perched on the table, Jackie took Grace's hands in hers and squeezed tight. "Sounds like four years of hell."

Living with her father had been bad, and the realisation that her entire married life with Phil sounded worse than her childhood gnawed at her guts. How had she let it happen?

"What do I do?"

Jackie looked long and hard at her. Grace could tell she didn't want to say the words. They had to come from her own lips. Talking about it made her feel like an idiot for putting up with it for so long. Like somehow it was her fault and she should've dealt with it from the start.

Grace picked at the label on the bottle, unable to meet Jackie's eyes. "You know what, Jackie? The only reason I stayed all these years was that I didn't make an effort with my first marriage. I walked out on it when it'd got too tough, so I vowed to make the next one work."

Jackie rose and stacked the empty plates. Grace got up to help, too, grabbing the empty bottles. "I have to leave him, don't I?"

Jackie froze, the cleaning up forgotten for a minute. "I just want to see the old Grace again. If that's what it takes—"

Grace's shoulders dropped. "There's only one way off this merry-go-round, isn't there? I have to get off for good."

Jackie smiled for the first time. The smile transformed both the angry and saddened looks Jackie had conveyed to Grace since they'd reunited the day before.

"And get as far away as I can," Grace added with conviction.

"That's my girl," Jackie said with an armful of plates as she led the way to the kitchen.

Grace grabbed the few remaining things on the table and followed. "But how will I manage? I don't own much, and I have no money?"

"The old Grace I knew easily worked three jobs."

"But this Grace has two small children. If I go as far away as possible, I won't have my mother to help."

"There is always someone who'll help a person in need." Jackie turned away from the sink and put a wet hand around Grace. "Even you can see you have to leave. Look at the state you're in. That bastard of a husband doesn't care that you nearly died. He was too busy going out while you were in hospital. And he changed the locks on the house. What sort of sadistic bastard does that?"

Grace nodded; her tears these days never far away. "I know, I know."

"Good. I'll loan you the money to help you leave. You can give it back to me when you're on your feet again."

Tears trickled down her cheeks this time. She wasn't a crier. Never had been, but she was at her lowest. She wouldn't need Jackie's money, though she was grateful for the offer. There was only one thing she owned, and it would break her heart to sell him. There was no other choice.

"Where should I go?"

"What's the furthest point from Perth on the map of Australia?"

Grace pictured a map of Australia. She immediately recalled a conversation she'd had on her European holiday with two mates travelling together. They lived in Innisfail and, in their own words: 'we couldn't live any further away from you and still be in the same country'.

"Cairns." The closest airport to Innisfail was Cairns, and she clearly remembered the two blokes insisting she visit them if she ever found her way on that side of the country.

Jackie dried her hands. "Cairns, huh?" Like all of a sudden it was *too* far away.

"Yeah, Cairns. You said I should choose a place as far as possible."

"Yeah, I did, didn't I?"

Grace giggled at the irony. It was a crazy reaction to the enormity of the discussion, but she felt lighter by the minute—in a crazy, dizzy way. She straightened her back and heard bones popping as she did so. No more slouching for her. It was amazing how a decent sleep and a proper meal could make such a difference.

On the spur of the moment, she gave Jackie a great big hug and then spun around a few times with her arms held out wide. When she stopped, she grabbed the sink before real dizziness threatened to land her on the floor. "Thank you so much for saving me, Jackie. I'll never be able to repay you."

A couple of tiny tears rolled down Jackie's cheeks. It must've been a shock to see how much her best friend had changed in only a few years. The ectopic pregnancy scare changed a lot for Grace. It was the wake-up call she needed, and she planned on staying awake for a long time yet—without Phil.

⁂

Selling Command, the horse she'd come to love so much, hurt like blazes. Her hard work and care earned her two thousand dollars. It was enough to pay some of her bills, buy airfares for herself and two children and still leave her with six hundred dollars. This was the total of what she had. Two children, three suitcases and six hundred dollars.

In the six weeks since Jackie helped put her on the road to salvation, she'd moved back in with her mother. She was never staying another night under the same roof as Phil. He didn't seem to care. That hurt too, but she pushed it aside. Anger put new words between them, and Phil telling her he was glad she was going only strengthened her resolve to make a better life. She had her freedom, and no amount of money could ever buy that.

Chapter 29

Present Day

Erin straightened her laptop screen and checked the camera was working. She fiddled with the hem of her shirt. In exactly two minutes, she'd be chatting with her grandfather online. After Grace had learnt they had the right Larry, things escalated quickly. One phone call had confirmed everything. Yes, he was the Larry she'd known, and yes, he was Erin's grandfather.

Two days later and after lots of messages between Erin and Katherine, the cousin she never knew existed, her grandfather was to appear on her screen any minute.

Erin drummed her fingers along her thigh. Katherine was a couple of years older, married with two young children and owned a busy agricultural supplies business with her husband.

Waiting for the call to connect had her heart racing. She hadn't uttered a word to her mother about learning of her grandfather's whereabouts, and her hand clenched around the mouse, nervous about what she was about to learn.

She gasped when a man's face appeared. Her first impressions were strong, proud and outback tough. It showed in the way he held himself. In the lines that crisscrossed his cheeks and met at the corners of his eyes. Not an ounce of excess skin, and what he had was sunburnt brown from a life lived outdoors. His thick grey hair looked like he'd run his hand through

it many times that day, but his initial worried look transformed into an
enormous smile when her face must've appeared on his screen.

"Erin! My God, I'd pick you anywhere." His deep, gravelly voice
soothed as he spoke.

Someone's arm blocked the view for a few moments. Erin assumed it
was Katherine, making last-minute adjustments to the sound and camera
position.

"Really?"

"If you don't look every inch your great-grandmother, Liz, I'll eat my
hat."

Erin laughed and all the nervous tension eased from her body. "I'll need
to see some proof of that to check you're telling the truth."

Larry's smile slipped, and every line and wrinkle on his sun toughened
face told a thousand stories. "Your mum never showed you one?"

Erin's smile dropped. "No."

Larry shook his head. "Stubborn as a mule, that one." He tried to
resurrect a crooked smile, but it wobbled instead. "Wonder who she took
after?"

Erin chuckled. "I'm guessing you?" Her mother was as stubborn as they
came, but it worked with her father because he had more than enough
patience for both of them. She leant forward and stared into the camera
lens. "Grandad, what happened?"

His eyes darted to his left, presumably towards Katherine. When they
turned back, he asked, "She never told you anything?" Erin detected a note
of sorrow in his gruff voice.

"No, nothing at all. That's why I went searching for you. I need to fill
in the gap of my history, my family's story." She could only see the top of
his shoulders, but they visibly drooped at her answer. "I was hoping you
would tell me?"

He perked up again. "You're not having a blue with them, are you?"

Erin gnawed on her bottom lip, debating how much to say. "No,
nothing like that. It's just that I haven't turned out how they wanted me

to. I'm supposed to be a doctor like everyone else in the family on my dad's side, but I can't seem to achieve it."

"Yeah? No joke. All doctors, you say?"

"Yes. Nothing like a bit of pressure. Since I don't take after dad's side of the family, I hope I took after yours." She paused, trying to find the best words to explain how she felt deep inside her soul. "I was looking for some answers as to why I don't fit in."

Larry snorted. "What the heck does that mean? Since when do you have to fit in anywhere? Just be yourself, and you'll get on fine. What about your brother?"

"How do you know I have one?"

"I have my sources, young lady." His deep, chesty chuckle brought a smile to Erin. She doubted anything got past this man. "Is he a doctor too?"

"He's nearly there, just another year to go."

Larry nodded but didn't comment. Did he have regrets about not being able to share their lives? Did he blame himself or Rosemary for taking away the opportunity to watch his grandchildren grow up and be part of their lives?

"So, what do *you* want to do with yourself? You could always come over this way and learn to jillaroo. Do you enjoy working with animals? We're very much a bunch of outdoors people, and if we're not working on the land, we're working with animals."

"I seem to be good with animals. I work for a vet clinic and recently changed from med studies to vet studies."

"Goodness me, my girl. Way to go."

Erin's chest pumped at the encouragement. "It'll still take a few years, but I'll get there this time. Some of my med degree can go towards it, so it won't be a total slog."

"You can still come over this way. There's always a need for a vet."

"I'd love to come and visit you all. I feel like a part of me is missing, and this might be what it is."

Larry dropped his eyes. He had his elbows on the desk and his fingers knotted together at the bottom of the screen. "If your mother hadn't been involved in that accident, none of this would've happened. She was moving to Queensland anyway, for her medical degree, but she refused to tell us the truth before she left."

"The truth about what?"

The audible sigh came across clearly when his eyes lifted. "It was an accident with a group of friends that went very wrong. One of the young kids slipped down a waterfall and was killed. We know your mother wasn't to blame for the death, but she refused to tell the police anything, and I wouldn't take a bar of it. All she had to do was describe exactly what'd happened. She wouldn't, and I drew the line. I'll admit I was angry and hurt that any daughter of mine would do this. When I put my foot down and demanded she volunteered a statement to the police or not come back, she—"

Erin let out the breath she wasn't aware she was holding. "—she chose not to come back?"

"Yeah, I guess so."

"Oh, Grandad, I'm so sorry."

"Not your fault. I thought I'd done the best I could as a father, setting the right example, teaching the kids how to face their problems honestly, no matter the outcome. In the end, it made no difference. She was more worried about any slight against her name that would risk her one chance to study medicine. She was adamant she'd done nothing wrong, and I just wanted her to explain it. In the end, it"—he sniffed and dabbed his nose with the back of his hand—"it broke us as a family."

Someone's arm blocked the front of the screen and obscured Larry's face. Then the same arm wound around Larry's shoulder before the screen moved to the person sitting beside him.

"Hi, Erin. It's me, Katherine. Grandad is a little overwhelmed, so I'll give him a moment."

Erin's jaw dropped. It was like looking in a mirror—the same honey-brown, shoulder-length hair and matching hazel eyes. The same high cheeks and button nose in a heart-shaped face. "Oh my God, Katherine, how many more of us are there?"

Katherine must've understood what she meant because her delightful laughter rang through the laptop speakers and, for the first time, Erin experienced what everyone else did when they heard her laughing. Erin had been told before her laughter made people stop and stare. Until that moment, she'd never really understood why.

"Well, let me see. Your mum has a brother and a sister. My dad is the brother, and I have three brothers. Our Aunty Anne has a couple of daughters and two sons. But it's just the two of us that look exactly like great-gran Liz. "

"Okay, I need to see a picture of great-gran Liz."

"Coming right up. Have you got your phone handy? I'll message it through."

"That would be great! Thanks."

When the phone buzzed with an incoming notification, Erin swiped and tapped, downloading the black-and-white image. She gasped, and Katherine chuckled. It was a photo of Liz with a hand-scrawled note, *Elizabeth, Age 21*. They could be triplets.

Something tugged inside her chest. There was this invisible cord that firmly attached itself to her heart and the woman in the photo. Erin couldn't suppress the enormous well of disappointment that she'd never had the opportunity to meet Liz. Rosemary had no right to keep her from this side of the family. How unfair and selfish.

"Believe me now?" Katherine asked.

Erin hoped her nod conveyed the message. She was too busy looking at every detail of the photo. When Larry spoke again, she looked up again.

"Thanks so much for trying to find us, Erin. It means the world to me."

Liz had passed away ten years earlier, but Katherine had assured her during the week that Larry was well cared for after the unexpected passing of his wife only a year ago. He still enjoyed a very active and busy life.

"I might come over for a visit," Larry continued. "It'll be grand to catch up with Grace too. I couldn't believe it when she phoned the other day. Thought I was hearing things. That young Gracie was some girl back in the day. Fearless, gutsy, with a competitive streak a mile long and a crazy side that left you scratching your head. Your great-grandmother adored her and thought the world of her. Some days she wished she could've done more for her but it wasn't always possible. It'll also make my day to meet you in person and not over these screens. I—"

Erin swallowed back emotions she wasn't used to.

"I should've tried finding your mother years ago. It broke your grandmother's heart, but I was a stubborn old fool who didn't deserve her and it's too late now to make it up to her."

"Oh, Grandad, don't say that." Erin blinked back tears.

"Hey, an old man can confess his sins."

On the edge of the screen, Katherine's arm wrapped around Larry's shoulder again and squeezed it.

"How about we do this again next week?" Erin suggested.

"I'd like that, love. It'll give me something to look forward to."

"I'm also going to talk to Mum about this."

"Now, you don't go doing anything that'll cause problems between you."

"I won't. I promise."

"Okay, I'll let you two chat. This old man will go shed a couple of tears while he has a shot of scotch. Thanks again for finding us. It'll help ease the guilt that is always sitting here."

She could only see the tips of his fingers against his chest. She swallowed the lump lodged in her throat and blinked back the tears filling her eyes.

As Larry rose from the chair, he said, "Don't do anything you'll live to regret. It's not worth it, love."

Erin assumed they wanted her to be cautious about what she told her mother. She'd think carefully about it, but the unsolved mystery was like an itch she wanted to scratch. It would be hard to hold back the questions.

"So, Erin—"

She pushed aside all her worrying thoughts and enjoyed a few more minutes chatting with Katherine. When they signed off, they set a date for the following weekend.

With the reunion complete, it was time to prepare for the barbecue and Grace's epic quest to get back on a horse. Erin had prepared two cakes earlier, so all she had left to do was shower and dress. Her hands shook, and her stomach churned as she turned the laptop off and stood. She stretched her arms above her head and took a couple of calming breaths. As long as Tom hadn't changed his mind, she wanted him to know she was ready to take things a little further.

Chapter 30

Present Day

Grace's daughter, Natalie, handed Erin a can of beer and told her to relax and mingle, but instead, she lingered in the shadows, feeling a little out of place as close family and friends continued to arrive.

Tom's work ute was parked down by the stables, and she itched to walk over and say hello. Resisting, she sat on one of the upturned wooden crates placed around the lawn for seating. Others had found seats, too, and their laughter and chatter began in earnest around Grace's homestead yard.

"Oh, there you are. Glad you could make it."

"Was there ever a chance I wouldn't?" She rose and embraced Grace like an old friend, comforting and ... natural. "You look great, and those riding boots are to die for!"

"Thanks. I'm nervous about everyone here. I have some very special friends I'll introduce to you later. Julie drove up from Innisfail and Gary and his wife have come over from Perth. Dear me, whose idea was it to invite so many people to watch me topple off my darling Eve?"

Erin chuckled. "Eve doesn't let *me* fall off. It won't happen to you."

"This is the longest I've ever gone without riding a horse. I'm not ready to give up my stirrups yet." A thinking-frown look appeared on her face. "Am I being a silly old woman?"

"No," Erin said with conviction.

They both turned when someone called Grace. She gave them all a smile and a wave.

"Off you go. They're waiting for you."

"I will, but first, thanks for coming," Grace said, resting her hand on Erin's forearm.

"Of course. I wouldn't have missed it. Between your nerves, are you excited?"

Grace's face lit up, and there was a twinkle in her eye. "Getting on any animal has always excited me. But yes, today is extra special. Eve has been waiting patiently, just like I have. Tom volunteered to ready her, and they should be here any minute."

At the mention of Tom, nerves fluttered inside her stomach. Erin smiled despite her body's overreaction. "I'm sure it'll all go how it should. Where do you plan on riding?"

"We're saddling up three horses, and I just want to ride around the homestead, maybe do a few little jumps. Just a taste of what I've missed out on this past year. Anyone who wants to join me is more than welcome. Do you think you'd like to?"

Erin gulped. She *was not* ready for any show jumping. She laughed at the absurd idea and then took a sip of her beer. "Maybe not today, but thanks."

Grace gave her an understanding smile and patted her shoulder. "Can I promote you to official photographer, maybe?"

Erin jumped at the offer. Being useful was akin to being wanted in her books. "I would love to do that for you. Do you have a camera, or would you like me to use my phone?"

"I have a camera. It's charged and ready to go. Give me a sec; I left it on the patio."

Erin remained on the lawn and watched the mingling crowd. There were a lot of RM Williams boots and a stack of Akubra hats in various colours and states of wear and tear. After hearing Grace's stories, she sensed this crowd knew how to party and had been doing so for many years. There would've been some good times had amongst them all, with a lot of boot stomping and fun had the old-fashioned way. An entire generation ago.

Grace returned with the camera. "Here you go. It's a fairly standard digital one. If you have any questions, Peter can help if I'm busy."

"I'll be fine. I'm pretty good with a camera. Now off you go; your friends are waiting."

A remarkably tall woman, Grace strolled away dressed in slim-fitting riding pants and a pale pink pressed-stud long-sleeved shirt. Despite her age, there was a glimpse of the stunning woman she'd been in her youth.

During one of their interviewing days spent pouring over photos, one particular image of Grace stood out. She was in her early twenties and showed a striking resemblance to the late Princess Diana. Even her hairstyle had mimicked the princess's.

Even though Erin had been only a toddler when the princess was killed in that infamous car accident, who hadn't seen images of the princess? Erin had immediately remarked on the likeness to Grace, but she had only responded with a shy smile. In hindsight, and after Erin had done the numbers, Princess Diana had not existed in a royal sense when that photo was taken, and no connection would've been made all those years ago.

Despite Grace's serious illness over the last year, Erin saw a woman who no longer resembled that twenty-something princess look-alike, but someone a lot older and wiser standing amongst her friends, but still able to carry herself in a regal manner.

Erin turned when a cheer went up from the crowd. From the direction of the stables, she spotted Tom and Grace's young grandson leading three horses towards the large gathering. She fumbled with the camera, not even close to having it ready to record such a momentous occasion.

It didn't take her long before she got busy with the shutter and started taking shots. She fancied herself a bit of a photographer and did her best to forget that one jibe from her parents that 'photography wasn't a career choice'. At the time, it had hurt—she had been desperately questioning what she was doing and trying to find her place in the world.

For one shot, she zoomed in on Tom's face. He held the lead around Eve's neck and was looking at Grace. Erin couldn't hear what was being said, but whatever Grace said caused Tom to laugh at the exact moment she pressed the shutter. She gasped at the perfect timing. She wanted nothing more than to stop what she was doing and look at it. It took every ounce of control not to. Instead, she ground her jaw tight and continued with the task. If anything, she wanted first dibs on that photo.

She took photos as Tom helped Grace into the saddle and zoomed in to catch her expression as she held the reins and nuzzled her face into Eve's mane. It was so natural, like she'd done it a thousand times before, and she probably had. Grace's face lit up brighter than the afternoon sun in the far corner of the western sky.

At one point, Tom rode beside her and then Natalie joined her as they walked over to the jumps. Others wanted to share in the occasion, too; it was as though everyone wanted to be a part of the history of Grace. That's how much she was loved and respected by everyone there.

When the sun lost most of its intensity for the day, it signalled the end of the ride for Grace. There was a loud round of applause as she dismounted, Erin capturing the moment the dust swirled around Grace's silhouette against golden hour light, the stables in the background. She checked the screen on the back of the camera—another postcard-perfect image.

The delicious aroma of barbequed steak and onion wafted past Erin's nose, causing her stomach to grumble. The guests were gathering around the food-laden tables. She was about to join them but found herself watching Tom make his way towards the stables, the three horses in tow. Alone. Before he got too close, she took a set of shots.

He stopped when he drew level with her. "Hey," he said and flashed her a brilliant smile.

"Hey, back." She itched to take another shot but was too busy smiling.

"Want to give me a hand?"

She didn't need to be asked twice. Nodding, she stumbled over her feet and followed behind.

When Tom led the horses inside, Erin drank in the smell of hay and all things horse, not so invasive on her nose these days, set the camera on a bench and helped with untacking and removing the bridles and saddles. Tom placed a bucket of water in front of each horse and handed her a brush. In silence, they brushed them down. They hadn't done anything too strenuous, but it was something Erin noticed Tom did to unwind.

"Okay, I think that's enough for now, he said. "How about we wash our hands and join the party? I'm starving."

"Me too!" Erin gave Eve a final scratch behind her ears before latching the stall door closed. Eve poked her head over and nudged Tom's shoulder, looking forlornly back at them.

"I don't think she wants us to leave."

Tom chuckled and pointed to the camera on the bench. "May I?"

The single bulb hanging down from the rafters cast shadows across the stables. Tom switched on the flash and took a close-up of Eve.

"Grace will thank me one day," he said. When his hand rested on her shoulder, it zapped with his warmth. "Now, one of you and Eve."

Instinctively, Erin wound her arms around Eve and rested her cheek against her nose. Erin's eyes were half closed when the shutter clicked, and they flicked open when she realised. Eve suddenly lost interest in what they were doing and moved back into the stall, snorting a few times.

Tom still held the camera at the ready, but his gaze blazed into hers. She licked dry lips. This was the moment she'd been waiting for, and somehow, her tongue had gone and done a runner.

"Can I take a shot of you?"

Erin gulped. He could have anything he wanted. What was a photo anyway? She nodded.

"This first."

Huh? His mouth was millimetres from hers before she realised what he meant. The moment his mouth touched hers, and for those precious few seconds, everything in her world felt right. When he pulled back, she wanted to protest and demand he kept going, but before she uttered a single word, he snapped another shot.

They stood staring at each other, the camera dangling from Tom's arm. She looked down when he placed it on a bale of hay. A rush of warmth filled her chest when Tom wound his arms around her waist and pulled her in tight; their bodies pressed together.

Now was her chance to declare her changed intentions. If she didn't do it now, she may as well just walk out. After all, *she* had followed Tom to the stables.

She breathed in a lung full of air and tightened her hold on his shoulders before slowly releasing it. "Tom, kiss me again."

His arms dropped, and her legs wobbled without his support.

"Thank Christ for that." The shock must've been too much for him because he stumbled back and tripped over the bale of hay. He fell onto his butt, and a burst of laughter erupted from him. "Do you have any idea how hard it's been to see you, work near you, talk to you, and *not* touch you?"

He laid back against the hay-covered ground. "Get down here, girl, and let me show you what a kiss is."

He reached for her hand and tugged on it. Dropping awkwardly, she laughed. Tom froze for a second at the sound of her laughter before winding his arms around her waist. She didn't hesitate to link her fingers behind his neck.

"Kiss me, Tom. Please, now."

"Hey ... what? That's what I plan on doing."

"Stop talking, Tom. It's called kissing. What don't you get about it?"

Tom laughed some more with her, rolling them to the side, but their laughter stopped abruptly when their gazes locked. Lust, compassion and apprehension flickered through his eyes. His tongue touched her first, and she gasped at the delicious invasion. She glimpsed a smile on his face before it vanished, his mouth fastening onto hers. Shivers travelled up her arms and down her spine. She nestled in closer, closed her eyes and drank in the sensation of kissing someone whose image had invaded her every waking moment since meeting him all those months ago.

Tom pulled back abruptly, and her heart jolted at the sudden withdrawal.

"Are you sure, Erin? Kill me quickly if you have to. Just take me out of my misery if you don't want this to happen."

She groaned against his mouth and tightened her hold around his neck. She was more than ready for this. "This feels so right. You're nothing like Nic ..."

"Don't you dare mention that scumbag near me," Tom growled, sliding his hands down her back and gripping both sides of her backside. Then he relaxed and sighed. "I'm sorry, I didn't mean to come across so grouchy. Every time I'm reminded of how he hurt you, I want to strangle him."

"He's gone, Tom," she whispered. "Dad told me this week he's been transferred to a Melbourne hospital. I'm finally free. I haven't been able to rid myself of the fear of confronting him again. I ... I'm ready to live again."

She was also ready to end their misery. Ready to feel the spark again that gave purpose to her life, confident she wouldn't experience a second Nicholas. She smiled shyly and cradled his head. "Not exactly where I pictured us getting it on for the first time, but hey—"

"Hey, what?"

"You're going to have one hell of a job getting every stick of hay out of my hair, so I'm presentable for the barbecue happening outside."

"That's if I let you out of here."

His hands firmed on her backside before pushing her up against his jeans.

"You will. I bet you're starving. *And* I have some delicious treats for after dinner."

Tom groaned and rested his forehead against hers. "Okay, you win. The smell of the cooking meat was doing my stomach in ages ago."

Erin chuckled. "I'm also the official photographer. I'm probably missing some of the best crowd shots."

"Okay, okay." Tom rose from the hay and reached for her hand to help her up. Then he went in for a slow, leisurely kiss until a groan escaped his mouth. "This has to be continued later."

After a quick dust off and checking for hay in their hair, Erin collected the discarded camera and put it around her neck. "Yes, please," she pleaded.

Chapter 31

Present Day

"Here, Grace, thank you for being so cooperative while I was doing the research." Erin handed over a small gift she'd hidden in a brown bag, then settled back in the timber chair in Grace's open-plan kitchen.

Grace did the usual thing of touching and prodding it first. "I have a feeling it's a framed photo. I wondered where the camera went. I knew I could trust you with it."

"I can't put anything past you," Erin said cheekily. "Anyway, I've downloaded all the photos, and they're on this memory stick." Erin placed it on the kitchen table. A few great shots of Tom she'd kept for herself. "I better give you back the camera, too." When the camera was sitting beside the memory stick, she added, "You can send photos to your friends now."

Grace gasped when the final piece of wrapping paper was removed, exposing the photo of Grace on top of Eve. The sun was perfectly positioned so not too much shadow obscured Grace's facial features. It also left Eve looking majestic and beautiful. Erin fell in love with the shot the second she'd swiped over it.

Erin looked across at Grace and noticed tears building up around her eyes. She reached across for the box of tissues and pulled out a couple for Grace. Passing them across, she hoped the photo stirred up some good memories for Grace.

"Here, let me put it up here near this trophy." Erin took back the frame and walked towards a shelf. She picked up a trophy to move it to one side and took a moment to read the plaque. "Herbie Rains Memorial Maiden Camp Draft. First Place."

Erin fingered it and left a streak through the light layer of dust. "Does this belong to you?"

This perked Grace up. "Oh, that day. What a lark."

Erin carried the trophy back and set it on the table, hoping it would bring back more wonderful memories for Grace. Her storytelling skills were exceptional and always transported Erin to another time and place.

Grace grinned mischievously and shook her head. "I've only ever done a few camp drafts, but I loved every single one. I was lucky my grey mare, Tammy's Trio, was a talented horse and good with cattle." She chuckled, and her face lit up as the memories came flooding back. "My first camp draft at Mount Garnet. Wow, looking back, I had no idea what I was doing and was just winging it. I stuffed up the team's event, which was a shame, because the other two on the team were very good horse people."

Erin laughed as she stretched across the table for the kettle and filled her cup again. "Would you like a refill, Grace?"

Grace put her hand on a full belly. "No thanks," and settled back as a faraway look crossed her face. The one Erin killed for every time she wanted some snippet of Grace's past.

"That first experience was so much fun. I went and did a ten-day course and learnt a lot about the sport. That particular camp draft"—she pointed to the trophy—"was held over two days and had one hundred and thirteen competitors. Naturally, I drew number one hundred and thirteen." Grace stopped reminiscing and asked, "Did you know thirteen was my lucky number?"

"I don't think you've told me yet."

"Well, when it was my turn to go, a bloke by the name of Jack Coghlan asked me which one I was going to take. The cattle used for the camp draft were station cattle, which meant they were pretty wild with lots of speed. I pointed out a little brown fellow in the middle of the mob I had my eye on. I probably did about four-to-four good blocks on him before I called for a gate, but boy did this brown one have some speed. Well, so did

Tammy, and we made a perfect run around the first and second pegs and then straight up before putting a bend in him for the gate. I was given a ninety-three-point score from a judge who gave points away like it was his lunch money, so yeah, I couldn't be happier."

"I'm sure you deserved every one of those points."

"You're right; Tammy and I certainly did. Only twenty-four competitors made it to the second day. This big brindle patterned steer broke out of the mob and pretty much picked me, so I took him on. Man, he was wild and turned hard and fast many times facing the mob. At one stage, he even tried to jump the yard fence. My Tammy blocked him right to the fence, and when he turned the other way, I called for the gate."

Erin pictured the dust billowing and the frantic, sweat-drenched work Grace put herself and her horse through. The life Grace chose for herself was as distant as Mars compared to Erin's privileged, safe life. Regret pressed against her chest as she questioned whether she was living her life to the fullest.

"I remember hearing what a cowboy said to the judge positioned near the gate. 'Pity she picked him cos she'll never get it out'. Well, we came out of the gates at a flat gallop after I got myself in position to put a bend in it. The judge called out twenty-three out of twenty-four. As it turned out, none of the other finalists got one around, so I won the trophy."

"What a fearless woman you are. Remind me not to go horseriding with you."

Grace waved a hand and laughed the compliment away. "That woman was a lot younger and probably more crazy than fearless."

"But I'm close to the same age as you were, and trust me, I have absolutely no intention of ever doing anything requiring so much stamina and guts."

"Yeah, but you'll do other great stuff. I know it."

Erin wasn't so sure about that. It took a certain type of person to do the things Grace had done over her lifetime. Not everyone was born with the same character, and Erin was okay with the fact she'd never do anything so wild or dangerous. She took hold of the trophy and put it back in its place.

Everything in Grace's home had a story and a place. She positioned it near the newest frame when the telephone rang.

Erin handed Grace the phone, gathered the used mugs and empty plate of muffins and made for the sink. It'd been one week since the barbecue, and Grace was still eating left-over sweets.

The party reminded her of Tom. He was never far from her thoughts. She hugged the newness of it close to her heart. She hadn't shared him with her family yet and wanted to wait a while longer.

It was sometimes awkward sharing the same workplace, but the occasional touch of hands and the lingering looks as they went about their hectic days couldn't be ignored. The week proved extra busy after hours with Tom called to attend to some unexpected emergencies. With another vet scheduled to work the weekend on-call shift, Tom promised her the weekend together. This sent a delicious shiver over her.

"Hey, Erin, guess who that was?"

Erin spun around. "Tom?"

"Nope, but I noticed a spark between you pair at the party. It was your grandfather, and he's coming to visit next week and asked if he could stay here."

Her heart boomed. She could no longer avoid talking to her mother and needed to do it sooner rather than later.

"I told him you were visiting today, and he sends his love."

Erin found her voice again. "That was a fast decision. We're talking again tomorrow, so no doubt we'll discuss it then."

"We've had a few phone conversations since I first made contact. Said he's getting too old to die with regrets. I imagine it has something to do with your mum?"

Erin nodded.

"And I'm guessing she doesn't know about this yet?"

Erin continued to nod.

"How about you hold off from saying anything to your mum until you talk to Larry tomorrow? Your cousin, Katherine, is coming with him and only staying a couple of days. Then your uncle will come and help Larry return home. Maybe you should discuss how to go about this with them first?"

Erin took a deep breath and folded the tea towel neatly over the sink. "I have to admit, I've been putting it off. I don't want to upset Mum, but I need to know more about her side of the family."

Grace came closer and put her hand on Erin's shoulder. "Every family has a falling out at some time. Believe it or not, I need to make an effort to patch things up with my brother. We were so close once, but things went astray a few years back over a stupid misunderstanding. Larry's right. We get old too quickly to die with regrets."

"I don't think I could handle having a falling out with my family. Sure, they can be annoying, but ever since I split with Nicholas, they seem to be starting to understand. For the first time, my parents are willing to accept my choices. My other grandparents are special too. I don't want to wreck anything there either."

"Your family sound like very reasonable people. I'm sure they don't want to lose you either. Don't forget, if you ever need a sounding board, I'm always here."

Erin smiled and pulled the plug from the sink. "I still can't believe you know my grandfather. What were the chances of that?"

"There's a reason for everything that happens in your life. Some people call it fate. I call it the path we're destined to take. You have no control over it. Life will take you over whatever path it wants you to go on. You either show courage and survive it, or—"

"—you die and get relegated to where all the boring people are shoved to and forgotten about."

Grace laughed heartily at Erin's summation.

"But thanks, Grace. I'll have to get my head around Grandad coming and the family reunion with long-lost cousins, but I better be off. I'm meeting Tom for a swim. He wants to do some riding later this afternoon. Is that okay with you?"

Grace quirked a brow. "Of course it is. This is Tom we're talking about, isn't it?"

Erin smiled, her heart beating faster just hearing his name.

"You pair have really hit it off. I'm glad your previous bad experience didn't leave you too afraid to try again. I was in the same boat when I met Peter. I kept putting him off, believing I didn't need another man in my life. Hell, my previous marriage was a disaster. But eventually, you get a sense that everything is right. Not only that, but you're a different person because of your experience. You'll never go back to being that person. You're stronger, surer and you'll be damned if another man controls you like the last one."

Erin chuckled. "Well, Grace, since you practically threw us together at every opportunity, you should be patting yourself on the back knowing all your hard work has paid off."

Grace's laughter tinkled around the kitchen as a slant of the sun poured in through the window and lit up her face. What a well-lived face. Those eyes had seen so much, and that mouth had spoken many well-meaning words. If the number of friends who made the special effort to witness Grace ride a horse again was anything to go by, Erin wasn't the only one who'd noticed what an incredible person she was.

"By the way, I've finished the medical report they wanted me to do."

"Oh, that's okay. I still expect you to visit me. You have to do a lot more riding to catch up to Tom's skill level. It'll also give me a good reason to get out there and join you." A cloud hovered across the bright midday sun and temporarily dulled it.

"And with your grandfather coming," Grace continued, "I bet he can teach you a thing or two. He certainly taught me a lot when I was a kid."

Erin took in everything about this kind-hearted woman. Regardless of her failing health and the many risks she'd taken over her life that could've resulted in instant death, here she was, still doing the best she could for everyone else.

"Thanks, Grace. Meeting you completely changed my life."

"Hey, hey, enough of this sentimental stuff. Are you trying to make me cry again? Get over here and give me a quick hug, and then go meet that hunk of a man I know is waiting for you."

As she put her arms around Grace, Erin swallowed, hiding any evidence of tears. Yes, it was time to grab her life and run with it. Risks and all.

Chapter 32

28 Years Old

"How was school today, Colin?" Grace wrapped her arms around Colin and squeezed hard.

"I have a second new friend. His name's Michael."

She kissed his forehead and released him. "That's great. See, Mum told you it was easy to make friends."

"Yeah," Colin replied, ripping off his sneakers. "He's invited me to his house on the weekend. Can I go?"

"Let's wait and see. I'll talk to his mum first."

Grace had played down Colin's nerves about starting a new school, but she understood his reluctance. Thank goodness it sounded like he was fitting in and making friends.

She bustled around the tiny kitchen in her two-bedroom flat in East Innisfail, making his favourite after-school snack of peanut butter and strawberry jam sandwich. She enjoyed the afternoons when they were all together. It was a special time for the three of them before she left them in the care of a babysitter and went to work at the Cane Cutter Hotel as a barmaid.

She wasn't complaining. Arriving in Cairns with only the name of a sister of a girl she knew in Perth, she was more than grateful this family had let her stay with them for their first week. During that time, she contacted the two mates she'd met in London and took up their suggestion to live in

Innisfail, where the rent was cheaper. The town seemed to be a great place to bring up the kids.

A kind neighbour had given her a shopping bag of fresh juicy oranges from their laden tree. She peeled three of them, putting them into plastic bowls. Fruit was always in abundance in her neighbourhood and shared with those in need. With her meagre wages, she was slowly adding to the flat. It no longer contained only two chairs, a bed frame and a big plastic plant. She'd added a table and second-hand lounge and the op shop was an excellent source for cutlery, crockery and a few pots and pans. Somehow, she made her earnings stretch. Rent was always paid first, food next, then some money put aside for electricity, fuel and babysitting.

Sometimes panic overtook her when there were only five dollars left in her purse, but she'd come a long way. Being frugal was how she could afford to add more furniture to her tiny flat. It wouldn't be long before she could afford the six-hundred-dollar car she had her eye on.

"Snacks are ready," Grace announced. Colin joined her at the table, and Natalie, who was nearly four years old, climbed up onto her lap for cuddle time. Grace ran her fingers through the blonde strands of Natalie's hair and pulled them away from her mouth.

It was hard for Grace to look at her beautiful daughter and regret the life she shared with the man who'd fathered her. She couldn't deny they were all more relaxed with their everyday home life. The new friends she was starting to make were easing the pain of the transition.

"So, Colin, what did you learn that was new today?"

She gave Natalie another hug before getting her to sit in her own chair while Colin told her about his day. Then she reached for her orange, thinking ahead of what she needed to do before leaving for work.

"One last swim, kids," Grace called, stacking plastic buckets and spades into an old cotton tote.

The four children scampered down to the gentle waves at Etty Bay. With a new set of wheels, Grace and her new best friend, Julie, often went on outings with their children on the weekends. Sometimes Julie's partner came along, and other times he didn't. It didn't matter because it was the perfect escape from the flat and into amazing nature right on their doorstep.

Grace experienced nothing like it in Perth. They were so spoilt for choice in Innisfail, and it was all free. Swimming holes, creeks and rivers to explore, waterfalls to visit. Some fuel for the car and a packed picnic and the scene was set for a relaxing day.

Grace lay on the towel and soaked up a few more sun rays in the minutes before packing up and heading home. She and Julie kept an eye on the kids as they frolicked near the water's edge. Julie's daughter Rowena was nine, and her son Adam was four. With their ages so similar, it was easy for the kids to enjoy each other's company.

"So, Grace, I've been meaning to say that I should introduce you to some friends of mine. They do some showjumping and that sort of thing."

Grace perked up and raised herself on an elbow. "You know someone who does showjumping?"

"They're a young couple, George and Sandy. How about I take you up to their place next weekend?"

A stirring started in Grace's chest. She'd been too long away from a horse. It was a lifetime since she last rode Command. It was hard to erase the memories of the terrible day she handed him over for a couple thousand dollars. She couldn't fathom what she'd do to ride a horse again.

"You wouldn't mind?"

"Er ... duh ... you're my friend, right?"

Grace chuckled. Julie lived a few houses down and they'd clicked barely two weeks after Grace and the kids moved into the flat. With the children of similar age, they all got on well. It felt natural to do things together. Julie knew her history with Phil, and in such a short space of time, Grace considered her a good friend. "Yes, we're friends, and I'm grateful for it. I would love to meet this George and Sandy."

"Done. I'll talk to them during the week."

"Mum, quick!"

Grace and Julie sprang to their feet when the kids yelled out. Which one was in trouble was anyone's guess. As they made a beeline for the water's edge, it was Natalie, scared of a little crab that had bitten her toe. Grace relaxed. Nothing a good hug and kiss couldn't fix.

***

"Let's stop for a pub lunch. You up for it?" Julie asked.

Another day off, another day discovering a new swimming hole. "Why the heck not. I could do with a cold drink. It's stinking hot in this place." It'd been three months since Julie introduced her to George and Sandy, and from there, her circle of friends expanded. She'd learnt about the Mount Garnet Rodeo and the Mareeba Rodeo and itched to visit them both during the coming year.

"Will the Cairns Central Hotel do?" Julie asked, scanning the street for a car park.

Grace wasn't familiar with the local pubs in Cairns and shrugged. "You're driving today with the roomier car. You choose."

An hour later, they had the kids settled with their chicken nuggets and chips and were sitting back enjoying a steak and a lemon squash.

"Either of you ladies interested in buying a raffle ticket? The prize is a meat tray."

Grace looked up into the face of an attractive man. He sported muscled arms and looked to be almost bald. When he smiled, his face creased in all the right spots, giving him a youthful look, making a mockery of his baldness. He was unwilling to take his eyes off her, which sent an unusual flutter through Grace's chest.

"They're three for a dollar. Interested? All money raised goes to the local footy club."

Grace sucked her drink through a straw and raised an eyebrow. "Make it four for a dollar, and I might be interested."

"Jeez, you know how to drive a hard bargain."

They both laughed, reminding Grace she was still young and deserved the attention of a good-looking man now and then. She pulled out a dollar note as another young man sidled up to the bald one and pretended to whisper to Grace. "Watch him. It didn't take him long to notice you sitting over here. I reckon he's keen to ask you out."

The bald man's cheeks turned a lovely tinge of pink, causing Grace and Julie to exchange looks and stifle a giggle. "What's your name?" Julie asked.

The second man answered, "Peter. Captain and coach of the North Queensland NRL and a bloody good player," before sauntering off to sell more tickets.

A piercing scream which sounded familiar had Grace and Julie on their feet. Chairs scraped back, they rushed to where the four kids played near a side entrance leading to an outdoor garden.

Blood was trickling down Natalie's forehead. "Quick, grab me a couple of serviettes, Julie."

Grace took a dazed Natalie in her arms as Julie pressed the napkins against her wound. The unexpected splash of blood made Grace's heart pump painfully.

"I'll call an ambulance," Peter said, standing by her side.

"No, no, I don't think it's necessary. She'll be okay in a few minutes."

"No way. I'm not taking any chances. I see enough injuries on a football field. Concussion, breaks, stitches required, you name it. I insist. It won't hurt to check her out."

After taking a deep breath, Grace realised what he said made sense. Natalie was looking pale, and the bleeding hadn't eased. She turned a grateful smile his way and said, "Thank you."

It took the ambulance about fifteen minutes to arrive and, in that time, she learnt Peter was a construction project manager and coached and played football. Somehow, she let slip where she worked.

Over the following months, she received Peter's occasional phone calls at work. Initially to check Natalie's recovery from her stitches and then to ask if he could visit. Her answer was always no. Why spoil a good thing? She liked the idea of a man in her life, but she didn't *need* one. She hadn't recovered from the last one. Everything was working out as it should, and she was okay with doing it alone.

Not only was she working at The Cane Cutter, but in true Grace style, she was also waitressing, selling advertisements for the local newspaper and making beds. Which was where she found herself face to face with Peter at the Black Marlin Hotel in Innisfail. With an extensive renovation about to begin on the hotel, the last person she expected to see involved with the project was Peter.

Surrounded by his bosses and staying at the hotel while the project got underway, Grace couldn't help but smile at Peter's cheeky grin when he asked, "Can I take you out to dinner?"

She stood there with her hands on hips. This bloke had tried and tried to get her to give an inch. She wasn't interested in another man but having dinner with an adult, a man no less, would be nice. She also wasn't inclined to embarrass him in front of his bosses, so she conceded defeat. "Okay, this once only."

When he chuckled, which was deep and throaty, he looked younger, and she had to admit he was okay on the eye.

She turned away, trying to keep the smile off her face. She even hummed a little as she prepared beds for the next round of guests. Even though he'd cornered her in front of his colleagues, she could've refused his invitation. But something compelled her to say yes, despite the odd feeling of fear refusing to go away. She'd gone against her gut feelings about Phil after *their* first date.

She roughly squashed a pillow into place beneath the sheets. Never again. One date only, and if the vibes were off, there wouldn't be another. But until then, she could do worse for company for one night out.

Chapter 33

29 Years Old

"Woohoo, here we go." Grace put the phone receiver down and danced around the kitchen.

"Where are we going, Mummy?" Colin asked.

Natalie sensed her mother's excitement and jumped up and down, too.

"We're off to Mount Garnet." Grace took her daughter's hands, and they spun around like a game of Ring-a-ring a Roses, their infectious laughter spreading to Colin, who watched his mother's and sister's antics with amusement.

"We won a raffle prize," Grace announced.

"What's that?" Colin had a question for every occasion, and Grace loved his curiosity.

Grace stopped for a second to get her breath back. "It's when you buy a ticket to win a prize, and they pick out one ticket to be the winner. Today, they picked out mine. We won."

"What did we win?"

"Good question, Colin, my clever boy." Grace wrapped her arms around him, squeezing him tight before squirming free.

"Mummy, I'm hungry," chimed in Natalie, not to be forgotten.

Colin freed himself from Grace's clutches and sat at the table for lunch. Grace had to deal with that immediately, or she'd have an uprising.

"We won a tent and some camping equipment, so we're going to drive Mummy's trusty Holden out to the rodeo at Mount Garnet. Who wants to come?"

Both Colin and Natalie chorused together with a huge, resounding, "Meeeeeeeeee."

With bread and Vegemite in hand and a couple of cheese slices, Grace stopped her lunch making to look at her kids. Natalie wouldn't understand what going to a rodeo meant, but Colin would have some memories stored away. What a godsend of a gift to win. It was a timely reminder she was due back on the rodeo circuit. Something she had missed terribly. What trouble could she brew up?

"Okay, everyone, eat your lunch, and I'll start organising our trip."

Another shout of joy from the table enabled a sigh of relief to escape her lips. She reflected on the fact a happy mother made for a happy house. She'd not heard from Phil other than to sign the divorce papers, and she still kept Peter at a distance. The vibes were good between them, but she was being cautious. Peter was a regular visitor to their home and on some weekend outings between his football commitments. So far, she hadn't put a stop to it. He was busy with football on the Mount Garnet weekend, so it'd be her and the kids. She was okay with that.

◦✽◦

Grace inhaled the dry dust of Mount Garnet and held it in for a moment, enjoying the memories it elicited. The landscape had rapidly changed within thirty minutes of leaving Innisfail. From the lush greenness of the tropical coast, heavily laden with sweaty humidity, it changed to sparse eucalypt forests with tufts of brown grass. Hot, dry and to die for.

Grace set up camp with the new tent she won, with Colin and Natalie helping to hammer in pegs and roll out the sleeping bags. Their eyes were round with wonder at all the unfamiliar sights and sounds. Already the atmosphere was buzzing and the rodeo hadn't started yet. Cowboys of all shapes and sizes were setting up their gear, and even though she didn't recognise a single face, she felt right at home.

"Well, if it isn't Grace Lucas. What the hell are you doing here?"

Grace spun around and gasped. "Good Lord, what the heck are you pair doing here? Can't a woman go anywhere?" Grace recognised Mark and Brett Botell immediately.

"Hey, hang on a minute; there's actually three of us here. Kevin's running around like a headless chook putting in nominations for some events."

"So, you three still the best exports from WA?" Grace asked with a teasing smile.

The brothers laughed, reminiscing about their bull-riding days. These three were top-ranking cowboys and nice guys.

"You been doing anything lately?" Mark asked.

"Nah, not for a couple of years. I've been busy with these two." She looped her arms around Colin's and Natalie's shoulders. "I'm dying to get back into it, though."

"God almighty, that's all we need. A woman causing more trouble than she's worth."

Grace laughed with the brothers, having missed this camaraderie of her rodeo days. "I haven't even started in this neck of the woods. Just wait until I do."

"So, tell me," Brett asked, "you gonna be riding as a woman or a bloke?"

Grace cringed at the fuss created with Deat all those years ago. She was never ashamed of what she'd done, just angry at being caught out. She thrust her hip out and clamped her hand on it. "Think I could get away with it these days?"

"Not bloody likely. You're too damn pretty to look like a bloke," Mark remarked.

"Thanks, guys. How about we catch up over the weekend?"

"Sure thing, Grace, we've got lots to organise now."

They gave her a quick hug and left to do the many errands required before the rodeo started. Grace turned to the kids and offered them a hand each. "Who wants to go for a walk?"

"Yes, yes, yes," they both chanted.

"Anybody hungry? We could buy some hot chips."

They both nodded enthusiastically. It was a stupid question to ask. Kids, she was learning, were hungry, thirsty or needed to go to the toilet. It didn't matter in which order it went.

She tightened her hold on their hands and took them into the crowded rodeo, the atmosphere thrumming with excitement.

She stopped for a moment. *Electric.* That was a better way to describe it.

⁂

The torrential rain woke her up. Grace sat up in the tent and checked for Colin and Natalie on either side of her. She touched each of their arms as they slept inside their sleeping bags and the bags were wet. *Holy Shoot!* How long had it been raining? After a big day of catching up with her WA friends and a full itinerary of rodeo action to watch, they'd all worn themselves out and fallen asleep like the dead.

Dampness seeped past her pyjamas, and her toes wriggled in liquid. *Damn!* There was water in her sleeping bag.

"Colin, Natalie, wake up!"

The Holden was parked beside the tent, but she still had to transfer the kids into it without getting drenched. The sleepy kids woke to the loud noise but came awake when Grace shone the torch to reveal two inches of water in the tent.

"In the car, quick. We'll clean this up in the morning." Thank goodness she left everything in the car except for the sleeping basics. She couldn't believe it, though. How often did it rain in Mount Garnet? No doubt the locals would welcome anything, but really? On this weekend of all weekends, there'd be people sleeping in the backs of utes, on the ground and in tents. At least the car was dry. In a tangle of arms and legs and pillows stuffed between the front and back seat, they slept the rest of the night well enough. And in the morning, they woke to a perfect blue sky and a blazing sun.

Grace couldn't believe how many people she knew through her years with the Australian Rough Riders Association (ARRA) in Western Australia. She caught up with a few of them. These riders were some of Australia's best, and her inspection of the bulls left her with no doubt their quality was also second to none.

She'd been hugely disappointed when she checked with officials if she could do any riding. As she was no longer a member of the ARRA, it was out of the question.

As this was the final rodeo under the ARRA banner, it was time for Grace to check out the new organisation, Australian Bushmen's Rodeo Association (ABRA), and enquire if there was an avenue for her to become a member and compete. She might be defeated this time, but she wasn't hanging up her hat yet.

She turned to Kevin Botell as the day neared its end. "Hey, Kev, since you've got a week before your next ride in Townsville, how about you blokes stop by Innisfail with the kids and me? I can show you around, and I'm happy to feed you all."

A week later and a house full of guests about to leave, their reminiscing stirred up something proper in Grace. She stood in her driveway with Peter by her side, his arm securely around her waist, watching them drive away.

"You enjoyed their company, didn't you?" he asked, nuzzling behind her ear.

Grace took comfort in his arms. "It was so good to talk rodeo. I can't believe it's been so many years since I last rode."

The kids scampered inside, leaving her alone with Peter. They enjoyed more and more time alone, and she slowly let her guard down. Peter turned to face her and placed a gentle kiss on her mouth.

"What can you do about it?"

Grace thought about this, remaining close to Peter as their foreheads touched. "I'm not sure. I have to suss out what this new association means and whether women can compete in the same competition as men or not. Pointless having a women's competition because there's none of us around."

Peter chuckled. "Trust me to find the only woman in this country who wants to ride bulls."

Grace smiled and let Peter kiss her again. This time it was long and sensual. A delicious buzz ran along her arms.

She'd wait for the Mareeba Rodeo. It was only a couple of months away, and she could delve a little more into the rodeo association. She wasn't about to sit back meekly and wait for them to come to her.

Chapter 34

Grace tucked her top neatly into her shorts and walked around to the back of the chutes at the Mareeba mini rodeo. Her heart pounded with excitement. She wasn't sure what to expect when she did the two-hour drive. New association, new rodeo rules, but nothing changed the electric atmosphere of a rodeo, making her skin tingle. The smell of animals and their leathery hide intermingled with the pungent odour of manure. It was everything she loved.

She breathed in the dry air of Mareeba, sweetly filled with the sweat brewing from the growing crowd. It did it to her all the time. She couldn't help the way her heart hammered, beating faster to let her know she was where she belonged. Crazily, an action-filled rodeo ground was where she was most at peace.

Thanks to Julie's introduction, her new showjumping friends put her back on a horse, exercising as she should. She was fit and healthy again, ready for action.

She spied an official-looking person holding a clipboard and, with some trepidation, approached him. "Ah ... excuse me."

In looking up from his clipboard, the man did a cursory glance from her long, exposed legs up to her chest before settling on her face. "Yes, how can I help you?"

"What are the rules about riding a bull?"

The man's jaw dropped, but to his credit, he recovered quickly. "Depends who's asking. Who wants to ride?"

Grace gave him a cheeky smile. "Actually, I'd like the chance to ride."

The man gulped. Grace had heard rumours that with the anti-discrimination laws almost in place, denying a woman the same rights as a man would no longer be tolerated. But Grace knew better than to mess with the men at a rodeo.

"Ah …" he stalled and twisted around, looking for a way out. When he turned back to Grace, he checked to ensure he had it right. "So, you want to ride a bull?"

Grace nodded and continued to smile at the man's discomfort. She wouldn't bring up the anti-discrimination laws just yet.

"Okay." He stalled for a moment. "This is the deal. Go to the official tent, and if they agree with what you want to do, pay your twenty-dollar day membership. Then, if you want to ride, put in your nomination and be sure you're wearing the right gear. Don't turn up at the chutes in that flimsy gear because you'll be turned out on your ear."

Grace chuckled in relief. Nothing could keep the smile off her face. She was in! Twenty dollars, that was it. In her excited haste, she stumbled towards the official's tent but stopped short when realisation dawned on her. She wasn't prepared for a ride. She hadn't expected to be allowed near the chutes, let alone on a bull.

With Peter busy coaching football and Julie minding the kids, she'd made the trip to Mareeba to check out the new association and its rules. As a mini rodeo, it was small compared to the major events on the circuit. She'd hoped with a smaller crowd, she could ask more questions. Never in her wildest dreams did she expect to be allowed to ride.

She frantically inspected the crowd congregated around the chutes. Eyeing the cowboys lounging around or leaning over the rails, she spotted a tall cowboy who looked about her size. She'd done nothing like this before. Heck, if she got away with it, it'd undoubtedly go down in the books.

She approached the cowboy wearing a black Akubra, her throat thick with nerves. "Hey, cowboy."

It took a couple of times before he turned around to acknowledge someone was talking to him. "Hey, do I know you?"

"Not really." Grace swallowed.

"So, what can I do for you?"

Grace put up with the full all-over glance that started at her face and travelled to the bottom of her well-toned legs. "Ah ... could I borrow some gear from you?"

He turned away from the arena, hooked a booted leg on the bottom rail and folded his arms. He studied her face, then asked, "Some gear? Like what?"

"Your boots and if you have a spare pair of jeans."

His expression grew thoughtful in the bright morning sun. "What the hell for? You want to climb into my jeans?"

Grace groaned internally but put on her best convincing smile. "I want to ride a bull, and I didn't come prepared."

"Holy shit. You wanna do what?"

Grace straightened and put on a confident air. "You heard, cowboy. I want to ride a bull. I've come to the right place, haven't I?"

The cowboy let out a low laugh and swore too. "This I have to see. So, what else do you need?"

The cowboy loaned her a pair of jeans, chaps, boots and spurs. Some other cowboy watching the exchange offered her his rawhide bull-riding glove. She could wear a long-sleeved tracksuit top she had in the car.

"What's your name, cowgirl?" the cowboy called after her as she left for the official tent.

She twisted around. "Grace Lucas."

"I'll be watching you, Grace Lucas."

"You do that, cowboy. It won't be my last time."

When it was almost time to call it a day, Grace's number was called. She'd spent most of the day doing stretches and psyching herself up for the ride, leaving the socialising until afterwards.

Finally, it was her turn to clamber into the chute and climb the bull. It bucked as it was supposed to and flicked dust upwards, snorting rage through its nose. The chute boss wound the rope around her gloved hand. Someone shoved a hat on her head as she tightened her hand against her pelvis. She took a deep breath, hanging onto it for a couple of seconds as they readied the bull.

Sounds filtered past her. The man on the PA conveyed her name to the crowd and told them she was a woman. She tuned out, wanting to concentrate on the heaving, heavy mass of flesh twisting and writhing beneath her. The sun seared the back of her long-sleeved track jumper, and sweat trickled down her shoulder blades. She pushed aside all the sounds and discomfort in the sweaty jumper and concentrated on what she had to do.

When the bull settled for a mere second, she gave the chute boss the nod. The gate opened, releasing them both. The seconds drew out to feel like hours as her body reawakened and remembered the graceful flow required of it and swung into action.

Her free hand flew into the air, her body at one with the wild animal, until about the fifth second when one filthy twist by the bull dislodged its unwanted rider. Grace fell to the sawdust-filled arena as a pickup man winched her up and out of harm's way. She spat out a mouth full of dirt before hoisting herself up and over the rails.

Her heart thundered. She didn't make the eight second bell, but hell, she hadn't even expected to ride that day.

They made another mention over the PA that she was a woman and unexpected cheer bombarded her. She'd done it. Unofficially, she'd competed against men in a competition where other women competitors were unheard of.

Heck, she wanted this exhilarating feeling to go on and on. She wanted the chance to ride as many bulls as she could fit into her lifestyle.

There were a couple of familiar faces near the penned animals and she went to join them. She would happily hand over the gear she borrowed and shout the cowboy a beer. The rodeo was nearly over, and they would all make their way to the bar.

For now, she wanted to bask in the success of her ride. But next time, and there would be a next time, she wanted her ride to be official. No more skulking in the background of a male-dominated sport. Women could no longer be ignored or discriminated against, and this was where she wanted to be. Her sights were set on the next Mount Garnet Rodeo, where it was an official event and where her ride would count, regardless of how much time she made.

An hour later, she handed a cold beer to the cowboy. "Thanks for loaning me the gear."

"Any time. That was some almighty ride. Are you all there in the head?"

"Most days." Grace laughed, others crowding around and joining her. She *was* crazy, but it was what drove her adrenaline-starved body. Before her marriage to Phil, she'd survived on different events most weekends. Hell, even going back as far as her pony club days, she'd been doing this stuff to sustain her mental health.

"Hey, I know you."

Grace looked over her shoulder at another cowboy who was vying for a spot at the bar. Grace sipped on her soft drink and smiled.

"You're Peter Luppi's girlfriend."

Grace nodded and shoved her way over to make room for him. "You know him, do you?"

The cowboy shuffled himself into the space beside her and rested his elbows on the bar. "Can I buy you a decent drink?"

"No thanks, I'm allergic to alcohol."

"No shit." He looked at her as though she had two heads, then continued, "You rode a pretty mean ride today. How the hell did you get mixed up with that Luppi?"

She chuckled before taking another mouthful. "He won't leave me alone."

The cowboy took an extra-long slug of his beer and plonked his glass on the bar a little too heavy. He leant closer to Grace and, with a strong alcohol breath, said, "I'd hate to see such a bonny girl like yourself getting hurt after riding the wildest bull on the day, but I don't suppose you know Peter is married and still living with his wife?"

His words were slightly slurred, but the bombshell he dropped detonated something that left her paralysed. She doubted anyone else had heard the whispered words, but the sweet lemony taste of her soft drink immediately soured in her mouth.

She licked suddenly dried lips and turned his way. Red flames of anger feathered their way around her body, lighting up her skin. She could barely get the words out between her fiercely drawn lips, but she owed this cowboy a massive debt of gratitude. Pasting a smile on her face, she said, "Thanks for telling me. I didn't know, and I owe you one."

He nodded and gave her a wink before squeezing her hand. "So, I'll see you on the circuit again?"

She stumbled off the bar stool incapable of responding. The shock of the news made her outstanding achievement pale into insignificance. She left her unfinished drink and shouldered her way out of the enclosed bar and past the crowd enjoying the end-of-day celebrations. Tears shimmered behind her eyelids, but she'd be damned if she let a single one drop. Instead, she clamped her jaw, determined to reach her car in one piece.

She berated herself the entire way home. How did she fall into this trap? She'd been so determined to live her own life, her own rules, her own way. Then Peter came along and persisted and promised a possibility. *He's married?* She slammed her fist against the steering wheel, unable to believe she'd been had so easily, again. Was she always doomed to fail when it came to men? God, how she hated them!

Reaching Innisfail, she detoured home first before going to collect Colin and Natalie. She had one phone call to make before planning her next step. It was easy to locate a phone number in the Cairns directory. She knew what suburb Peter lived in, and it listed his number with his initials. Before she thought twice about what she was doing, she dialled the number and hoped she could hear the conversation over her thundering heart.

When the phone call ended, Grace slid to the floor and tucked her knees against her chest. She wrapped her arms around them and rocked back and forth. Peter's wife confirmed everything. Yes, she was married to Peter and still sharing the marriage bed.

Now she could face Peter. She didn't give a hoot if she put a spanner in the works of his marriage. She checked the facts, and everything matched up. The random cowboy at the rodeo had told her the truth. It wasn't too late to detach herself from this disaster and shove bloody Peter out the door and all the way to hell.

She roused, knowing she had to fetch her children.

From as far back as she could remember, horses had soothed and calmed her. Then she smiled for the first time since learning of Peter's betrayal. A fresh reminder of her amazing feat flashed up, taking centre stage in her mind. By the next Mount Garnet Rodeo, she'd be ready. She had to be fit and healthy, and nothing would stop her from having a go. Her ride in Mareeba had spiked her adrenalin sky-high, and she desperately wanted to go there again.

She also wanted the comfort of her children around her. Somehow, they always made her realise that some things in life were more important than others. Having unconditional love from them would help purge the hole Peter created with his lies.

She flicked a hand across her eyes to wipe any evidence of tears and grimaced harder. To hell with men. She could do without this rot. Glancing around her living room for her Winfield Green's and lighter, she sought comfort in a cigarette before leaving to collect the kids.

It was the next day when she confronted Peter. She asked him to call around in the middle of his working day. Natalie was at kindergarten, and Colin was not due back from school for a couple of hours. There was no way she would subject her children to angry voices between two adults. They'd suffered enough. She'd protect them from any reminders of the ugly domestic violence they used to live with if it was the last thing she ever did. At this hour of the day, it was enough time to have her piece with Peter.

She flicked the remains of her cigarette and stubbed it out when Peter knocked on the front door. He smiled and looked happy. He had the best of both worlds. Her world and the one he went back to each night. Did he think she asked him around for some intimate time alone? She couldn't wait to wipe the smile off his face for good.

She led the way inside, not having muttered a word or hello. The first thing Peter did was to reach up and kiss her.

She slapped him away and stood firm.

"What the heck?" he asked, taking a step back.

"Yeah, you can ask, you lying, cheating bastard."

Comprehension dawned.

"Want to tell me about the wife you're sharing a house and bed with?"

He reached for her hand, and she batted it away. "Grace, it's not like that, and who told you this?"

"Um"—Grace tilted her face up in serious contemplation and tapped her chin—"let me see. Someone at Mareeba mentioned it, and I phoned your wife to confirm."

Alarm had his eyes opening wide. "And she told you that? She's lying, Grace. I swear it. She's lying."

"About what? The living together or sleeping together."

"Can we sit down and discuss this?"

"How about not? How about we stand right here and discuss it?"

"Okay, have it your way." He let out a frustrated sigh. "Yes, I'm still married, but we're only sharing the house for the sake of our daughter."

"Oh, how nice. You have a daughter and didn't see fit to tell me."

His gaze narrowed in on hers. "And I'm not sleeping with my wife. Our relationship ended a long time ago. I promise you it's the truth."

Grace lifted her brows. Was it the truth, or was he only telling her what she wanted to hear? She rolled her shoulders to ease a little of the tension. It wasn't spectacular news, but it was something. Still, she'd need a little more detail before deciding if he wasn't a complete arsehole. "So, when were you planning on telling me?"

Peter stalked past her towards the kitchen table. He sat and rested his face in his hands. Grace reluctantly followed.

"I've found a place I'm going to move into in the next couple of weeks. When it was sorted, I was going to tell you everything."

"Everything? Are there any more secrets?"

"No, I promise. My marriage has been bad for a long time, but I didn't know how to move on until you came along. For the first time, I glimpsed light at the end of the tunnel. I knew I needed to work towards it if I ever wanted to find some peace in my life."

Grace slumped into a chair and tapped her finger on the tabletop. Neither spoke for a few extended seconds.

"Will you forgive me, Grace?"

Her tapping continued. She wasn't sure how to answer. Learning of his wife had cut swiftly across her chest. It had damned well hurt.

She took a deep breath and let it out before she answered. "Sort yourself out and prove to me you've moved out of the marital home. Don't come anywhere near me until it's done. I don't care how long it takes. Then take the necessary legal requirements to get a divorce."

"Fair enough. I should've started this years ago when things soured between us."

Peter stood and went to her side of the table. He reached for her mouth and gave her a lingering kiss, which reminded Grace of all the good times they'd shared. "I know when I'm onto a good thing, Grace. I won't let you go."

"We'll see. Now go before I change my mind and send you packing for good."

Peter grimaced.

Grace rested her hand on his cheek. "I'm sorry for slapping you. There's no ... I ... I shouldn't have hit you."

"I deserved it," he said and turned and let himself out of her flat.

Was she right to make demands? She wasn't going to be some third wheel responsible for tearing apart a marriage if the wife still thought there was something to save.

She'd get over him if she had to, but God almighty, he'd already left his footprint on her heart. She hoped to hell and back his marriage really was over, so they had a fighting chance of being together.

With Peter gone, she aimlessly walked around her flat, already missing his presence. It vexed her that she had to deal with this stuff. What did it tell her about Peter? What did it tell her about herself? Couldn't her life be straightforward and normal?

She stopped wandering and stared outside the living room window. This out-of-the-box thought had her grimacing as she collapsed onto a cheap beanbag purchased for the kids. If she wanted boring and straightforward, she was in the wrong body. She had about six months to prepare for the Mount Garnet Rodeo, and that was as far removed from boring as anyone could imagine. This involved gyms and strength training every day. The dilemma with Peter would hopefully sort itself out in that time.

She wasn't going to allow him to make any excuses. If he tried dragging it out, she would move on. This wasn't the first crossroad she'd negotiated, and with a sense of despair, she hoped there weren't too many more to face in her life.

As she stepped outside and closed the front door to collect Natalie, Grace looked at the sky. Was fate looking down on her, heaving great belly laughs at how naïve she was?

Chapter 35

Present Day

"Look at you go."

Erin lost herself in Tom's vivid green eyes and lazy, masculine smile. The slow and steady swing of Eve's rump beneath her was a soothing balm. "Eve's probably the only horse I'll ever be able to ride."

"Nah, you're a natural."

After swimming in the frigid lake, they'd decided to warm up in the afternoon sunshine and enjoy a horse ride together. When they reached the edge of a small patch of the forest close to Grace's homestead, Erin dismounted on her own as Tom taught her. She *had* come a long way.

With the horses tethered and chewing on grass, Erin turned to find Tom's eyes feasting on her.

"Has it really been a week?" Tom asked, dropping his gaze as he gathered the horse blankets in his arms.

Erin nodded. She hadn't forgotten his words at the party: 'to be continued'.

Tom spread the blankets in the shade of the tree canopy. "What a crazy week. They'll need to employ another vet if this workload continues."

"I know. It was nonstop, you poor thing," Erin added.

They could talk about work now that it was something they shared. But work wasn't what they were interested in that afternoon. The anticipation had been building all day. All week. This was their promised weekend together. She swallowed, getting distracted by the cosiness of the horse blankets and what it might lead to.

Tom straightened, a look of uncertainty coming over his face. "Erin?" He reached for her hand as a frustrated groan escaped his lips. "It's been killing me all week not being able to be near you. Will you put me out of my misery?"

The gentle tug on her hand wasn't unexpected. Tom cushioned her as they landed on the blankets. She burst out laughing, breaking the awkward tension between them. Tom visibly relaxed and smiled, tucking strands of her hair behind her ear.

When her laughter stopped and Tom's smile slipped, she reached up and gently kissed his eyelids before trailing a line of kisses down his stubbled cheek and onto his neck. With the blankets coating them with the familiar hint of leathery hide, there was still enough taste of the lake on Tom's skin. The perfect combination.

Tom groaned quietly and found her mouth. This was the promise to continue what they'd started. She was more than okay with that, and he moved in relaxed sync with her. She moaned when his tongue lazily slid between her lips, and he chuckled at her reaction. Then his mouth began a journey of discovery and found her sensitive spots. Her hands and mouth followed a trail of their own. Heat pooled between her legs and sent tremors along her skin. It was her body aching for more from Tom. She looked forward to it one day.

The next hour dwindled while they discovered each other and committed it to memory. Erin could stay in this spot forever.

When the sun dipped a little lower, a cool breeze lapped over their private Eden, and Erin shivered.

Tom must have felt it too because he pulled away and sat up, still holding her hand, his chest heaving in time with hers. "Easy to lose track of time, isn't it?"

His thumb caressed her skin in maddening circles, distracting her thoughts as she languished on the blankets. "It is. Thanks for sharing the day with me."

Tom chuckled before groaning in frustration. "Erin, you know I've wanted this for a long time."

She accepted his grimaced-laced smile with one of her own and knitted her fingers with his. "Me too."

"You mean that?"

Erin smiled cheerily before admitting, "Yes, I do. From the first day you showed up to save me from those damn horses trampling me."

Tom laughed and ran his hand up her arm. "Hmm ... that long, hey?"

"Yes, and don't pretend it was any different for you."

The fading sun highlighted a cheeky glint in Tom's eyes. "Okay, I'm not going to lie. I wanted you from the very first time I heard you laugh. You're one of a kind, Erin."

Heat suffused her face at the compliment, and she dropped her gaze from his probing one.

"So, you good with us working this out?" Tom asked, giving her hand a gentle squeeze.

She looked up again. "I thought we were doing just that. Do you mean we have to repeat all this?"

Tom chuckled and tugged on her arm until she sat up. "Come on, girl, we better make tracks. You've got a big week coming up. Are you nervous about meeting your grandfather?"

At the reminder of what the next week would bring, she rose on unsteady legs and stretched out the kinks. She'd already told Tom everything while they'd swum.

"I'd like to meet him," Tom said, ploughing a hand through his hair.

"And I'd love for you to be there." She looked down as Tom gathered up the blankets, feeling lucky to have found him. She couldn't wait to show him off. It felt right to start with the grandfather she never knew. She'd wait with bated breath to see how he and Katherine reacted to Tom's presence, then introduce him to the rest of the family.

"Thanks. Now let's saddle the horses," Tom said, getting to his feet.

"Did you have any plans for tomorrow? Would you like to meet my dog, Lacey?"

"I'd love that. How about a hike near the dam? Dogs are allowed to swim there."

Erin nodded as she reached for one of the horse blankets and draped it over Eve's back. Then it was a matter of putting on their riding boots and helmets and re-saddling the horses. This they did quietly as the coming dusk brought out the new forest noises of another night approaching.

"Hey, Erin," Tom whispered, "look up there."

Tom pointed to the tree canopy. At first, she didn't see anything. He put his cheek against hers and pointed a finger at what he wanted her to see. Her vision adjusted to the changing light, and a lump on a branch came into focus.

"A Lumholtz tree kangaroo," he continued to whisper, "found only on the Tablelands. They're rare and special."

Erin knew of the species but had yet to see one in its natural habitat. She gasped when it moved, and a second one became visible beside it. "How lucky is this?"

His hand cradled her neck and gently massaged it. "Nah, I think I'm luckier."

Erin leant back into his bulk and smiled. A mere six months ago, her life was a trap with no way of escaping. A dead end with no solution. She'd had the courage to take one step and instigate some change.

Was she on the right track now? One could never be sure or complacent. But one had to keep finding the right path that *could* lead to that elusive happiness.

She was on the job and didn't hesitate to turn around and give Tom a long and lingering kiss before the saddled horses got too restless.

※

"Hey, Grandad," Erin said, stepping into Grace's living room.

Larry arrived four days ago, and it'd been a whirl of activity after work to spend as much time as she could with him. Katherine had left to go home the day before, vowing more visits.

"Well, if it isn't the world's most beautiful granddaughter."

Erin laughed and gave Larry a good hug. Then she swallowed the lump in her throat like she did every day since meeting him. She'd experienced a sense of things falling into place when his arms had wound around her for the first time and squeezed. A sense of coming home. Of feeling like she was in the right place. The familiarity of family, despite the many years lost. Nothing could dull it.

Erin took a step back and took another good look at him. With so many wasted years, she wanted to commit everything to memory. With her grandfather staying with Grace and Peter and his arrival a secret from the rest of her family, she had no choice but to visit him at Grace's house.

"Now, where's that young man of yours?"

"He's bringing in the goodies I baked last night. I'm feeling bad about how much cooking poor Grace is doing."

"Now, you stop that, Erin," Grace called out from the kitchen. "Larry and I have had the best catch-up these last few days. I wouldn't have it any other way."

"Hi, everyone," Tom called from the kitchen where he deposited the Esky full of homemade sweets.

"Dinner in about half an hour," Grace announced from the kitchen.

Erin turned to her grandfather and asked, "So, what have you been up to today?"

"What? Other than talking and eating too much?"

Erin took hold of his sun-bronzed hand and squeezed it. Every vein stood out on his hand as his heart proudly pumped blood around her tough and wiry seventy-year-old grandfather. He was such an energetic and spirited man that she had trouble thinking of him as old.

"Actually, Grace brought me up to speed on how she's been officially recognised as Australia's first woman to compete against men in open bull riding."

Erin froze.

"I knew she'd done a stack of rodeos in WA back in the day, but I thought women could only ride steers and broncs. I lost track of her antics when she left to come here."

"What?" Erin demanded attention. "What did you just say?" Her voice might've risen a fraction.

"Ask Grace." Larry shrugged. "Apparently, she's recorded in the Australian Women's Hall of Fame for being the first woman to compete against men in open bull riding."

Erin spun around and was confronted by Grace, Peter and Tom, all looking baffled. "Why has no one told me this?"

"I thought Tom told you," Grace said, pleading ignorance.

"Hey"—Tom's hands rose in protest—"I told you she was a remarkable woman, and you should ask her."

Erin tried to unjumble her thoughts and rearrange her tongue to speak again. She stuttered at first, "So ... so, let me get this straight. If I googled you, your name and what you've done would appear alongside some of the most remarkable women in Australia in the Hall of Fame?"

Grace shrugged.

"And in all this time I've known you, no one saw fit to at least mention this monumental detail. I mean, you told me about poddy calves and steers and bronco riding, but—" Flustered, Erin pounced on a framed photo she spotted months ago. "This"—she pointed to it—"this is you, isn't it?"

Grace nodded.

"And all this time, I thought it might've been Peter." Erin took a moment to study the grainy photo. It showed a rider coming off a ferocious-looking bull. The bull was huge, and she could *just* make out a number thirteen branded into its rump. She took a closer look at the rider and studied the tall shape of Grace as she slid off the bull's back. Who would ever contemplate such a thing? Erin rubbed her arm when goosebumps appeared.

"I suppose Grace hasn't told you the lark about the fake boobs, either," Peter asked.

Grace chuckled from the kitchen, and Larry added, "This sounds like a Grace thing."

"I wasn't there, but I've heard it retold a few times. Come on, Grace, better share with them what a larrikin you really were," Peter suggested with a laugh. "And we need to do something to wipe the scowl off Erin's face."

Erin relaxed and allowed herself a laugh. "I suppose I was only employed to record her medical recovery. Nobody told me to expect so much more. Certainly nothing about wearing fake boobs."

"When did this happen, Grace?" Larry asked.

"Good God, it was on one of those show runs. Such a heap of fun. I was forty-six when I pulled the fake boob stunt, and I should've known better. But it was such a crack up." Grace laughed at her memories as she put a lid on the pot and turned the stove down.

Grace started to wash some lettuce for a salad, and Erin left the grainy photo to help.

"It was about 2000, and the show run started in Brisbane and finished in Cairns." Grace shivered like a cold draught had passed over her. "It can get bloody windy and cold in some of those southern towns, especially when you're bunkered down in a horse float in only a swag. But still, the bunch of friends who did the circuit with me each year were a great lot to be around. We all got on really well. We used to go out for dinner somewhere when we arrived in a new town and did a lot of drinking, soft drink for me, dancing, joking and laughing. We lived by the attitude 'go hard or go home'."

Erin smiled, not doubting Grace's partying ability at all. "How many towns and stops are we talking about?"

Grace paused at washing the lettuce. "Well, after Brisbane, there were towns like Warwick, Toowoomba, Roma, Taroom, Bundaberg. It was at the Gin Gin Show where the fake boob stunt happened."

Tom took a seat on a stool at the kitchen island bench and rested his elbows. "Why am I not surprised that Grace was the party animal?"

When Grace laughed some more, Erin looked across at Tom. It'd been a long time since she'd let her hair down, and she would be well out of practice. Maybe a little encouragement and advice from Grace might help her come out of her shell. She shook her head and brought her attention back to the story.

"It wasn't hard," Grace continued. "I'm allergic to alcohol because it sends my body into toxic shock. So, I relied on my great dancing and singing skills. Also, my great arm wrestling skills. It was easy to down a huge competitor if they had some drink in them."

"Only a woman like Grace," Larry added. "Let me guess, Erin, she hasn't told you how she pretended to be a male rider so she could compete against men?"

"What?" Erin spluttered. "You did that?"

Grace's laughter rang through the kitchen and living room. "That's a story for another day. I know I've rambled on about a lot of things, Erin, but that one just hasn't come up yet. I shouldn't brag about it."

"Jesus Christ. It's going to take the rest of our lives to unravel who the real Grace is." Tom added, giving Erin a wink.

"Hey, back to the fake boobs before I forget what really happened and start making it up," said Grace.

Everyone laughed and Erin revelled in the contentment of being around these special people. It felt natural, and she didn't have to be someone else to fit in.

Erin took over the salad-making duties so Grace could tell her story. But competing as a male? She wanted to hear *that* story and would bring it up one day.

"I bought the fake boobs from a novelty shop and put them over my bra. Then I put on a stock collar, as they call them, that tucks into the front of a riding jacket. I buttoned it up and rode over to the ring. I remember riding past two blokes, Ronnie and Geoff, who were standing by, and I told them to 'keep an eye on us; you don't want to miss anything'. They assured me they would be watching. Then I rode over to the judge's wagon and Father Paul was there. He used to love following the shows around and helped with the scoring. When the judges rang the bell for my ride to start,

I rode away from the wagon with my back turned, so they didn't see me unbutton my jacket."

Peter chuckled, obviously knowing what was coming.

"After the first jump and as the course changed, my jacket opened up, and all you could see was me jumping with these huge hooters showing. I could hear the announcer spluttering words, and as I cleared a last jump, I heard him say, 'I think she's having fun with us'."

Larry and Tom cracked up with laughter, and it was hard for Erin not to join in.

"The funniest bit," Grace continued, "was seeing three older women staring at me with a look of shock on their faces. I heard one say, 'She doesn't know'. I was embarrassed for them, except it was so funny. When my ride finished, I rode past Father Paul and said to him, 'I guess I won't be going to heaven now'."

Grace paused, lost in her thoughts as a serene look came over her face. "I've never forgotten Father Paul's reply. He said, 'Yes, Grace, you will, because heaven needs people like you'."

"Aww, that was so sweet of him." Erin wiped away a stray bit of moisture from her eyes. She wasn't sure if it was from too much laughing or the thoughtful comment from the priest. No wonder Grace never forgot his reply.

"When I rode out of the ring, Ronnie and Geoff and quite a few of the other spectators were in fits of laughter. I know they referred to me as 'the old bag on the grey nag', but they all agreed if there was ever a title for the biggest larrikin of them all, it belonged to me."

Lights from an approaching vehicle lit up the inside of the homestead.

"They've arrived," Peter said.

Erin ignored the new arrivals, not sure who else Grace had invited for dinner. She was still trying to get around the fact that she finally understood why Grace was so loved and treated so special. Not forgetting she was also famous. With the salad made, dinner was close to being served. She took the lid off the pot and inhaled the delicious aroma of curry. She'd ignored the hunger pangs making noises in her stomach for the past half hour, but now, with the promise of food, she was more than ready to eat.

When the chatter and laughter quietened down, Erin looked up.

Larry walked to the stove and tugged on her arm gently. "Grace spoke to your parents and invited them to dinner tonight."

Huh? Mum and Dad? She hadn't seen them for a couple of weeks but kept in touch by phone. A shudder jolted her to attention when the news penetrated her skull. "Here? To see you?"

"After we spoke about how to approach this, I didn't want any of the blame to land on your shoulders. If there was a further fallout, it had to be with me, not you."

Suddenly light-headed, it threatened to land her on her face.

"Hey, are you okay?" Tom entered the kitchen and wound his arms around her. "I didn't know about this either." He tightened his hold and braced her.

This was too sudden. She hadn't prepared herself, and neither had she said anything to her parents. They weren't going to take this secrecy well, and her heart plummeted at the angst about to be created between them.

She looked at her grandfather and the sad lilt to his mouth. Gently releasing herself from Tom, she went to him. "Oh, Grandad, are you sure about this?"

Larry took a deep breath. When he released it, the look of weariness on his face frightened Erin.

"Sure as I'll ever be."

Chapter 36

Present Day

"Rosemary, Brian, a pleasure to meet you."

At Peter's welcome, Erin turned towards the front door. "Mum, Dad …" she spluttered.

But her mum only had eyes for Larry. She walked over to her father and stood hesitantly in front of him. On wobbly legs, Erin retraced her steps back to Tom and his embrace, giving her mum space.

"Oh, Dad, I've been such a fool." Rosemary wrapped her arms around the proud old man and shed tears on his shirt. Larry patted her back with his large hand, trying to comfort her, unable to keep his tears at bay.

When Rosemary took a step back, she looked into her father's face and said, "Dad, I'm so, so sorry for everything. I'm so ashamed—" she whispered through her tears.

Larry nodded, his Adam's apple bobbing up and down as emotions struggled to stay confined.

"Please forgive me, Dad." Rosemary tightened her hold again and shed more tears.

Erin gulped as she watched the scene. The reunion looked so painful.

"I never stopped loving you and Mum, and I'm sorry I wasn't there for you both." Rosemary hiccupped and wiped her face with her sleeve. "I don't even know where to start." She rested her hand against her chest before scrunching it closed. "I've kept everything so tight inside here." She tapped against her chest. "But it's time I told you what happened, isn't it?"

Larry nodded and swallowed at the same time. This was the reason the fallout occurred. They had to return to that moment and make it right, or they would never move forward.

"Dinner's ready. How about you tell your dad about it while we eat?" Grace hesitantly suggested. "News of any sort is always better on a full stomach."

This brought a murmured consent from Larry as the others gravitated towards the table. Erin remained standing, wanting to help Grace serve dinner.

Rosemary came up to her and gave her a hug. "I'm so sorry for keeping this a secret."

Erin swallowed roughly. "I should have told you sooner about finding Grandad."

Rosemary shook her head before squeezing Erin's hand. "I'm so glad you had the courage to do it. You're a much stronger person than me. Thank you darling, I really needed this."

Erin nodded and they both turned back to the others.

Before taking a seat, Larry approached Brian and put his hand out for a shake. "Nice to meet you, Brian. Thanks for taking care of my daughter all these years."

Brian reciprocated the shake, nodded and exchanged pleasantries.

With everyone seated and dinner spread across the table, Larry spoke to Rosemary. "You don't mind sharing your story here? I don't know how much Brian knows about the accident at the waterfall, but I've told Erin, Peter, and Grace about the young man's death."

Rosemary shook her head. "It's so long ago I'm not sure it matters anymore."

"I've told Tom," Erin volunteered, and Tom squeezed her hand under the table.

"Who's Tom?" Brian asked.

Larry gestured towards Tom. "This fine young man here. If you're lucky, he'll take good care of your daughter for you."

Erin blushed at the pointed stare both her parents gave her.

"Ah ... Erin, did you want to tell us any—"

Larry cut Brian off. "We'll get to Tom later," he urged. Erin could tell he was impatient to learn Rosemary's version of the events.

Brian nodded but continued to sneak glances at Tom before turning his full attention back to his wife. When her dad wrapped his arm around Rosemary and gave her an encouraging squeeze, Erin released a shaky sigh of relief. She and Tom were off the hook, for now. How did she answer her father's question? There were no excuses for keeping Tom from them.

Everyone served themselves some food, but Erin doubted Rosemary or Larry would get a mouthful in until the story was told.

Her mother fumbled with her cutlery, then gave up trying, setting them back on the table. "I've never told anyone what I think happened that day. Brian knows a version of what happened, but I could never bring myself to say out loud what I thought I saw."

Rosemary paused for a moment and reached for the glass of water next to her plate. She swallowed roughly and then put it down. "Dillon died at the waterfall. And I knew for a fact Dillon and Jack were both in love with Sally. As Sally's friend, I knew she was most in love with Dillon. My anguish was caused by not knowing if I saw Jack giving Dillon a nudge, causing him to topple over."

Erin gasped quietly. How horrible to carry that uncertainty all this time.

Rosemary rubbed her hand over her mouth before dropping it to her lap. "You know how you think you see something, and you look back on the events and think, no way, I didn't see that. So, you begin to doubt yourself. You tell yourself over and over you didn't see it. It was only a figment of your imagination. There's no way Jack would purposely do that to Dillon. How could I accuse a man of murder and condemn him to a life in prison if I wasn't one hundred percent sure? I remember it was very windy on top of the waterfall because, at one point, I grabbed a small shrub while we waited for the others. They hadn't quite reached the top yet, except for us three. Jack claimed he reached out to stop Dillon from going over when he realised he'd lost his footing and was about to fall too. Who was I to say the story was different?"

Rosemary's bottom lip quivered; a stray tear slid down her cheek. "Except, I think my gut instinct was the right one. Before I had time to second guess myself, I knew what I saw."

Everyone stopped eating for a moment and let the truth of Rosemary's words sink in. Brian continued to knead her shoulder before squeezing her closer to his side.

Nobody moved until Larry sniffled into a tissue. "Why didn't you say so?"

"And condemn a man to a life behind bars when it might've been false? Oh, Dad. I was so confused. I refused to say much in my statement because I couldn't trust myself not to bring it up. What *if* Jack saw Dillon slip and was trying to help him?"

"Did Jack ever speak to you about it?" Larry asked.

"No, never. I left soon after to come over here. I kept in touch with Sally, but she never recovered from Dillon's death. Then a year later, she told me Jack had died in a car accident. He was drunk and driving at a ridiculous speed when he hit a tree. After that, I didn't see any point in bringing it up. The longer I avoided the subject, the quicker the years sped by."

"Your disappearance from our lives devastated your mum," Larry murmured.

"It's too late now to tell her I'm sorry, isn't it?"

"Yeah, she passed on a year ago."

Rosemary used a tissue to wipe the moisture around her eyes. She sniffled and wiped her nose as well. "I'm so sorry, Dad. I'll never forgive myself for not being there for you. This entire saga has tortured me for years. What if it was murder? I should've done something about it earlier, but I didn't want anything to sully my chances of a medical degree. In my immature mind, I was trying to plot the best path for everyone concerned."

Her tears started again, and she apologised with a sob. "I didn't mean to break yours and Mum's heart."

Tom squeezed Erin's knee underneath the table. This jolted Erin into taking another breath. So enthralled in the story, she'd forgotten to breathe a few times. She looked down at her plate and realised she hadn't eaten anything.

When Erin flicked her glance up, her mother was looking at her. It was hard to describe the sinking sensation surging down towards the pit of her stomach. There was such a look of sadness on her mother's face. Erin wished she could undo the duplicity of the last few months and, in doing so, take back this moment.

Sure, the whole scenario surrounding the death on the waterfall and keeping it locked away was sad enough, but with her version revealed to Larry and the culprit concerned no longer alive, it was more likely a noose had been removed from around her neck.

No, the sadness would be targeted at her. Rosemary was probably more frightened history was about to repeat itself. Her own daughter was excluding things from her and doing things behind her back. This had never been the case before. She'd always spoken openly to her parents—until she moved in with Nicholas and things went awry. Keeping Tom a secret would add fuel to her fire of uncertainty.

"Erin, how did you find your grandfather?" A lopsided smile appeared on Rosemary's face, and to Erin, it resembled an apology. An 'I'm sorry you couldn't come to us and talk about this' apology.

Words jammed in her throat. Should Erin remind her mother how the subject of her family had always been a difficult one?

"To answer that," Larry chimed in first, "we'll have to explain how Grace fits into the story. Trust me, this will take us all night." Relief was clear on Larry's face when he chuckled. It was obvious a huge burden had been lifted from his shoulders. It would never erase the heartache of losing their daughter from their lives all those years ago. Neither would it take away the pain of losing his wife without her ever having this reconciliation.

Erin finally found her tongue. "Be sure to mention that Grace is Australia's first ever female to compete against men in open bull riding. Just in case it's forgotten along the way," she added, pushing aside that niggle of annoyance at not being told sooner. Grace would never have bragged about such an achievement.

Everyone laughed except Rosemary and Brian.

"Did we miss something, dear?" Brian asked.

Rosemary looked confused for a moment. "I'm not sure, but someone will be bound to tell us."

Erin could finally relax as the laughter continued around the table. Nerves had made it impossible for her to eat more than a couple of mouthfuls. Now it looked like the worst was over. She wasn't about to lose her parents. She'd gained a grandfather, made terrific friends in Grace and Peter, and met a man for whom she was not only good enough but a prize to be treasured.

For a moment, she felt like jumping up and proposing a toast to her life. Instead, she squeezed Tom's hand resting on her thigh and reached across to kiss his cheek. "Thank you for being here," she whispered.

"I'm not going anywhere," Tom whispered back. She caught the sparkle in his eyes just before his mouth found hers and kissed her.

Only when Larry deliberately coughed louder than usual did Tom pull back and chuckle. Erin sat entranced with her mouth open, wanting the kiss to go on.

"If you young ones want to go for a walk after dinner, I'll do the washing up," Larry offered.

More laughter erupted, breaking the spell over Erin. Heat raced up the back of her neck, and she looked down and fiddled with her fork. Everything would turn out okay. She still had to explain to her parents why she'd kept Tom a secret. And nightmares of running into Nicholas still worried her from time to time, despite his relocation to another state.

That aside, she was prepared to take the good with the bad, knowing total goodness sat beside her. With Tom by her side, she would make it through the tough times. His declaration that he wanted to stick around had set off a flutter inside her chest that wouldn't rest.

More confident of her future now than she'd ever been, she gave Tom's hand another squeeze and looked across the table. "Grace, will you tell us about your Hall of Fame ride?"

"Before or after Larry tells his story?"

"Ladies first." Larry declared.

"Oh, alright." Grace pouted, and everyone laughed.

Erin picked up her fork and ate heartily. She couldn't wait to hear this story and looked forward to Larry's too. Grace had entered her life at a critical point. Her stories of hardship, tragedy and triumph had given her the courage to change the direction her life had taken. She would be forever grateful for this.

Chapter 37

30 Years Old

"I'm coming with you this weekend. I can help take care of the kids," Julie said as she stirred sugar in her tea.

Grace looked up from stitching the XXXX lager label on the back of her pressed-stud shirt. "Really? You'd do that?"

"Oh, for God's sakes, woman." Julie leant back in her chair and spread her arms out wide. "Yes, I would."

Grace smiled. Sometimes she forgot the power of having a wonderful friend. "Thanks. I'd appreciate that." She winced when the needle pricked her finger. Her hands shook slightly with the coming anticipation. "I've rented a van in the caravan park at Mount Garnet this time. We can squeeze you in. I don't want to go through what we did last year when all hell broke loose and it bucketed down with rain. There's only camping at the rodeo ground, and this time I'll need a good night's sleep."

Julie laughed and took a sip of her tea. "Me too, I bet."

The four kids played soccer in the backyard while Grace enjoyed a cuppa with her friend. It'd been one hell of a hectic six months, but she was ready. She was also quietly nervous. "What I wouldn't do for a drag on a cigarette to calm the nerves."

"Don't you dare," Julie warned. "You're so much healthier, and I haven't heard that horrible cough of yours in ages."

"Yeah, I know. It was tough, but the smoker's cough was the boot I needed to give up the damn things."

"And a good thing too. I must admit I wondered whether you'd be strong enough to give them up cold turkey, but stupid me, I'm talking about the strongest woman I know here. Should've known better, hey?"

Grace chuckled, finishing up the last of the stitches on the label. It'd been damn hard to give up smoking. But a promise at a party to give them up after being told how bad her cough sounded was the push she needed.

Grace smiled, recalling how it had all happened. She was being a smart arse that night, and after some provocation, she threw the packet of Winfield Greens outside the window in the pouring rain. Someone called out that she probably had another packet in the car. She did and, after some persuasion, went to retrieve it, and they pulled it apart, declaring she'd never smoke that pack either.

She knew very well there was a full carton on top of her wardrobe at home, and how would she cope with that temptation? But she gave them her word she would try to give up, and in her books, if you couldn't stand by your word, you couldn't stand for anything.

This dogged attitude got her across the line and carried her past many frustrating and cranky days when it would've been so easy to have one drag to calm her nerves.

One day turned into one week and one week turned into many months. At another party with friends, she was sitting around people who'd been drinking and smoking most of the night. With her sense of smell so altered from not smoking, the stench of the cigarettes was enough to churn her stomach and put her off ever lighting one again. And good riddance to an expensive habit!

"How'd you manage to get XXXX to sponsor you at Mount Garnet?" Julie asked.

"Peter organised it for me."

"Oh, I see. Does this mean he's back in the picture?"

"He will be soon enough. His divorce is nearly finalised."

"Hmm," came Julie's response.

Grace looked up. "He's done everything I asked of him. You don't trust him?"

"No, no, I do, and I know you did the right thing when you told him to hightail it until he sorted his life. I just wish he'd been honest from the beginning. But"—Julie shrugged—"I haven't been in his shoes, so I don't know why he made the choices he did." She winked at Grace. "Two more strikes and he's out, though."

Grace nodded, grinning. She missed Peter's company. Despite going to the gym four to five times a week, fitting in work shifts and taking care of the kids, she missed the intimacy they'd shared. He was relaxing to have around, and it had been tough without him. But in a way, not having the distraction of Peter was a blessing in disguise. It left her able to concentrate fully on her goals.

Once the rodeo committee had accepted her nomination, it'd made all the hard work and loneliness worthwhile. She was primed and ready to go. "I was planning to drive up Thursday afternoon. Can you take Friday off work?"

"Yep, already sorted. I knew you'd want to be up there by at least Friday."

Grace put her shirt down and gulped down the rest of her tea, the liquid swirling around her stomach. It was actually happening. A whole crazy year in the making from when she swept into Mount Garnet a year ago and inhaled the excitement of being at a rodeo again. And the crazy dream that one day she'd climb onto a bucking bull, hold on and be acknowledged for it.

She was mostly packed and sorted, so there was nothing to stop the adrenalin buzzing through her. Licking her dry lips, she focused on her new pressed-stud shirt lying on her lap. She fingered the XXXX label. This style of shirt was one of the requirements, so if a rider got hooked by the bull's horns, it would pop open and reduce the risk of injury.

"I also want to be there in case you get hurt," Julie added solemnly.

Grace glanced up and swallowed past the lump in her throat. "Thanks heaps." There was an understanding between the two women. Both mothers and both with small children dependent on them. The danger of what she did always lurked in the background. She never forgot that her children needed her to take care of them and her heart swelled at Julie's gesture. Now and then she allowed herself to dwell on the dangers of what she did. With Peter still at arm's length and the football season in full swing, she hadn't invited him to Mount Garnet.

But she could finally allow herself a small sigh of relief. With Julie's presence, she could concentrate on preparing for her ride without the distraction of worrying about the kids.

That aside, she'd never let potential danger stop her from doing what she wanted. "I do think about how badly hurt I could get. But you know what, Jules? If you can't live dangerously, why bother living at all?"

Julie laughed as she rose to leave. "Oh, great. Spoken like a true daredevil. I knew you'd say something like that. Anyway, I better take my kids home and do some housework this afternoon."

"You don't want to bring them with you this weekend?"

"No, not this time. Maybe next year. They'll stay over with Mum."

"Okay, I'll swing by Thursday afternoon to pick you up."

"Done deal, girl. Now let's go get this dream of yours."

⟨⟩

The promise of heat and the potent smell of eucalyptus did it for Grace every time. She stepped outside the rented van and inhaled deeply the fragrances that came with the dry landscape. A world away from the wet and tropical Innisfail, being in a place like Mount Garnet made you appreciate a clear blue sky. Only a thin smattering of high-level clouds tarnished the blue sphere, and it came with a weird early crispness that would turn into a sweltering day.

She turned back towards the van and poked her face inside. "Okay, so who's ready to check out the rodeo grounds and all the stock?"

"Coming," Julie said while Colin and Natalie packed up their colouring in books and pencils.

It was only a few minutes' drive to the rodeo ground, and Friday was the day they unloaded the steers and bulls and assembled them into pens. They found a spot to set up their camp for the weekend, and with Julie's help, she put up a tarp to give them some shade during the day.

"Who wants to check out the bulls?" asked Grace.

"Meeee," chorused both Colin and Natalie.

"Ready when you are," Julie chimed in.

Cowboys of all ages wearing an array of coloured checkered shirts and Akubras crisscrossed their path as they meandered towards the pens set up to corral the animals. Grace leant against the timber beams and watched the unloading of the bulls. "They look like top-quality bucking bulls this year."

"How can you tell?" asked Julie.

"Look at how huge and powerful they are." She wiped her clammy hands down her jeans. Her heart sped up just looking at them. One particular bull caught her eye. The massive Brahman snorted in the pen and kicked up a spray of dirt. The breeze carried its scent in their direction, and Grace let it settle over her. The number thirteen was stamped on the bull's rump. "Wouldn't you shit yourself if you drew number thirteen?"

A cowboy chuckled beside her, catching her attention. She turned in his direction when he spoke. "All these bulls are owned by Groverner, and he's their feature bull. They call him Double U, and yep, he's their meanest."

Grace's adrenalin spiked that little bit further as she anticipated the possibility of having to ride bull number thirteen. She eyed him and the other bulls carefully. The cowboy's assessment was correct—only bull number thirteen etched fear along every nerve in her body.

For the rest of the day, as they meandered around the camp grounds catching up with friends she met the previous year and some she knew from Perth, Grace kept stealing glances back at the bulls. She'd have to ride one of them, and excitement mixed with nerves churned in her stomach for most of the day.

She had to believe she was ready for this. Physically, she was as fit as she'd ever been. Yes, she was worried about the dangers, but nothing could stop the infectious anticipation of what she was about to do, and it spread to those around her. They gave her encouragement, support and the occasional slap on the back—their way of showing her that she had this.

The day dwindled faster than Grace expected, and when darkness descended, they joined friends around a campfire. These people were the life and blood of a rodeo and knew how to share a good joke and laugh.

As Grace helped the kids toast marshmallows, she gathered all the memories and held onto them tight. This was what she'd remember the most about the weekend. The camaraderie and companionship between people with a common interest. She looked up and memorised the clear sky where a million stars dazzled back at her. Could she imagine one of them might just belong to her?

Some of the other bull riders were there, too, and while they teased her good and plenty, she didn't miss the hint of respect hidden behind bad jokes and laughter.

She put an arm around her children and squeezed them tight. When they complained, she eased off and laughed. She loved her children more than bull riding, but she could no longer deny her body the adrenalin rush it required just to survive. It was time to call it a night, get a good night's sleep and ensure she was in the best condition possible.

Grace strode back to their camp set-up and dropped on her backside. "My name's been drawn, and I'm in the first half of the bull rides."

"What does that mean?" Julie asked.

"It means my ride will be part of the morning events, so I won't have to hang around for most of the day waiting."

"Is that a good thing?"

Grace laughed. "Well, it'll help settle my breakfast a lot faster."

She'd enjoyed a solid breakfast of bacon, eggs and toast and was ready for action. Much to her relief, it would happen sooner rather than later.

"You go and do what you have to. I've got the kids under control. We'll watch the morning events, and then I'll take them to the loo and buy them some food."

"Thanks, Jules." Grace wanted to spend some time behind the chutes doing stretches and push-ups to limber up. She wasn't worried about the ride because she believed she could do it, but warming up helped her focus on the task ahead. "They'll be calling out the chute numbers soon too. I better go check out which bull they've given me."

"Good luck, Grace. You got this. Listen out for us because we'll be cheering the loudest. Won't we, you two?"

Grace smiled when Colin and Natalie gave an impromptu cheer as she swooped down to give them a fierce hug. She didn't want anything to happen that would take her away from these two. They needed her, and short of the bull landing on her heavily, she would survive with a broken bone here and there. She'd done it before and it hadn't killed her.

"Okay, you pair, behave for Julie. I'll see you after the ride."

"Go Mummy. I love you." Colin wrapped his thin arms around her neck and hugged her with all his strength. He'd always been her little man and constant support during the roughest days with Phil. Her stomach clenched. She had so much to make up for. Colin deserved so much more, and she believed she was working hard enough to give it to him.

This, of course, meant Natalie needed her hug, too. Her adorableness never failed to blow Grace away. How had she gotten so lucky?

"Who wants a hotdog?" Julie winked her way, allowing Grace to leave and sort her stuff out.

"Thank you," Grace mouthed as Colin and Natalie jumped up and waved their arms with excitement. The promise of a hotdog had done it.

Chapter 38

Grace gathered behind the chutes with the other riders, waiting for her name to be called out.

"Grace Lucas!"

"I'm here," she called, raising her arm.

"Your bull is in chute number three," the chute boss called out.

Grace took a step back to have a better look at the chute. A muscle in her stomach momentarily tightened. The number thirteen was clearly branded into the bull's rump. *Damn.*

She smiled despite her thundering heart. Her comment about a rider shitting themselves if they drew that bull came back to haunt her. It didn't surprise her, though. Number thirteen had always been the standout number in her life. Fate was at it again, and landing bull number thirteen was exactly what was supposed to happen.

With the chute and bull decided, it was time to let tunnel vision take over and make her final preparations. Spurs on boots, chaps on legs and lots of rosin on her gloves and chaps. She warmed the rope and gloves with the rosin, pulling the rope with her gloved hands and pumping up the muscles in her arms.

"Grace Lucas, time to climb up," someone called out.

She was so focused on what she was required to do that she missed the announcement over the PA system. As she stretched and climbed up on the chute, the friendly face of Les Bell appeared, an acquaintance from her days on the rodeo circuit in Western Australia. It'd been a pleasant surprise to run into him again.

"Here goes, Les."

He gave her a soft tap on the shoulder. "You've got this, Grace."

She used all her strength to block out the sound of the cheering crowd when it was announced that she was Australia's first female allowed to ride a bull in competition. All those early years of fighting for the right to compete. All those times she'd hidden her gender and ridden as Deat Lucas. All those frustrating times when she wanted a fair go and the chance to prove she could do it. If she had to compete against men, so be it. The day had finally come, and she hoped with all her might there'd be plenty more days like this one.

She switched her mind back to the confined space of the chute and forgot about all the possibilities this first ride could lead to. As Les helped her tie the rope around her hand, the man in charge of the stock said, "You've drawn a really good bull here, and he'll probably start to spin to the left once he's three bucks outside the chute."

Grace nodded and murmured a thanks. Once she was tied down, she slid onto the back of the bull, supporting her weight on the rails on either side of the chute. More comfortable with her right hand tied down, even though many riders preferred to tie their left hand, she slipped down lightly on the bull's back and moved right up on her hand, making sure her forearm was as tight as possible against her hip.

This was part of her tunnel vision training. The closer she could stay to her hand, the easier it was to follow the movement underneath. Aligning her body's flow with the animal's rhythm was like dancing together. That's what made the ideal ride, except it was a lot harder in practice because the bull had a mind of its own. She would give it her best shot.

There was no turning back now. She sucked in a deep breath. She was tied in, warmed up and all the hard work she'd done over the past year was about to pay off. There was only one thing left to do. With a nod, she shouted, "Let him out!"

The chute opened, and the bull exploded underneath her. Everything went black as though a giant bolt of lightning had struck her. It quickly cleared, and the need to harness the bull's power if she wanted to hang on became her priority. *It's just eight seconds.*

She kept her hand tight against her hip and rode with the movement of the bull as each second ticked by. Each one felt like fifteen seconds, but at four and a half seconds, Double U got the better of her, and she hit the ground hard, her shoulder taking the brunt of the impact.

Grace rolled out of the direction of the bull and scrambled to her feet. The cheer from the noisy crowd penetrated her senses. The man on the PA system announced how everyone was watching history in the making. That she, Grace Lucas, was the first woman to compete in open bull riding.

Picking up her bull rope, she walked back towards the chutes, doing her best to stem the disappointment that she hadn't made it to the eight seconds.

One cowboy shouted, "Good ride, Grace."

"Not good enough," she answered as she climbed through the rails and sat at the back of the chutes to watch the rest of the first round of bull rides. She needed some time alone to put what just happened into perspective. The elation would come later, but not until she processed every nanosecond of those four and a half seconds. She hadn't come anywhere close enough to the eight seconds, and this would haunt her forever.

⁂

Peter cheered until his voice was hoarse, and still the crowd hadn't quietened. The guy next to him let out a series of wolf-whistles as the masses rose for a standing ovation. He wanted nothing more than to race across the arena and take Grace in his arms. She'd be disappointed in her time, but then she'd come alight at the amazing first experience of riding in a competition and being recognised for it.

He straddled the timber rails of the arena and used his hands for balance on either side. There was never a chance he would miss her first official ride. He'd used every excuse he could muster to be away from football for one day. His plan had always been to turn up and surprise her.

He shuffled over when one of the pickup men climbed the arena fence near him. Peter was close enough to stretch his hand out for a shake. "Peter Luppi's the name. You're doing a terrific job out there."

"Thanks, mate."

"Did you just see that ride by Grace Lucas? It was some wild ride."

"Sure did. She's some woman, isn't she? Tough as old boots and not afraid of anything."

"I'm going to marry her someday."

The pickup man turned on his side and raised an eyebrow. "Now, why would you want to do that?"

Peter chuckled. "Because she's crazier than me."

The man angled his face and asked, "What did you say your surname was?"

"Luppi."

The man burst out laughing. The loud hum of the crowd, along with the music pulsing out of the PA system between rides, added to the bombardment of noise around them. "With a surname like that, you'll both get on bloody amazingly."

It took a moment for his meaning to sink in, but when it did, Peter doubled over laughing, too, before he jumped off the arena rails and searched for Grace.

Peter found her behind the stalls, leaning against the rails with her rope wound over her shoulder. "Grace!" he called out.

She swung around at the sound of her name, and her mouth opened. "Peter, you're here?"

"As if I'd miss this great day. Get over here, and let me give you a hug."

Grace dropped the spurs she was holding and wrapped her arms around his neck. He squeezed her hard and filled his lungs with everything Grace. "I'm going to marry you one day, Grace," he whispered close to her ear. "You just wait and see. I'm nearly there."

Grace chuckled, and Peter gently pulled back. Enough so he could kiss her—in amongst the dust, the chutes, the bulls, the music blaring out from the PA system and a hundred cowboys all cheering. If this was where Grace was most at home, then it would be his home too.

⁂

"I need a few minutes to gather my gear." Grace accepted another tingling kiss from Peter and a hug from her kids as the rodeo ended for the day. Her heart swelled at the effort he'd made to show up. She didn't doubt it required some wrangling to get out of his football duties, and putting her first hadn't gone unnoticed. "I won't be long, and then we can go back to the van park and prepare dinner."

As Grace walked off, she couldn't deny Peter's presence buoyed her spirits. There'd been congratulations all round from many spectators, but it was Peter by her side and his confirmation of how great her achievement was that pulled her out of her initial disappointment. At the end of the day, it wasn't the eight seconds that mattered. It was the recognition that she could do this as a woman, and she had. Peter had reminded her of this all afternoon.

With gear in hand, she detoured to the empty grandstand and sat on one of the top seats. Nobody would miss her for a few minutes. She took a deep breath before exhaling and looked around the arena. The smell of sawdust overpowered her senses, creating new memories that would carry her through the years. A lump formed in her throat, and she swallowed it back. Her hand tightened around the rope she held. It'd taken most of the day for her achievement to sink in, and nobody could take it away from her.

She'd done it and was proud of her efforts. It hadn't happened overnight but over a lifetime of love and passion.

Lost in thought, she remembered her young self at a rodeo many years ago. Back then, she wanted to meet someone like herself when she grew up.

She blinked furiously as emotions swirled inside her chest.

I am that someone.

Having a Go

We met many years ago, although it seems a few
The years have passed us quickly by, the good times generally do,
You would be the toughest that I've seen, you never know retreat,
In a fight or on a bull you'd be the one to beat.
You bend a beast around a course and put it through the gate,
Then jump a solid 6ft fence on Skity he's your mate,
And you don't mind teaching others the skills that you possess,
But what a shock it was to me to see you in a dress.
Now anyone that hears this poem might think that you're a bloke,
And that I threw the dress thing in to have a little joke.
But if that's the way you're thinking, no girl could be that strong,
Well you're more than sadly mistaken son, I'm telling you you're wrong.
Cos this girl that I have wrote about is everything and more,
That you will find within this verse and that's for bloody sure.
I've seen her get upon a bull that nobody could ride,
We tried to talk her out of it, but she just yelled outside.
The bull exploded from the chute and went into a spin,
She didn't budge a flaming inch it looked like she could win.
Scorn soon turned to panic as cowboys watched in awe,
The girl who dared to tread their turf should be against the law.
Now the whistle can't be far away and it doesn't seem quite fair,
They think about the prize money and the buckle that she will wear.
Then the bull at all four feet off the ground flung his head about,
One horn clipped her on the chin and almost knocked her out.
A roley that was in her ear was catapulted forth,
Her vision cleared just in time to see it heading north.
She reached out with her free hand and plucked it from the ground,
The whistle went the judges cried no score,
She's touched down.
Well the cowboys breathed more easily, at least she hadn't won,
How could they ever live that down and spoil all their fun.
So she picked her rope up off the ground and headed for the gate,

One cowboy yelled, 'Bad luck, Di.' She grinned, Next week mate.'
Reporters swarmed behind the chutes and asked if she knew,
That she was the first to ride the old bull, Double U.
Her reply was simple, she didn't really know,
The only thing she is sure about,
She had a bloody go.

Graham Heffernan

AUTHOR NOTE

The Bikini Tree Story

This story is inspired by *Dianne Lucas Luppi,* Australia's first female to compete against males in open bull riding. With no females to compete against, Dianne had no choice if she wanted to experience the thrill of competition. The road she travelled wasn't always smooth, but she refused to give in and was lucky enough to live her passion. She still does to this day.

Now, how did I find this remarkable woman? This is a story in itself.

I'd read some amazing books inspired by someone or something, and I wanted to write one myself. So, like all budding writers, I went to Google and searched: 'famous Australian women'. Lots came up, and most of them you'll find in the Women's Museum of Australia (formerly called, Australian Women's Hall of Fame). I made lists and read what I could on a select list that interested me. But I kept returning to this one woman purely because what she'd achieved had been done in my backyard.

My first step was to contact the Women's Museum of Australia and ask for any information they could offer, and if they agreed, would it be okay for me to use her inspirational achievement to write a story. A reply came the next day, citing that the curator was away for three weeks and all contact would have to be made through the curator. This kindly person could send me an old newspaper clipping and a short write-up they held on file for Dianne.

The newspaper clipping was of Dianne and a young girl during the clerk of the course days at the Cairns Annual Amateurs. I immediately recognised the young girl because I went to school with her sister, Maree.

After sending a text to Maree, I received an immediate response. 'I think you're looking for Dianne Luppi from Lake Eacham. Give me ten minutes, and I'll find her phone number.' I couldn't believe my luck. This famous woman lived in *my* backyard. Barely a ten-minute drive and five of those minutes required opening and closing a gate.

With nerves roiling in my stomach, I made the phone call, and Dianne's immediate response was that she'd been told for many years that she should have her life story recorded. I explained that this wouldn't be a biography but a story inspired by her life. And what a life she's lived so far.

It still stuns me that I'd never heard of Dianne or her achievement. Over thirty years later, Dianne and her husband, Peter, continue to live in their perfect patch of paradise, surrounded by family and friends and horses, of course. Her achievement is recorded in the Women's Museum of Australia, and by the time she rode her last bull in Rockhampton on the day after her 34th birthday, she was still the only female competitor and also the oldest competitor. She landed hard on that final ride and could barely catch her breath. She never let on that it hurt because she knew the usual response would be that women shouldn't be allowed to ride bulls. A couple of weeks later, when she went for a medical check-up, she learnt the fall had caused a big hematoma to form on the main artery to the heart. If it'd burst, it would have killed her. Once again, she'd escaped serious injury.

<hr>

In Far North Queensland, one of the roads connecting the picturesque Atherton Tablelands with the coast is the Gillies Highway. For any kid in the back seat of a car driving down the Gillies—it's a living hell! Nineteen kilometres of continuous curves and trying to hold in the contents of your stomach is a running battle for the entire way.

Back in the late sixties, or early seventies, a local charter bus driver decided to dress up a tree with a bikini. Another attraction to show his bus full of tourists who had just spent a glorious day on the Tablelands. The sight of the bikini tree will forever live in my memory as the highlight of what was otherwise a torturous drive down the Gillies. It was three kilometres from the end of the range and the sight of the bikini tree meant the ordeal was nearly over. Each trip you would wait expectantly to see what colour bikini it was wearing.

Fast forward about twenty-five years, my boyfriend (now husband) and I decided one day to stop on the way up and paint the bikini tree. I vividly remember painting it a bright red with blue polka dots. It was a thrill, and we did it without being caught. Not that it was a crime to do so.

For almost a year, it was a highlight of the drive to see 'our bikini tree' with our choice of swimwear. Until one day, we drove past, and it had been painted yellow. I remember being disappointed that our fifteen minutes of fame was over. I recall blaming the road crews. It looked yellow enough that it might have been the paint they used to mark the bitumen roads.

Fast forward another twenty-five years, and I find myself visiting Dianne in the early weeks of writing this inspirational story, and she's showing me lots of photos in her fabulous home (yes, completely filled with horse trinkets). Towards the end of the visit, she handed me a photo and said, "You have to do this at least once in your life."

It was a photo of Dianne and her daughter and friend painting the bikini tree. The breasts had been partially painted, but the unpainted portion clearly showed remnants of a bright red paint job with blue polka dots. Dianne's reasoning for using the yellow paint was in honour of the song, 'Itsy Bitsy Teenie Weenie Yellow Polka Dot Bikini'.

I couldn't believe it. I'd never considered taking a photo of our paint job all those years ago, and now I had one, still showing our efforts. And I'd found the thread that connected both myself and Dianne. Just tenable, but there.

Sadly, the bikini tree succumbed to fire in 2009. Forty fabulous years after its inception, it finally fell to a charred death—a sad day for all Gillies Range drivers.

This story was a joy to write, and I hope it inspires many women to follow their dreams and passions and never give up.

If you'd like to look at a photo gallery for Dianne, please go to this link:

https://francesdallalba.wixsite.com/francesdallalba/eightseco ndsgallery

THANKS FOR READING

Thank you for reading **Eight Seconds.** I hope you enjoyed it. This style of book veers slightly from what you're used to from me, but I really wanted to write a book inspired by someone incredible. I was fortunate enough to find her in Dianne Lucas Luppi. I hope you agree with me.

While there is a lot of fiction in this story, the very threads that made this story real and breathed life into it, came about from sharing cups of tea, emails, phone calls and memoirs Dianne had already recorded. I could have filled another three books with the things Dianne has experienced over her life.

It's not every day you get to meet a person in real-life, who has achieved such greatness, that others deem it important they become part of the Women's Museum of Australia. Dianne is one such person. A tough lady, who never gives up and now faces challenges of another kind as she negotiates a path to stabilising her health.

And finally, I want to thank Dianne for being so patient. This journey started a few years ago, but with everything worthwhile achieving, it takes time to come to fruition.

Together with Dianne, we created a gallery of photos which you can find at this link.

https://francesdallalba.wixsite.com/francesdallalba/eightseco ndsgallery

ALSO BY FRANCES DALL'ALBA

The **Australian at Heart Series** tells the stories of four interconnected siblings.

<u>Little Blue Box – Book 1</u>

Regrets, lies, and earth-shattering secrets. When Ella learns the identity of her biological father, nothing will stand in her way. Not even his power. When things don't go to plan, can one little blue box put Ella and Zane back on the same path? This second chance contemporary romance is filled with suspense, emotion and a life-changing sizzling romance.

<u>The Stone In The Road – Book 2</u>

Emotional, passionate and heart-wrenching. This suspense-filled captivating romance will have you dancing in the rain and smiling through your tears. Set in tropical northern Australia, we don't always get to choose our path.

The Silk Scarf – Book 3

An unravelling silken scarf ... mysterious gold ... a breathtaking romance.
An emotional and unforgettable contemporary romance set in Australia.

Rustic Denim Love – Book 4

Forgotten secrets ... blazing fires ... burning love.
She's busy and diligent, doing the best she can to save her crumbling family.
He's funny and witty, with a solution for every problem.
This one may just beat him.

Link to read more and BUY.
**https://francesdallalba.wixsite.com/francesdallalba/australianathe
artseries**

Sway of The Stars Series will share the stories of a group of friends.

The Shooting Star – Book 1

Hidden treasures ... broken spirits ... tangled love. A modern-day treasure hunt where hidden treasures will tangle their love and break their spirits. Duty or love, or can they have both?

The Glittering Star –Book 2

Shimmering waters ... towering giants ... buried mysteries. She's the no filters chick. Funny, full of life and always ready for a good laugh. Until her mother drops a bombshell. He's the environmental warrior. Passionate, driven and determined to save the world. Burnt once before, he's moving on and doing things his way. So how did they end up hand cuffed together on day one?

The Giving Star – Book 3

Endless roads ... timeless discoveries ... unbreakable love. She's packed up her life ready for change, with one regret still hanging over her head. He's working his way back from hell, adamant he's never going there again. But one stumble, one discovery, and one hotbed of attraction ... and the entire game plan changes.

The Priceless Star – Book 4

Forgotten treasures ... a perilous ransom ... shattered hopes
She's chasing answers long buried since the war.
He's content with a steady working life. Until he's not...
Sent to Far North Queensland to research a wartime mystery, Lucia Levorico escapes her privileged life and finds unexpected passion with reserved local, Theo Mather, under an outback sky – until a sudden goodbye and a devastating worksite tragedy tear them apart. When a ruthless ransom plot targets Lucia's wealth, their only reprieve will come from sharing the unravelling of a wartime mystery and its priceless treasure. Unless they're willing to fight for what they have.

Link to read more and BUY.
https://francesdallalba.wixsite.com/francesdallalba/swayof the stars

Eight Seconds, is a standalone story inspired by Australia's first female open bullrider. She pushed past the barriers and succeeded in a male dominated sport, creating a new legend showcased in two Australian halls of fame.

Triumph, hardship, true grit ... and one crazy dream.
An inspirational story about one woman, with one dream, and one almighty driving passion.

Link to read more and BUY.
https://francesdallalba.wixsite.com/francesdalla lba/eightseconds

Jack& Eva, is a standalone contemporary romance set in tropical North Queensland. It showcases our unique and adorable Lumholtz tree kangaroo and the valuable work done by Dr Karen Coombes in her care and continued research of them.

Broody meets bubbly ... and a bunch of cuddly tree kangaroos.
When the tempest blows over, will Jack and Eva be able to find a way forward, or are they destined for a train wreck with a bunch of furry animals caught up in the middle?
Fall in love with our adorable tree kangaroo while reading an emotional and passionate contemporary romance set in Australia.
Link to read more and BUY.
https://francesdallalba.wixsite.com/francesdallalba/jackandeva

ABOUT THE AUTHOR

As a contemporary romance author, Frances loves nothing more than losing herself in a good romance. She's all about helping you forget the housework, or the bus to work you're going to miss, if you don't put the book down now!

She's devoted to giving her readers an emotional, passionate, possibly some ugly-cry, fairly steamy love story, that'll melt your heart and have you fighting for the happy ending right until the end.

Frances sets her books in North Queensland. She makes no excuses if some of her settings include amazing lakes and waterfalls, stunning views from tops of mountains, spectacular outback scenes, or crystal-clear creeks shadowed by tropical rainforest.

When she isn't writing, Frances is climbing mountains, searching for waterfalls and swimming across lakes. She loves to exercise, would prefer it if someone else cooked dinner every night, and never notices dust on the furniture.

She lives with her husband in tropical Far North Queensland, Australia, and uses her great baking skills to tempt her family to visit home often.

Say hello to Frances
Visit her website: https://francesdallalba.wixsite.com/francesdallalba and subscribe to her newsletter. It will keep you up-to-date with everything happening in her author world.

Follow Frances on Facebook, Instagram, Bookbub, TikTok, and Goodreads. To do so, click on this link: https://linktr.ee/francesdallalba

Still have a question?
Ask her at: https://francesdallalba.wixsite.com/francesdallalba/contact

Leave a Review

Did you enjoy this book? The best favour you can do for an author is to leave a **review**. If you'd like to leave a review, go to your place of on-line purchase of the book, or search for the book on **Goodreads** and leave a review. Thank you.